PRIDE AND DESIRE

ANA CRAVID'

Cover design by Dri K. K. Design.

ISBN E-book: 978-2-487170-00-1
ISBN Paperback 978-2-487170-01-8

LAZARUS TAXA

In paleontology, the Lazarus taxon refers to a taxon, typically an animal species or group, believed to have vanished from existence but is unexpectedly rediscovered alive. Alternatively, it describes a taxon absent from the fossil record for a substantial stretch of Earth's history only to reappear later. The past always comes back to haunt us.

The soft glow of the dim lights made the place less overwhelming, even if the cacophony of various perfumes intensified her nausea. Rob still hadn't recovered from her trip from the hotel to the event. Her stomach was still churning, making her regret her choices that night. If only she had not been late, she wouldn't have needed to take the car provided by the event organizers. She could've taken the tramway and saved herself from all the effects of her motion sickness. Now, she had to grapple with the consequences. Nausea always brought along a throbbing headache. With any luck, at least that was her hope, it would subside before she took the stage.

She had grown accustomed to such gatherings, mingling with the owners of the world who, in a bid to polish their tarnished images, tossed a few million here and there to address the problems they themselves had caused. Not to resolve them, of course, but to slap a bandage on a gaping wound. Just last year, a billionaire had donated a million dollars to her organization to combat the effects of rising sea levels on her island. This same billionaire and his multinational corporation were among the primary contributors to CO2 emissions. They could have easily implemented internal policies to reduce pollution, but that would have been expensive. So instead, they tossed some money on the issue, garnered favorable publicity and called it a day. Rob still accepted the money. Pride isn't something one can always afford. And that's why she was there, her stomach churning and head throbbing, amidst people she largely despised, all for the sake of money.

As the singer took the stage, her voice barely reached Rob's table at the back of the room. Part of her was grateful for that, though she couldn't help but feel a pang of cynicism. That singer was earning a hefty sum for her performance, far more than the donation Rob's organization would likely receive, despite a rather mediocre show.

"Do you want more sparkling water?" Omali offered.

"I'm okay."

"No, you're not. You look weird."

"It must be the make-up."

"Nah, don't even. I did a good job on your make-up. You were perfect when we left the hotel."

"Don't worry. I'm going to be okay."

"Just don't puke. Last time, you embarrassed me in front of my friends. If you embarrass me here, that will be it."

Amidst the pain, Rob found a reason to smile. Her sister was a cliché, a regular sixteen-year-old who was embarrassed by her older sibling. Omali looked beautiful, with her short locks styled in a loose way and bold, jet-black eyeliner that swept outward in fierce, winged arches. Her septum ring and her spiked choker contrasted with her soft, delicate features and her warm brown skin glistened even in the dim light.

Rob kept her eyes closed, focusing on breathing exercises to ease her discomfort. The ovation that followed Alison Bic's performance interrupted her process. She stood up and joined the applause, playing her part. When the opening speeches began, she excused herself to the bathroom, hoping to splash some water on her face for some freshness, some relief, but as she looked in the mirror, her make-up reminded her that was out of the question. *Beauty really is a prison,* she thought as she inspected her face. She was still amazed at how the contouring transformed her round nose into a slender shape and accentuated her high cheekbones.

How she wished she could turn back time a few hours and decline her sister's request to do her makeup. If she had said no, they wouldn't have been late, and if they hadn't been late, she wouldn't have opted for the car, sparing herself from the nausea and throbbing headaches. And if, by some chance, she had a headache, she could simply splash her face with cold water for a bit of relief. As she rifled through her bag searching for lip gloss to touch up her makeup, she stumbled upon a solitary tablet of doliprane buried at the bottom, nestled among her small sewing kit and sanitary towels. She swallowed the pill on the spot, cupping her hands under the faucet to gulp down water, being careful not to smudge her makeup. It would be ironic, wouldn't it? To ruin that makeup that had ruined her evening. The price she had paid, and was still paying, was too steep to even risk it.

She took a deep breath, reassuring herself that the evening could only improve from there. After smoothing out her dress and applying a fresh coat of lip gloss, she returned to the room where the distribution of humanitarian awards and checks had already commenced. The checks—those were the only things on her mind.

"You feeling any better?"

"Don't worry, I won't make a scene."

"They've already called two people up. The president of COA even cried on stage."

"Ugh, really?"

"I know right."

After numerous interventions, awards, applause, and speeches, it was her turn. The sequence of events unfolded predictably at the ceremony. She knew that POLO, an organization dedicated to the preservation of indigenous lands and peoples in South America, would precede her. She knew she would be awarded the Health Action of the Year for her organization's efforts in combating HIV in her country. She knew she would be receiving a grant of 5 million Swiss francs from one of the event's organizers, The Universal Funds. She knew she would have precisely one minute and thirty seconds for her speech. In that brief time, she knew she had to smile, convey her gratitude, showcase her organization's impact, and persuade the influential attendees to lend their support.

"And now, to present the Health Action of the Year award, please welcome to the stage James Collin," the host announced.

She remained seated, fully aware of her impending recognition. James Collin, representing TUF, would take the stage, delivering a preamble about Rob's organization and its notable achievements in the past year. Then, he would invite her to ascend the stage to accept the award and the oversized check on behalf of her organization.

"Where is James? Did something happen back there?" the host quipped, his tone light with curiosity.

A lean and tall figure emerged from the backstage, catching everyone's attention. The host handed him the microphone.

"For those of you who don't know James, I'm not him..."

Her heart skipped a beat. Suddenly, everything seemed to freeze, and the background noise faded away, leaving only the sound of her own heartbeat echoing in her ears. She squinted, trying to discern his face through the haze of her myopia, but even if his features were blurred, his voice rang out clear and unmistakable.

"James had a last-minute, um… Issue, so I was asked to step in. I wasn't involved in the process, so forgive me if I don't get everything right."

She stood up, her movements automatic as if drawn by an invisible thread, and began to weave through the crowd, her senses honed on his voice, guiding her toward him.

"The TUF financial award and the Health Action honor go to Candjá, represented by its founder, Robinson Kwame Frades."

And there she stood, at the forefront, amidst the gaze and applause of all, though she still couldn't hear. The silence enveloped her, almost absolute, with only faint murmurs attempting to penetrate it. Yet, all she heard was his voice echoing in her mind. When he ceased speaking, a ringing persisted in her ears and thoughts. *Snap out of it, Rob. Snap.* With a deep breath, she plastered a smile on her face, bracing herself for each step toward the stage. Each stride felt like a journey, her legs akin to cooked noodles on high heels.

The host handed him the award, and he approached her, extending it without a word. It was as if her body was merely a vessel, devoid of a soul. In a state of astral projection, she observed her own faltering, her hesitations, even the tremble in her hands—memories destined to haunt her on sleepless nights. She stepped up to the microphone and delivered her speech in under a minute. It wasn't what she had planned, but it was the best she could muster given the circumstances. With the award in her left hand and the giant check in her right, she hurriedly retreated from the stage, eager to evade the imagined stares fixed upon her.

Back at her table, her cheeks were on fire. She wanted to convince herself that she had made a mistake, that it couldn't be him, but she knew better.

"What happened?" Omali asked, concern etched on her face. "Rob, what happened?"

"Nothing."

"You walked up to the stage like you'd seen a ghost."

"I have a headache. I want to go home."

"Are you sure?"

"Yeah."

"Okay then, let's go."

"Let's wait until the next performance. We can slip out without drawing attention."

Time crawled as they waited for the next singer to be called on stage. When the moment came, Omali and Rob slipped away, counting their steps to avoid drawing attention.

Once outside, they retrieved their coats and made their way out of the building.

"Which way?" Rob asked Omali, who had been tasked with downloading the city's public transport app earlier. "What's taking so long?"

"The service is terrible. I can't download it."

"But I told you to download it while we were at the hotel. You could have used the Wi-Fi."

"I forgot."

"Ké kua, Mali."

"I'm doing my best, okay? It's not my fault the service sucks, and you're the one who wanted to leave early."

"What difference would it make if we left later? I'm cold," Rob said, her voice laden with frustration.

"I'm cold too. Don't rush me."

Rob sighed, her arms crossed as she hugged the oversized check, her right hand still holding the award.

"Do you need any help?" a deep, warm voice asked from behind her.

Rob didn't dare turn around. She was certain that the voice

was in her head, and even if it wasn't, she would have preferred to pretend it was.

"Can I use your phone? We're trying to download the TPG app to figure out which tramway to take to get back to our hotel," Mali asked the stranger.

"Mali!" Rob scolded, her voice sharper than intended.

"What? Do you prefer we stay here freezing?" Mali retorted.

The man stepped closer. "Where is your hotel? Maybe I can help."

"No, thank you. We don't need your help," Rob said, turning around. And there he was—the Lazarus taxon, the coelacanth.

LONG TIME NO SEE!

She took a deep breath, focusing on the cold to distract herself from the whirlwind of emotions coursing through her.

"Hi, Rob. Long time no see!"

"Hi, O'Neil," she replied, her voice hoarse, almost stuttering. She could attribute the tremor in her voice, her unusual expressions, and even her demeanor to the biting cold. It was the Swiss winter displaying its majesty that night, paralyzing her, not him.

He approached her and went in for a hug. She didn't reciprocate, her arms remaining folded across her chest, maintaining a certain distance between them, yet not enough. The scent of his winter perfume remained unchanged. At that moment, it felt as if no time had passed at all.

"Look at you! You're so… It's great to see you!" he said, gripping her shoulders. His wide smile only added to her confusion. *Did he forget?* No, it couldn't be that he forgot. If that was the case, his disregard for her would be even greater than she had imagined.

"So you two know each other. Great," Omali said, dryly.

"I'm sorry," Rob said. This is my sister."

"This is Omali?" he asked.

"Oh, now he knows my name," Omali remarked.

"I can take you two to your hotel. I'm parked not too far from here," he offered.

Rob shook her head. "No, we're good."

"No, we aren't. Rob…" Omali pleaded.

"My motion sickness is still kicking my ass. I can't add to that," Rob explained.

"Then let me take you to the tram station," he suggested.

"I'm sure you have a lot to do."

"What're you talking about? Rob… It's me," he said with a reassuring smile.

She looked at him, puzzled. *What does that even mean?*

"Lead the way," Omali said before Rob could say anything.

The trip to the hotel felt interminable. She found herself repeatedly checking her cell phone, only to remember that it had no reception nor internet. Whenever their eyes met, she looked away. When they finally arrived at the hotel, she handed the room card to Omali, who immediately went upstairs. Both stood in silence, waiting for Omali to disappear from sight.

"It was really nice to see you, Rob. Are you coming to the afterparty?"

"I was hoping to, but I'm not feeling well."

"When will I see you again then?"

"I don't know."

"For how long will you be in Geneva?"

"A week."

"We can go out tomorrow then. Let's catch up."

"Why?"

"What do you mean why? We haven't seen each other in years."

"I don't know. Tomorrow is Sunday. I made plans to do a bit of sightseeing with Omali."

"Tomorrow night then. Please. You won't regret it. I'll pick you up at 8. It will be like the old times."

Rob smiled awkwardly, unsure of what to say. It was a goofy smile that betrayed her confusion. As he hugged her goodbye, she closed her eyes, relishing in the moment. She didn't return the hug, but deep down, she didn't want him to let her go.

* * *

THE WATER from the shower wasn't enough to cleanse her soul. She remained disoriented, in shock, replaying all the scenes of that night in her head, searching for meaning in the details, between the lines.

"What's your code?" Omali shouted from the hotel room. "Rob, what's your code? Rob..."

"What?" Rob said, Omali's voice finally reaching her ears.

"What's going on with you?"

"I'm fine. I'm just tired."

"I changed your SIM card. Now you have service. What's your code?"

"97-86-75."

Omali entered the code into Rob's phone and ensured that the service was functioning properly.

"You have a bunch of notifications."

"Thank you, Mali. I'll check that later."

Rob settled into a chair facing the mirror, beginning to braid her hair to preserve her curls overnight and prevent shrinkage.

"Let me do it," Omali offered, reaching for the jar of shea butter.

"Thanks," Rob replied, passing it over.

"Who was that guy earlier?"

Rob looked at her through the mirror, trying to figure out if there was any intent behind the question or if Omali was just making conversation.

"We used to work together."

"You guys seem close."

"Do we?"

"I don't know. The way he hugged you."

"Well, yeah, we were close. It was a long time ago. He was a good friend."

"Must have been. He remembered my name."

"We used to work at *Les Enfants de Demain* when I lived in France."

"Turn your head a little bit," Omali said with nonchalance, as if she were scarcely listening to her sister's words.

"He asked me out, like, to meet. I don't know yet."

"When?"

"Tomorrow night."

"You should go."

"I don't want to leave you by yourself."

"I'm not going to do anything crazy. I don't even know anyone here. You said you were going to trust me more."

"No, I said I would give you the chance to regain my trust. Besides, it's not only about you. I don't know what possibly we would have to talk about."

"I'm just saying, he seemed pretty happy to see you. And he escorted us to the hotel. Would be a shame to not thank him."

"Just say you want to get rid of me."

"I just want you to have fun."

"Riiiiight…" Rob said, with suspicious eyes.

"You do you. I'm just saying…" Omali trailed off as she finished the last braid.

"Thank you. And I'll think about it."

Rob donned her bonnet and settled onto her bed. In the quiet hours of the early morning, the unexpected encounter continued to weigh heavily on her heart. After some thought, she reached out to her friends, Angelina and Makeba. First, she messaged Angelina, then copied and pasted the same message to Makeba.

Guess who I saw today? O'Neil. Crazy right? He works at TUF. He was nice, I think. Idk...he acted as if nothing ever happened. He asked me out. Not like a date or anything, but just to meet up.

Not long after, she had her first answer from Makeba.

How was it? Seeing him for the first time in years?

Idk...Scary, I think.

Are you going to meet him?

I don't know yet. Maybe???

What do you think?

How did you feel?

Idk. I felt weird, I guess. But I also was feeling like shit because of my motion sickness, so Idk...

You didn't pack medication for motion sickness?

I forgot. And our flight was delayed, so I didn't have time to buy anything.

Look, follow your heart. You're not the same person you were seven years ago. You are doing better.

Do you still have feelings for him tho?

No!

Do you think I'm that stupid?

You having feelings for him wouldn't be stupid. You can't control that. Getting back to your situationship… That would be stupid.

But no one is doing that.

Right. No one is doing that.

Then go if you feel like it. It's okay to be curious, I'd be curious too. Just don't expect much.

How about you? How was therapy?

I fired the therapist.

After only one session?

I'll find someone else. Someone who doesn't tell me I need to move on.

I know I need to move on, but Sara was the love of my life. I don't like it that he told me I need to move on in the first consultation.

I understand. But you need to find someone else.

Therapy is helping Mali a lot. I'm sure it will help you if you find the right person.

How's Mali doing? Is she behaving?

Yeah. She is a bit moody.

She's always moody.

True that.

Thank you, Makeba. I'll try to get some sleep now.

You should try to get some sleep too.

You know I don't sleep.

But go on, get some sleep.

THE CONVERSATION with Makeba provided the validation she sought, a reassurance she desperately craved. Her curiosity felt justified. That was the sole reason she agreed to meet him—she was curious. Nothing more. She repeated the mantra aloud: "Nothing more."

As she prepared to go out with Omali the next morning, her phone rang. It was Angelina. Rob took a deep breath.

"Hi Ange. How are you?"

"How dare he? How dare this motherfucker?" The sound of screaming children and crockery was always the background to conversations with Angelina.

"I can barely hear you."

"Wait, let me go to the yard. These kids keep on screaming… Kids, never have them, Rob. Never."

"I won't."

"So, O'Neil, what did he want with you, like, what happened?"

"It was just a weird coincidence. He is the one who handed me the award and the money. He apparently works at TUF. I didn't understand everything."

"And he asked you out? How did that happen?"

"I don't know. I left very early. Mali and I were trying to figure out the public transportation in Geneva and he helped us."

"And then he asked you out?"

"He just wanted us to meet. I don't think there is anything behind it."

"Yeah… No, you're not going."

"I think I'm going, Ange."

"No, you're not going. This son of a dog destroyed you. He broke you. You were suicidal at one point…"

"Depressed, not suicidal."

"You didn't shower for a week. You lost your job. You had to leave France."

"This is not going to happen. It's just dinner, or something. We'll eat and talk."

"I have two children now. I cannot pick you up this time."

"I won't need you to."

"See? I just don't get it. Why would you go? This man treated you like shit."

"Please, don't say it like this."

"How else? He treated you like shit. Zero consideration for you. Zero appreciation. Zero love. Not even friendship. What else do you have to talk to him about?"

"I don't like him, Ange. I will never like him again. I will not…" she sighed. "I could never, ever, I just… I'm curious. I want to know what he has to say. The way he acted when he saw me, it was as if nothing went wrong. He hugged me."

"And you didn't punch him in the face?"

Rob laughed.

"Violence is not always the solution, Ange."

"Violence is always the solution."

"I'm going to be okay; I promise."

"I wish you weren't curious. Fuck! After everything, I wish he didn't mean anything to you."

"He doesn't mean anything."

She didn't respond immediately. Rob hated Angelina's silence; it weighed heavily on her, filling the air with tension. She much preferred Angelina's direct, straightforward approach.

"I hope so. You need to take care of yourself."

"Always."

"If it were anyone else, I wouldn't be worried. But I know he is your exception. He broke your heart once…"

"I'm not the same person I was seven years ago. I'm stronger, I promise."

"You still shouldn't go, though."

"I'll punch him for you, what about that?"

"Promise?"

"I promise."

The conversation soon veered towards the event, brainstorming ideas for Candjá, and Omali. Before long, they said their goodbyes. Rob spent the rest of the day visiting Geneva with her sister.

As 6 o'clock approached, Rob began to prepare herself for her meeting with O'Neil. She had only packed one night dress and she had already worn it to the event. Normally, she wouldn't have minded wearing the same dress, but not the very next day and not with O'Neil. She opted for black pants paired with a sheer black blouse and heels. She experimented with various hairstyles before settling on leaving her hair loose. Adding earrings, a necklace, and a bold red lipstick, she briefly entertained the idea of letting Omali do her full-face makeup, but quickly dismissed it. The thought of feeling trapped, not being able to wet her face whenever and however she wanted in the name of beauty, was not something she wanted to experience again. After shaking out her winter coat, the only she had packed for that trip, to ensure it was clean, she glanced at the clock as 8 p.m. approached. The phone rang in her room, signaling O'Neil's arrival. She said goodbye to Omali, asked her to behave and left.

The elevator ride from the seventh floor to the ground floor felt like an eternity. Apprehension and fear twisted her stomach into knots, while her heart pounded irregularly, threatening to burst from her chest. When the elevator door finally opened, she hesitated, paralyzed by her emotions. *Snap out of it, Rob.* It took the arrival of another couple to jolt her out of her trance. With a forced smile, she stepped out of the elevator, summoning a confidence she didn't truly feel.

O'Neil was waiting for her at the reception. His eyes widened in surprise when he saw her, and for a moment, they both stood there in silence. She waited for him to speak, but instead, he simply looked at her, his expression unreadable, until a smile slowly crept across his face.

"What?" she asked.

"Nothing."

"You're being weird," she noted, furrowing her brows.

"We were always a bit weird."

"I was never weird."

"You were the weirdest person I've ever met," he teased.

"Okay, I guess I'm going back to my room now," she said, playfully.

He reached out and grabbed her hands, stopping her. "See? Weirdo," he teased again.

"I took motion sickness medication. What do you want us to do?" she asked.

"I planned to leave my car here and take the tram, but this makes things much easier."

"Well, today the tram intervals are longer, especially at night, so I bought medication."

"Let's go then," he said, leading the way.

They walked side by side. Occasionally, he stole glances at her, but she pretended not to notice.

IT'S ALL COMING BACK…

The waiter escorted them to a secluded corner table, softly lit to allow a view of each other and their meals. As they settled in, he returned with the appetizer menu, breaking the silence that had fallen between them. Rob found refuge behind the menu, though her mind was far from the words printed on its pages. A tumult of conflicting emotions churned within her. She yearned to engage with him as they once did, to reach out and grasp his hand, to embrace him and confess how much she missed him, if not as a lover, then as a friend, her best friend. Yet, simultaneously, she burned with the desire to confront him, to demand answers, to question his audacity in asking her out after all this time. She teetered on the edge of these personas, unsure of which to present to him. Lost in her contemplation, his hand reached across the table, gently touching her menu.

"Hey."

She slid down the menu.

"Campari. With lemon," she said.

"I knew it."

"No, you didn't."

"Yes, I did. You told me once how you used to steal Campari from your mother's cupboard."

"Mmm..."

"There has never been silence between us, or at least not awkward silence. What happened?"

"Seven years, O'Neil. It wasn't seven days."

"True. But do you remember what you once told me? You said we would be close forever. I still have the screenshot of this text saved."

"I'm not often wrong. That was one of the few times. I actually was wrong about you, a lot."

"No, you were not."

"What were you doing at the event yesterday?"

"I work at TUF."

The waiter brought their drinks and swiftly departed.

"I figured that much. But... How?"

To her friends, she hadn't heard from O'Neil in seven years after he vanished from her life, but secretly, she had followed him on social media under an alias for two years after their relationship ended. So, she knew many things about him. She knew that five years ago, he was working in Germany. She knew that five years ago, he had received a promotion, and five years ago, not long after that, he officially proposed to his girlfriend with a massive diamond ring.

"When I left *Les Enfants de Demain,* I started working in Human Resources for a multinational medical corporation. Guess where?" he asked.

"I'm not going to guess."

"You can guess. The last place I would ever choose to live in."

"Germany."

"See? You know me."

"Why were you in Germany then?"

"I sold myself to the higher bidder. The pay was really good."

"O'Neil..." she said, in an almost scolding voice.

"Yeah, I know. It was soul sucking. I was very unhappy but making a lot of money."

"We're all a little unhappy, so it's better to be unhappy with money."

"I was literally crying in my Bentley. But after three years, I found another job, first with the WPO and now with TUF."

He signaled the waiter, and they placed another round of drink orders. Shortly after, the drinks arrived. Rob took a hearty sip of her bitter and fruity beverage before promptly requesting another.

"Awnn... So after working with Germans for three years, do you like them now?"

"Oh, these perverts? I still don't."

"I love to hear about that white-on-white hatred."

"God, I missed you."

"I missed you too. Fuck, I didn't want to say it. I think I'm getting tipsy."

"You were always a lightweight."

"I hate your face," she muttered.

He grinned. "You used to say that a lot... That you hate me."

"What happened to James? He is my point of contact."

"I don't know. He was at the event and then he left. We aren't close. We don't even work in the same department."

"Mmm, I guess I'll find out at the meeting on Monday. He's supposed to be my monitor."

"Your monitor?"

"The giant check is just for show..."

"Yes. That's why I didn't understand why you took it with you."

"You saw me and didn't say anything? Gosh, I was so disoriented that I didn't even realize. I'll be taking it back. Anyway, they'll be making the wire transfer to my organization's bank account. And they'll send someone to shadow me for six months. They say it's for help and advice, but I think it's just a way of monitoring how the money is spent. Depending on that, I might be eligible for real financial aid, not just a one-time check."

"And James is the one doing the monitoring?"

"I want him to. James is a nice person. He's actually the one who reached out to me and told me about this opportunity. He's an idealist."

"You know what's crazy? I wanted to join TUF to do work that actually matters. But I'm stuck in HR. Again."

"Someone's got to do it, right? HR is important."

"Yeah, but last year for example there was an initiative to do some real work, and my project was not chosen."

"What was the project?"

"It was silly. One day I'll tell you."

"Can I ask another question then?"

"Shoot."

"Why did you ask me out?" He seemed confused. "You know what I'm talking about."

"Because I couldn't just accept that that's what we became. When I saw you walking to the stage, I froze. And then I grinned. And then I was scared. I didn't know what we were going to do, but I didn't think we were going to completely ignore each other, as if the year we worked together didn't mean anything. As if once, we weren't each other's world." Rob cackled and then quickly brought her hand to her mouth in an attempt to stifle her laughter. "I knew I was funny, but not that funny," O'Neil said.

"How can you say this with a straight face?"

"Say what?"

"Why aren't we friends anymore? Why aren't we close as we used to be? What happened?"

"I left the country."

"Yes, O'Neil, you left. You left me. You just disappeared. You didn't tell me anything. You just left."

"I'm sorry. I should've opened with that. I'm really sorry, Rob."

"Why? Why did you do that?"

"Right now, I look at what I did and how I did it... I don't know. I know you want an answer, a clear answer. I know you want to hear something that makes sense, and you deserve to have some form of explanation, but I don't have any."

"You didn't love me, I get it. But we kissed. You kissed me. And the next day you were just gone."

"I loved you."

"You didn't. It took me a long time to understand that, but you didn't. You don't do that to people you love."

"When I told you I loved you, I wasn't being casual about it, I wasn't just saying it. But I also wasn't in the right headspace, I was confused. I still had feelings for my ex."

"No shit."

"To be honest, I was scared. I'm not trying to get your sympathy, but I was. I don't know exactly of what, but there was this anguish inside me..."

"If kissing me left you feeling this level of distress, I guess I do have sympathy for you. No one deserves this."

"It wasn't about you. Everything I told you, I felt it. I never lied to you."

"Why do I feel lied to then?"

"Rob..." He reached for her hands, but she recoiled. "I never meant to hurt you."

"I don't believe you. I think you meant to hurt me. There was no way you thought: 'oh, Rob is going to be just fine with me leaving, blocking her number, blocking her on all social media and cutting her off without an explanation.'"

"You're right. I don't get to claim ignorance. I knew how my actions would affect you. At that time, I just didn't think about it."

"Exactly! You didn't think about me."

Rob struggled to hold back her tears.

"I don't know what to say. There are no right words. Fuck, I hate that old me. I hate how young and immature I was."

"Don't blame it on your age. Don't do that. You were great, and then you were awful. None of it had anything to do with your age. I guess you made the best decisions for yourself. I guess I wasn't… I didn't mean as much as I thought, which is okay. I fantasized about confronting you so much. I spent nights imagining scenarios, my reaction, the tone of my voice, the words that would come out of my mouth. All of it disappeared when I saw you."

"I don't regret many things in my life, Rob. I really don't. I know I told you about some of my crazy university experiences, even my alcohol poisoning, all of it… I don't regret any of it. But I regret the way I acted. I regret leaving you."

"It's not that you left me, you know. It's that you just left. No words. Nothing. One day you were my whole world and the next, you didn't exist. I struggled. A lot. When I created that fake account and dmed you and you blocked me, I understood. Deep inside me, I knew you didn't want anything to do with me and I knew I shouldn't do it. I knew I shouldn't humiliate myself, but I just couldn't help myself."

"I don't even remember what was going through my head when I did that."

"You taught me a lot about myself. You leaving, I mean. I did things I never thought I would. I was pathetic. Desperate." She laughed, her sadness infecting every sound of it. "I hated that person. But I guess I had to be that person. It taught me humility. Being in love and stupid were in fact not beneath me."

"I owed you at least a conversation. A real conversation."

"No, you didn't. It took me a while to understand that, but you didn't. No one owes me anything, especially you. That's how things are."

"You're still hurt."

"I'm not. I promise. I was. For a very long time. Then a lot happened. I had to grow up."

"You are the one person I never wanted to hurt."

"You're funny." She laughed again, disguising her pain with a smile. "Can I tell you something though?"

"Yeah."

"I prayed that you'd end up loving someone as much as I loved you and that person would break your heart."

He cackled.

"I can't believe I got you praying. And for that."

"Please, tell me it worked. I prayed to the universe, did some witchcraft, some voodoo."

"Can't say it did. Your witchcraft is weak. Islanders shit."

"Take that back."

"Never."

"We have good witchcraft on my island. My uncle's dick…"

"Fell because he messed with his friend's woman. I knew you were going to bring up this example. Your uncle had impotence and wanted to blame it on witchcraft."

"You might be right."

Their laughter echoed in the room, punctuating the tension with a moment of levity.

"That's your first honest laugh. I missed that."

Rob searched for a response when a notification on her phone saved her. It was from Candjá's social media page, indicating that her sister had started a live stream. She smiled down at her phone.

"Is this Francisco?"

"What? No. It's my sister. She went live. She made sure that I didn't get the notification on my account, but I got it from my organization's account."

"Speaking of your organization, Rob, look what you've created."

"Yeah, no… Just, let's go back… How do you know about Francis again?"

"Francis? Who is Francis?"

"Don't play with me."

"Okay, I stalked your social media. Well, not yours since it's private. Your organization's. And I saw a picture of you two together, which led me to his very public profile and there was a bunch of pictures of you two. I gathered he is your... Boyfriend?"

"Mmm, yeah."

"Just to be clear, it wasn't really stalking. I was just checking. I was curious about you, about the life you created for yourself."

"No, I get it."

"I mean, anyone would be curious. Weren't you curious about me?"

"I felt a lot of things. Curiosity about your life wasn't one of them."

"What did you feel?"

"I don't know. Too much to put into words."

"Seven years. Doesn't even feel like it. You look exactly the same."

"I don't."

"You do."

"You look good. Not as thin as before."

"I started running, put on some muscles. Finished my first marathon two years ago."

"That's impressive."

"Yeah, being tall, skinny and pale wasn't a look."

"Yeah, tall, lean and pale is much better."

"You're mocking me?"

"I'm not, I swear. But I liked you skinny too."

"Your celebrity crush was Racine Carré Stromae, so, yeah, I know you liked it. Do you like me now?"

"You're not that different."

"You should see me naked then."

Seven years ago, that would have sparked flirting and teasing between them. She knew exactly the kind of banter he expected in response. However, that playful dynamic no longer existed.

They had both evolved into different individuals, navigating separate stages of their lives.

"I wouldn't know the difference," she said, dryly.

The disappointment flashed across his face for a moment, fleeting yet obvious.

"You still lift?" he asked.

"Of course. And I started getting into calisthenics recently."

"That's so cool."

"I expected you to have less hair. Damn, my witchcraft is really weak," she quipped, admiring his neatly trimmed buzz cut with a fade and line up.

He gasped in mock horror.

"I can't believe you tried to get my hair to fall out."

"Well, your hairline was already receding. I just wanted to speed up the process."

"That was my biggest insecurity. That's evil, Rob," he responded, half-serious, half-amused.

"It didn't work, so."

"It might. Good thing Türkiye exists."

They laughed so loud that a nearby couple shot them disapproving glances.

"Let's order."

The night passed in the blink of an eye. It was as if nothing was enough, not even eternity. On the way out of the restaurant, O'Neil began to sing, his voice like a duck choking on dried couscous.

"Please don't do this. Do not subject these poor people to your horrible singing, King Julien. They don't deserve it."

He laughed amidst his singing. They meandered, without direction, along the edge of the lake.

"Oh yeah, you used to call me King Julien. Why were you so mean to me?"

"You brought that on yourself by singing 'I Like to Move It' at

Jennifer's birthday party. And you and he are equally bad singers."

"I can't believe I let you bully me like that."

"I didn't bully you. I just said you sound as awful as he does, with his confidence."

"No one has ever criticized my singing as much as you."

"You were too spoiled by your parents."

"Yes, I was. But if you hated my voice so much, why did you always put my name on the karaoke list?"

"I never said I hated it. I loved to hear you singing despite your voice. It was endearing."

"Remember our last night in Strasbourg?"

"It's all coming back; it's all coming back to me now..." She sang the lyrics.

"We Celine Dioned that shit."

"We did. Many people regretted having ears that night, but we nailed it."

"Remember what the owner said?"

"You two shouldn't be allowed to sing. Ever. Your voices together are a crime against humanity," she said, trying to imitate the old man's thick Alsatian accent.

"He was exaggerating though. Come on. Me Celine, you Whitney. We can start a duo and sell records."

"Nooo. We would torture the world."

"I never knew my singing was that bad until that year," he said.

"That's why you needed me. I refuse to hype my friends and give them confidence when they have zero talent. You know these people who go on to singing shows and competitions and sound awful. It's not their fault. It's their family's and friend's fault because they never told them the truth."

"You saved me. I was about to start my application process to The Voice."

"I would pay to see that fail."

"Good to know that you were praying for my downfall."

"Then again, witchcraft from islands ain't shit, right? You're still standing and thriving."

He stopped. After some steps, she also stopped, looking at him.

"What?" she asked.

"I don't want to go home."

He sat down on a wooden bench on the edge of the lake. She sat next to him.

"Tomorrow is Monday."

"I don't want to go to work tomorrow either."

"Then stay here. Sleep here."

"I mean, if you join me, I'm down."

"Oh, no. I can't. I need a good shower and a bed."

"I have both at my place."

"I love hotels. I love not having to think about anything. My life every day is thinking. Things depend on me. But hotels give me the illusion of being taken care of. I don't need to think about anything, what to eat, to change my bedsheets or to dry the floor after leaving the shower with soaking wet feet. Don't get me wrong, I love the work I do. It's just…"

"Everybody deserves a break."

"Yeah… Yeah! So as much as I'm curious to see where you live, I'd rather go back to my hotel. Besides, this week is going to be crazy. So many workshops and meetings at TUF."

"Can we grab lunch tomorrow then?"

"I don't know if we're going to have the lunch break at the same time."

"I'll make it work."

"Okay then. But I need to go now."

"Do you?"

"Yeah. My sister must be missing me."

"I doubt that."

"You might be right. But I need to go. Besides, I don't think your fiancée would be too happy if I just showed up."

"What fiancée?"

"Seriously? Are we going to do that? I know that you went back to your ex when you left the country."

"How do you know that?"

"After trying to reach you and getting blocked everywhere, I created an account and stalked you for two years."

"That's not possible. My profile is private, and I don't accept people's requests unless I know them."

"That's why I created a profile curated to appeal to you: a Polish girl who went to the same university as you, majored in the same field as you. She follows your friends from Poland, and some of them follow her back because people can be shallow like that. I was actually surprised that so many of them followed her. It's the unspoken rule of 'follow for follow,' I guess. She posts inspirational quotes and, like you, doesn't like showing her face very much. She likes fashion and has a cat, like you. She posts pictures of her cat. Only after nine months of creating and curating this profile did I send you a follow request. You studied her profile; I knew you would. Her most recent post at the time was from three days before she sent you the follow request, and it was about her being lactose intolerant but still eating ice cream and suffering the consequences. You liked that post. I knew you would like it because you can relate. And you accepted her follow request and followed her back."

"What's her name?"

"Anna Olkiewicz. You can look her up. I bet she still follows you. I didn't delete the account. I just abandoned it."

He took out his cell phone and entered the app. He scrolled down the list of people he followed and there she was. Last update was five years ago. A picture of her orange cat. He had liked that picture.

"How did you know my friends from Poland?"

"Your account was private, but you had the friend suggestion feature enabled. When I searched for you, I could see the people you followed, and many of them had public accounts. It wasn't hard."

"Rob, you're scary. I thought she was someone I went to school with and didn't remember. Or someone I met at a party through friends, I don't know. Not even in a million years I would think it was you. You gave her a life and a job. You posted a picture of her Starbucks cup with her name on it."

"I found it in the trash. Anna is such a common name. I don't drink Starbucks, you know that."

"Exactly. That's why I could never think... This is some real shit."

"Yeah, it's embarrassing. I'm sorry. I was desperate."

"This is very calculating for someone just desperate. I'll never use the word stalk again. You earned it. It's yours."

"I followed your ex too. Well, not your ex anymore. Your fiancée. She had a public profile, so it was easy. I even liked the post she made about the engagement, showing off her ring. That was my last action actually. I liked the post, commented congratulations, disconnected from that account and never connected back."

"I don't know if I should be impressed or scared."

"Why not both?"

"In my defense, I didn't leave you to get back with my ex. We started talking about six months after I went to Germany. It wasn't anything serious. She was living in France, like, we were friends. My cat died. She was there for me. And then, one day, she told me she was going to Berlin for a gig. Instead of spending money at a hotel, I offered her my guest room."

"And let me guess, she ended up sleeping in your room."

"Not on the first night, but yeah, eventually. About a year later I proposed and that was it."

"Yeah… The whole stalking thing made me miserable, but it was like I was addicted to it. To my own misery. And then when I saw you happy, and your family and everybody was so happy I was like, damn, I don't need to be this unhappy. So I disconnected and never looked back."

"If you had, you'd see that our engagement didn't last."

"I'm sorry. Really, I'm sorry."

"It's okay. I wasn't heartbroken or anything. I think I only went back to her because of familiarity. She was my high school girlfriend, we had history. We were together for over five years. My father adores her. She knows my family, I know hers. But as adults, we were very different people. I knew this. We had broken up once because of it. But somehow, I forgot. And then the same things started showing up, the same problems, the same irreconcilable differences."

"It happens."

"Yes. Anyway, so that you don't have to stalk me anymore, I'm going to follow you. You can follow me back."

"I'm not going to follow you back. And I'm not going to accept your follow request either."

"Why not?"

"Just no. If when I wanted, you didn't want, I don't want it anymore. I don't need it anymore."

"You're kidding, right?"

"I'm not. Accepting this now would be humiliating."

"So this is revenge?"

"This is me having a little bit of self-respect. I begged you for this years ago and you didn't give me. I don't want it anymore."

"Fair enough. At least give me your phone number. We need to communicate. We need to find each other for lunch tomorrow."

"Oh, of course."

She gave him two numbers, her usual one and the one she had bought in Switzerland so that she could access the data and the network during that week. They stayed there for a while, in silence, before leaving for the parking lot of the restaurant where they had dined earlier.

FRIENDS

The next morning, Rob woke up early. As she got ready, she spoke aloud, rehearsing her interventions in various imaginary scenarios. It was a habit of hers—creating fake scenarios, arguing, answering questions, and fantasizing about situations, encounters, speeches, and interactions.

"Please, stop talking to yourself. I'm still sleeping," Omali said, her voice drowsy.

Rob resumed her self-talk in front of the mirror while she did her hair, this time in a lower tone. After getting ready, she called Francis. She had talked to him the night before when she got home after her dinner with O'Neil. She told him what had happened. 'Was it a date?' he had asked. 'No, of course not.' She had said, unsure of her own words.

"Hey, I'm sorry for calling you so early."

"Don't worry. We only have one hour of difference. I was already up anyway."

"I miss you," she said.

"I miss you, too. How did you sleep?"

"I slept fine. This hotel is really good. Four stars. So fancy, sometimes I forget how to act. I feel out of place."

"Nonsense. You are right where you should be. No one is more deserving of being there than you."

"Thank you for saying that. I'm a bit nervous about this meeting today. I haven't heard from James. I called, left messages and e-mails. Nothing."

"I'm sure he's okay. Bad news travels fast."

"Yeah... Yes, you're right. It's just that... I'm afraid. If something happened..."

"Don't overthink it, Rob. You always do that. Everything is going to be okay."

"What would I do without you?"

He stayed silent for a second.

"Are you going to see him today?" he finally gathered the courage to ask.

"You're talking about O'Neil?"

"Yeah."

"Yes. He works there. We'll probably grab lunch together. He might have information about James." Francis stayed silent again. "Francisco. Listen to me. I love you. Don't worry about O'Neil. He's just a guy I used to love."

"Don't say it like that. You know love is not trivial. He was a big deal, so much so that you told me about him on our first date."

"That was four years ago. I'm not that person anymore."

"You spent four years stuck, loving him."

"I spent four years stuck in heartbreak. It's different. But now I love you."

"I know you love me. I'm afraid you might love him too."

This time, it was she who remained silent, only for a few seconds. Her silence bothered her. The fact that he could be right bothered her.

"It's one week. No one falls in love in one week."

"Yeah, that's not what I wanted to hear."

"I'm sorry."

"Don't be. I've got to go now. I'm going to the clinic."

"Francis, I love you."

"I love you too."

* * *

AT AROUND ONE O'CLOCK, Rob and O'Neil met at a restaurant not far from the TUF headquarters. He was already there, waiting for her. They exchanged kisses and she sat down, removing her coat and scarf.

"What happened?" he asked.

"Nothing, I'm just… I got lost. The GPS took me somewhere very far from here."

"You should've told me. I would've gone to you."

"No, don't worry. I'm used to this. I'm always getting lost."

"Yeah, I remember. You're here now. Give me your hands."

She gave him her freezing hands. He stroked them gently, blew warm air on them and kissed them. She suddenly withdrew her hands before he could finish his maneuvers to warm them.

"It's warm in here. I'll be all cozy in a minute."

"Do you want us to order?"

"Have you ordered already?"

"Not yet, but I took a look at the menu."

She grabbed the menu in front of her and skimmed through the selection.

"I want onion soup for entrée and beef with rösti for the main course."

"I'll call the waiter."

"Do that. I'm going to wash my hands."

When she came back, she sat down at the table, this time calmer, the slight rosiness having already left her cheeks and nose.

"How was the meeting today?"

"It was awful. James is out. I don't know what happened."

"Yeah, about that, he had a stroke. That's why he left the event. I saw him leaving with his wife. I thought he was simply tired or having a headache. We were informed that he is at the hospital."

"God, is he okay?"

"I don't know."

"Fuck. This messes everything up."

"How so?"

"Can I trust you?"

"Yeah, of course."

"So, one of the things we are going to use the money for is to create a clinic for women, to deal with things that pertain specifically to women's health."

"That's great."

"Yeah, but women's health also means reproductive health, including abortion. In my country, abortion is not legal, but it's still performed. It's becoming increasingly dangerous to perform the act or to receive this type of care. So many women die… That's one of the reasons I'm building the clinic."

"But won't it be controlled by the government as a healthcare facility?"

"That's why I'm building it on an islet. You know my country is an archipelago. Last year, I negotiated with the government to purchase an islet. One of our benefactors gave me the money. I didn't buy it as a property for my organization; I bought it under my name so it would be considered private property. I opened a branch of my organization there. The islet is not very big, but big enough for a sizable clinic. We would provide transportation to and from the islet and the dock would be private. My country is poor. Our government doesn't have the means and would not try to find ways to go there, but even if they did, it wouldn't be that easy for them to access because it's private property and the law would give me some protection. Even if for some reason, they manage to get into boats and appear there, we would have time to organize since without tangible suspicion of wrongdoings or someone in danger, they are not allowed to just barge in without a warrant. I'm not a lawyer, so I don't know all the technicalities, but my lawyer has been planning everything."

"That's also great. What's the problem then?"

"I was going to use this money to set everything in place. To finish the construction work, buy machines, medications and hire doctors. But the thing is, The Universal Funds don't look too kindly on abortion. I think it's because of the founder's religious beliefs."

"No. What? I never heard... No."

"I did my research. TUF cut all connections with organizations that support abortion. The female employees aren't even covered in case of an abortion."

"You're serious?"

"Yes, I am. Have you ever read the staff health insurance plan guide? Abortus provocatus is not covered if based on personal choice. Only covered if the woman is dying and that is thoroughly checked before agreeing to coverage."

"How do you know all of this?"

"I do my research. Open your insured area, download your guide and check."

He did that and then, looked at her, surprised and embarrassed for being so surprised.

"I never knew."

"Because you don't need it. And of course, this is not something your female co-workers go around broadcasting, especially when the culture in the organization is so anti-abortion. Not only abortion is not covered, but only certain types of contraceptives are covered. Sterilization is not covered. That's why I wanted James to be the one doing the monitoring. If it's someone else and they report that we are providing these types of services, we won't qualify for more help from TUF. And we need the funds."

"Who decides who will be the monitor?"

"James' boss, Richard van den Brekel, I think."

"I don't know him, but I'll try to see if I can do anything for you, alright?"

"Thank you."

"Of course. It's very disappointing though. Like, why not cover abortion, sterilization and contraception?"

"They cover some contraceptives, but only under prescription."

"But why?"

"They are too busy covering Viagra, Levitra and all..."

"Wait, they cover impotence medication?"

"Yep. And without prescription. Limp dicks matter." He cackled and then covered his mouth, trying hard to suppress his laugh. "Now that you know, you can claim Viagra and be reimbursed."

"My thing works just fine. Thanks," he said, still laughing.

The waiter brought the soup.

"Fuck!" At the first spoonful, she burned her lips on the boiling soup.

"Slowly, Rob. It's not going anywhere."

"I don't want to be late."

"You just got here."

"But I wasted time getting lost."

"They won't kick you out if you're twenty minutes late. Slowly please."

"I'm going to tell you something you don't like to hear. You're being very French right now."

"Nooooo... Lower your voice. This accusation could get me killed. The Swiss don't like us. They think they are better than us. They call us frouze and they believe all we do is complain and be dishonest."

"How's the taste of your own medicine?"

"I'm not even fully French. That's not fair."

"Well, you're culturally more Gallic than Scandinavian."

"I mean, is culture that important?"

She laughed. "Are you denying your mother's side?"

"Every day. Left and right."

"Damn! I didn't think you had it in you. I guess your name should've been Peter."

"Not even my co-workers know I'm French. They think O'Neil is my surname, and not my name."

"To be fair, you have a weird name. Your surname sounds like a name and your name sounds like a surname."

"And I play on this ambiguity."

"The day they find out your surname is Thibault, you're done."

"I'll do anything to prevent this from happening."

"Oh Mr. Thibault, what do we have here? An opportunity for blackmail, I see. Oh, guess what? During my stalking time, I found out Thibault is derived from old Germanic Theobald."

"Oh God, no."

"Yeah."

"Germanic, not German."

"Close enough. It means brave people. Doesn't suit you. You're not brave."

"I was not brave. People change, you know?"

"If you say so… Either way, it's something that connects you with Germany.

"Gosh, I'll tell you one day why I left that corporate job there. You'll laugh so hard."

"Tell me."

"Not now. It's a long story. Tomorrow maybe, if you meet me at my place. I want to cook for you."

"No."

"I owe you a meal. Last time we ate together at your place, you cooked for me. And I told you next time I'd cook for you."

"That was years ago."

"It doesn't matter. A promise is a promise. And I've broken enough of them."

"No. I'd rather not. Thank you, though."

The waiter brought out their main course, clearing away the entrée plates in one fluid motion. They ate with a sense of urgency and left the restaurant at a brisk walk. O'Neil walked alongside her, ensuring she didn't lose her way. As they reached the building's entrance, just before she could say goodbye, he reached out and took her hand.

"I want to see you tonight."

"I can't. Tomorrow maybe."

"You're only here for a week."

"Exactly. I can't spend every evening with you."

"You're right. You're right."

"I have responsibilities. My sister. I can't leave her alone every night."

"Is she alone right now?"

"Yeah. She is. She got in trouble at school and got a week suspension, so I brought her with me. I'm not punishing her. She was right, but she was also wrong. It's complicated. She stays at the hotel; she studies and tonight we'll go out."

"Then let me accompany you two. Your sense of direction sucks. I don't want you to be lost, cold at 1 a.m."

"I won't be lost and cold."

"Rob, come on. You don't want to go to my place, cool, I get it. But you are in my city. Let me show you around. I would do the same for any of my friends. It's not a big deal."

"Is that what we are? Friends?"

"Of course we are."

"I used to hate that about you. The way you say big things as if you didn't know what they meant. Things like friendship, love. You don't know me, O'Neil. You can't say we are friends. Words have meaning. Friendship is a big deal."

"But I know you."

"No, you don't. And I don't know you either. Even if I knew you seven years ago, which is unlikely because through my rose-colored lenses, I only saw what I wanted to see, in seven years, you changed."

"I know you want to believe that what we had didn't mean anything. Maybe that's the lie that helped you move on. But what we had was real, and we don't have to deny it just because it didn't work. I knew you. I'm sure some parts of you changed. But I knew the essence of you, and that can't change. And you knew me too. With you, everything was real. I could be me, or rather the person I wanted to be, instead of just conforming to the path and the ways of my peers. That's the thing I loved most about you; you inspired me to be better. I don't think I ever told you this."

"No, you haven't. But it doesn't matter. Some things we should leave in the past, right?"

"We don't have to."

She sighed. "Are you any good at this tourist guide thing?"

"The best you're going to get for free."

"Okay then. I leave the meeting at 4:30. I'll go home, and you can pick us at 7."

"I'll see you tonight then."

Deep down, a sense of apprehension nagged at her, telling her she shouldn't have agreed to his offer. But even after all that time, saying no to him was not an easy task.

And that's why you should avoid him, dumbass.

OMBRE NOMADE

That week, which she had anticipated to be dull and filled with forced pleasantries among people she barely tolerated, turned out to be the complete opposite of what she had expected. She despised how his presence seemed to dictate whether her day would be good or bad. Even more frustrating was catching herself smiling at the mere thought of him—a silly, foolish smile reserved for those in the throes of love. So, despite the pain, she was relieved when the week finally came to an end. Perhaps relief wasn't the most accurate term, but she held onto the belief that things would eventually fall into place, and that was a comforting thought.

As they sat in the car on the way to the airport, anguish permeated the air. They had arrived too early and now found themselves on a bench, waiting in silence, each lost in their own thoughts, wishing for time to pass quickly and not at all.

Rob and O'Neil exchanged hushed words while Omali remained fixated on her cell phone.

"Why do I feel like the third wheel?" Omali said.

"Don't say that. If you want to talk to us, just talk to us instead of being on your phone all the time."

"Yeah, no. I want to stretch my legs. I'm going for a walk."

"Take some cash if you feel like buying something to eat."

Alone together, their bodies gravitated towards each other. She nestled against his chest, his gentle strokes tracing patterns in her hair.

"Time flew by," he murmured. She remained silent, unsure of what to say. She wished to prolong the moment, enveloped in his scent, relishing the warmth of his touch against her skin. Despite the wrongness of it all, she rationalized that since she would never see him again, it was permissible. So, she closed her eyes, allowing herself to indulge in the fantasy of what might have been.

"Next time you're here, I'll take you to my favorite Italian restaurant in Lausanne. They have the best tiramisu ever."

"I don't like Italian food."

"But you were always down for Italian before."

"I was down for whatever because all that mattered was to be near you. I can eat Italian, but I don't like it particularly. I don't actually know any black person who loves Italian food. We eat it, it's convenient, but it's mostly bland."

"You're asking to be murdered. Italians are very defensive when it comes to their food."

"Then it should be better, shouldn't it?" They laughed. "It's not like Italians care about my thoughts on their cuisine."

"Then what do you like? Besides food from your country?"

"I eat everything, but I really love Nigerian, Senegalese, Angolan, Gabonese..."

"And outside of Africa?" he asked. She raised an eyebrow. "There aren't many African restaurants here."

"I love Lebanese food, Syrian, Iraqi, Mexican, but real Mexican, not only tacos and burritos, oh, Brazilian. I like French too."

"Right..." he said, skeptically.

"No, seriously. I like Coq au vin, boeuf bourguignon, souris d'agneau. And magret with balsamic vinegar and honey sauce? Amazing."

"Okay then. Next time, I'll take you to one of these restaurants."

"There won't be a next time."

"If all goes well, you'll qualify for help from TUF, right?"

"Yes, but if I come here again, I don't want to see you."

"Why? I thought this was fun. It wasn't like before, but I thought this was... I don't know. Was I wrong?"

"I'm in a relationship, O'Neil."

"Yeah, I know. That's why I didn't flirt or make sex jokes as we used to."

"I can't fall back... I love Francis. I can't fall in love with you again. I don't have... I can't. I found myself thinking about you, excited to spend time with you even more than I was to attend the meetings and workshops."

"I mean, I'm way more interesting than those boring workshops."

"I'm not kidding. It's not fair to Francis. I love him."

"You only love him because we didn't work out."

"And you're only here today because things didn't work out with your ex. See? We're all someone's second choice. I'm yours."

"Don't say that, Rob. I'm here because seven years ago, I was stupid, and I lost the most important person in my life."

"You never looked for me. You never tried to find me. How can you say I was important?"

"I wanted to have all the right words to tell you, but I don't have them. All I have now is what I feel. And I know, it's not enough, it won't change the past, and it probably won't affect the future. But I don't want to do what I did seven years ago. I don't want to just give up."

"We're nothing now. You won't be giving anything up."

"You know that's not true."

As she turned towards him, a subtle shift caught her attention, not in his outward appearance, but in the way he carried himself. Years ago, their conversations, though perhaps deep, had lacked a certain gravity, a weightiness that now infused their every exchange.

"What?" he asked.

"You look older. In your demeanor, I mean. There's something..."

"Well, I'm thirty. I'm supposed to look older."

Seated cross-legged before him, she watched in silence, her gaze tracing the contours of his face, drawn to his deadpan eyes. Amidst the stillness, a bead of perspiration trailed down his neck, disappearing into the fabric of his black hoodie. She battled against her most primal desires, a struggle that had consumed her entire week. Her mind was a battlefield, resisting the persistent thoughts of him—of tracing her tongue along his long neck, his Adam's apple, savoring every inch of his body, and exploring his mouth with her tongue. He touched her cheek, a tender caress, gently brushing aside the curls that framed her features, and bringing her back to reality.

"You're so beautiful. I've been wanting to kiss you since I saw you."

Complicit in the silence, the space between their lips dwindled, inching closer until she could almost taste the warmth of his breath against her skin.

"We can't do this, O'Neil. I can't do this."

She got up and made her way to the bathroom, seeking refuge from her inner turmoil. She splashed water onto her face repeatedly, attempting to wash away the desire and the shame. She didn't think of herself as the kind of person who lies and cheats. Who would hurt another for nothing, yet there she was. With trembling fingers, she typed a message to Francis:

I love you.

She had never told him that she loved him as much as she had that week. As if hoping her love for him could somehow absolve her of her thoughts, of her feelings, of the fever in her body consuming every bit of her soul.

"Hey!" she said when she was back.

"Hey!" he said, rubbing his eyes to dislodge an eyelash that had fallen in.

This time, she sat down, maintaining a slight distance between them.

"Can you help me?" he asked.

She approached him and, with a piece of paper, carefully removed the lash from his eye.

"Thank you," he said, blinking quickly and tearing up.

"Now make a wish." She held the lash on her finger for him to blow.

"You know what I want," he said after blowing the lash. She recoiled, instinctively maintaining some physical distance between them.

"Did you know that your eyes aren't actually blue?" she eventually said.

"You haven't changed. Still diverting conversations and situations with random facts."

"I don't do that."

"You do. But hey, at least you're putting your master's in evolutionary biology to use. And yes, I know my eyes aren't really blue. You've mentioned it before."

"No, I didn't. Did I?"

"Many times. You know, blue pigment is rare in nature. No vertebrate produces blue pigment. Wavelengths and all that," he teased, mimicking her.

She couldn't recall ever discussing his eyes, but that wasn't surprising. She adored his eyes not because of their color, but because they were uniquely captivating. Perhaps it was because they were his, or perhaps it was the soft shade of blue they possessed—cerulean and warm, reminiscent of the ocean surrounding her island or the bright sky on a hot day. His eyes reminded her of home.

"I'm going to miss you, King Julien," she said after a long pause.

He took her hand and kissed it.

"I'm going to miss you too, Stalker."

* * *

THE WARM JANUARY wind welcomed her as she stepped off the plane. After enduring twenty-one hours of travel and numerous stopovers, she had finally arrived home. Francis enveloped her in a tight embrace as soon as he saw her, and she melted into it as if seeking refuge. Refuge from the chaos that had consumed her week, refuge from thoughts of O'Neil.

"Welcome home!"

"You guys, get a room," Omali said with disgust, still glued to her phone.

Rob kissed him passionately, as if she were trying to prove something, yet whatever she sought to feel remained elusive. With a smile, he pressed their foreheads together.

"I missed you," she said.

"Let's go home."

* * *

THINGS DIDN'T FALL into place as she had planned. She believed that distance alone would erase thoughts of O'Neil. It was meant to. Yet, two weeks had slipped by, and he still occupied her mind. She'd been forthcoming with Francis, divulging every detail of the time spent with O'Neil and even suggesting a break-up. After all, even if she hadn't acted on it, she had thought about it and wanted it. Though Francis was disappointed, her promise never to see O'Neil again provided him reassurance.

She confided in her friends as well, but not to the same extent. Her friends knew what she had gone through seven years ago. Admitting to certain things was embarrassing. Makeba hugged her, while Angelina wanted, albeit jestingly, to knock some sense into her. Despite it all, she convinced herself that everything was fine. Everything was supposed to be fine. O'Neil belonged in her past.

He sent messages that she chose to ignore, battling against every urge to respond. In the end, she decided to block his number, recognizing that her willpower would only hold out for a few days.

She was supposed to go back to her old life, to banish thoughts of him, but nothing stayed the same. She found herself pouring extra passion into her relationship with Francis, attempting to compensate for the lack of genuine emotion she felt. Each kiss with Francis triggered images of O'Neil in her mind, and as he lay atop her, she would close her eyes, picturing O'Neil's body instead. Waking up beside Francis, she couldn't shake the disappointment of not finding O'Neil there. It was a painful and cruel secret she kept to herself, striving to push thoughts of him away as much as possible. Out of sight, out of mind—or so they say. But it wasn't just her sight; his scent lingered, haunting her every waking moment. His winter fragrance, Ombre Nomade, seemed to permeate every article of clothing she had worn that week, resisting even her most diligent washing efforts. That nomadic shadow relentlessly pursued her, infiltrating her thoughts and robbing her of focus. She found herself inhaling the aroma from her clothes, reminiscing about the warmth of his embrace against her skin. To ease her guilt, she immersed herself in physical intimacy with Francis, having sex as much as he could, kissing him, touching him, hoping to drown out the memories, hoping to feel something, anything.

THE MONITOR

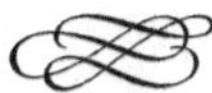

The plane was scheduled to arrive around 3 p.m., as Rob had been informed via e-mail from Alice Cooper, a colleague in James' department. At 3 p.m., Rob knocked on Angelina's office door.

"Ange, could you take me to the airfield?" she asked.

"Right now? I'm in the middle of something."

"Yes, the plane is set to land at 3:11 o'clock."

"Can't they just walk to the house? It's not very far."

"They've been traveling since yesterday. They're exhausted."

"You really should learn to drive. I can't keep being your chauffeur. You're not paying me for that."

"Please," Rob pleaded, her eyes widening like a child's.

"Fine. Let me save my work, and I'll be ready in a minute."

It was twenty-seven degrees outside. The windows of the pick-up were rolled down, allowing the coastal wind to tousle their braided hair. In less than ten minutes, they reached the "airport", though Príncipe only possessed an airfield and a modest structure for passenger check-ins.

The small aircraft, with a maximum capacity of thirty passengers, soon landed on San Antonio's soil. From her vantage point, she observed the passengers disembarking, scanning the crowd for Alice, whom she had only seen in a photo on her email profile. She squinted behind her prescription glasses with tinted lenses, straining to recognize any familiar faces. They should stand out amidst the primarily local passengers—individuals visiting family in Príncipe, residents returning home, and traders. Two white persons would undoubtedly catch her eye.

That's when she noticed him descending from the plane. She attempted to approach, but Angelina grabbed her hands.

"Where do you think you're going?" Angelina said. "We can't go any further."

"I think they're here."

"Yeah, and you think they're going to abandon society and start living in the airfield? Just wait. They'll come out soon."

"Ange… I think it's him," she whispered, the words carrying a weight she hoped would prove unfounded.

"Him? What are you talking about?"

"O'Neil. I think he's here."

"No way. That motherfucker wouldn't dare," Angelina scoffed.

"I'm telling you, it's him."

"Your myopia is playing tricks on you. You think too much about this guy. Forget about him."

Angelina's words provided a fleeting comfort. She embraced that falsehood which momentarily eased the relentless pounding of her heart. She replayed the lie in her mind, attempting to persuade herself, but her brain remained steadfast. In a matter of minutes, any hope of her being mistaken would be shattered.

"That's O'Neil," she uttered as he approached. Despite her efforts, her feet felt anchored to the ground, rendering her immobile.

"Oh, that's him?" Ange asked. Rob nodded. "Come!" Ange said. Sensing Rob's unresponsiveness, she reached for her hands. "You're okay," she affirmed.

"I have never left an airport so quickly in my life," O'Neil said, taking off his sunglasses.

"What are you doing here?" Angelina asked, directing her gaze at O'Neil.

"You must be Angelina. Rob told me about you. She also punched me for you."

"Why are you here?" she asked again.

"I'm the monitor. Alice and I will be working with you."

"You don't get to just…"

"Ange, could you please show Alice to the car? Alice, it's nice to finally meet you," Rob said.

"Likewise. I can't wait for us to start working together," Alice said.

She waited for the two to move away so that she could talk to O'Neil. Her legs more relaxed, she marched slowly to a corner.

"What are you doing here?"

"I told you, I'm the monitor. I know how important this project is to you, so I made the request to become the monitor. I talked to James. He helped me."

"Oh, is he doing okay?"

"He is doing better. Rehabilitation, eating soup, taking it slowly. Anyway, he recommended me to his boss and I'm going to be honest with you, there weren't many contenders. Most people don't want to come to a small unknown country in Africa. If I hadn't applied, they would've chosen someone who would be forced to be here, so out of spite, they would act in bad faith to fuck up everything you're trying to accomplish."

"I appreciate it, I swear I do. But I told you I didn't want to see you anymore."

"No, you said we wouldn't see each other anymore. Not that you didn't want to see me."

"It's the same. O'Neil, you know what you are to me. I can't…"

"And you know what you are to me. I messed up seven years ago. I'm not going to…"

"I'm in a relationship. I love Francis."

"I'm not going to force you to do anything. Now can we go? I'm very hot, I'm sweating even in parts I didn't know sweat."

The silence inside the vehicle mirrored the tension of the moment, but the ordeal would soon come to an end. In under ten minutes, they reached their destination. Angelina parked the car without uttering a word, but she noticed zero initiative from the two of them to get out of the car.

"So are you two not getting out?" she asked, annoyed.

"Oh, are we here yet?" Alice asked, surprised.

"I'm sorry, I didn't know we'd arrived," O'Neil said.

They retrieved their suitcases and followed Rob into the accommodation she had arranged for them, funded by TUF. Angelina remained in the car as Rob guided them to the residence—a three-bedroom house boasting a swimming pool and top-notch amenities.

"The house is exactly like the photos I sent. It has three bedrooms; you can choose yours."

"I'll take the room with the sea view."

"All the rooms have a sea view."

She guided them through the house, showcasing the well-equipped kitchen, the enormous living room, the cozy bedrooms, and the outdoor area complete with an outside kitchen, swimming pool, and vegetable garden. She let them choose their respective rooms and handed them their keys.

"Here are the keys to the gate, common areas, and your respective rooms. This smaller key is for the generator, which is near the outdoor kitchen. You are one of the only people here on the island to have a generator."

"A Generator? What for?" he asked.

"Power outages are common in the country. I..."

"Oh, yeah, that's a common problem in Africa. During my time in Chad, I experienced them frequently," Alice said.

"I don't know how frequent the outages will be. There's no warning or timetable. It happens and we deal with it. The generator has a good capacity, though it doesn't kick in automatically when the power goes out. One of you will have to go outside and use the key to start it. It's an older model but it's one of the best in the country. It runs on gasoline. The accommodation budget from TUF is sufficient to cover the fuel costs. It has a good reserve, but I recommend using electricity sparingly, on essentials like water and internet during outages. Sometimes gasoline can be scarce in the country."

"This is too much information," O'Neil said. "You'll have to explain to me how this all works later."

"I'll send someone."

"I knew the country was small, but I didn't realize it was this tiny," Alice said.

"Yeah, the country is small, but Príncipe is even smaller. It's only 142 square kilometers, and most of it is forest. The living area is even tinier."

"So, it's like Disneyland in Florida," Alice said.

"Yeah, size wise, almost that. The population is around six thousand here. That's why I need you to be careful. There have been people, foreigners who have caused trouble."

"Don't worry, we'll be on our best behavior," he said, giving her a playful wink.

"I'll leave you to settle in now. Feel free to take a shower, rest. You both have my number, and I've also bought local phone numbers for you. They're on the kitchen table. When you're ready, send me a text. My organization only has one car in Príncipe, and it's the one we used to pick you up from the airport. We mostly get around on foot here. Everything is nearby. Besides, the roads are very bad as you could see for yourself. It's quicker to get around on foot."

"Sounds good to me. I'm fine with walking," he said.

"Yeah, walking works for me too," Alice chimed in.

. . .

She left the house with a heavy heart, the weight of uncertainty pressing down on her shoulders. She closed the door behind her, took a deep breath and made her way to the car.

Angelina was standing outside, engaged in a phone call. Catching sight of Rob, she quickly dismissed the person on the other end.

"It's all set?" Angelina asked.

"I don't know what to do, Ange," Rob confessed, her voice tinged with apprehension.

"What do you mean you don't know what to do?" Angelina asked as they settled into the car.

"I still..." she trailed off. The shame that accompanied the admission of her feelings for him was almost suffocating. Acknowledging them to herself felt shameful enough, but to confess them to Angelina would be unbearable. Angelina had witnessed her at her most vulnerable, in the aftermath of O'Neil's sudden disappearance from her life. Rob had always prided herself on being the epitome of strength. Despite life's trials, she had always managed to persevere. But seven years ago, she had crumbled. She stopped eating, abandoned her job, and withdrew into the confines of her apartment whose rent she had stopped paying. She was also diagnosed with severe depression. Eventually, she was evicted. All this upheaval, all for a man. The mere thought of it made her skin crawl. If she could, she would erase every trace of that dark period, every memory of the person she refused to acknowledge as herself. She left her job at *Les Enfants de Demain* and returned to her homeland. It was then that Angelina took her in and nurtured her back to life. Months later, she founded her organization.

"Gosh, I hate him," Rob said, the bitterness evident in her tone. It wasn't a lie. Despite her love for him, there was an equal measure of hatred.

"God knows I won't judge you for it," Angelina reassured her.

"I don't know how to tell Francis about this."

"I know you two had dinner, but it wasn't a big deal. Even though I warned you against going to dinner with him. Dinner is too intimate, especially with someone like him. Now, I understand that maybe you needed to do this, but it could have been lunch," Angelina said her long version of I told you so.

If only she knew...

Angelina didn't know all of it, but Francis did. Rob had confessed, disclosing every detail—from the dinner to the conversations, the hugs, and the almost kiss at the airport. He knew, but he accepted it only because he believed O'Neil was gone from their lives for good.

THE VILLAIN

As she left work that evening, Rob's mind was still grappling with how to deliver the news to Francis. Upon arriving home, she quickly showered and gathered Francis' house keys. Before heading out, she knocked on Omali's bedroom door.

"Hey Mali, I'm going to see Francis, okay? There's food in the fridge," she said.

"Are you staying the night?"

"Just be good. I'm trusting you."

Francis was an obstetrician-gynecologist at the solidarity clinic established by Candjá in Príncipe. Rob prepared a meal for him and awaited his return. As she heard the gate opening, she rushed to the door, surprising him. The exhaustion etched on his face quickly dissolved upon realizing her presence.

"What are you doing here?" he asked, enveloping her in a tight hug and kissing her.

"Can't a girl surprise her man anymore?" she teased.

"You've been surprising me a lot lately."

"Not complaining, are you?" she quipped.

"Not complaining at all."

"Go take a shower. Dinner's ready."

"What did you make?"

"Your favorite."

As he freshened up, she set the table. They enjoyed their meal together, discussing their respective days and work. As she cleared away the dishes, he broached the subject of the new monitor.

"So, how was it? Did you get a good vibe from him? He might not be James, but maybe he'll be helpful." She paused, silently pondering her response as she began washing the dishes. "That bad, huh?" He surmised, wrapping his arms around her. "Let me take care of the dishes tomorrow. Oh, and guess what? Lili is bringing me crabs. I'll prepare them for you on Saturday."

She rinsed the suds from her hands and turned to him.

"Thank you," she said.

"Come with me," he urged, his eyes twinkling with mischief.

"Where are you taking me, Francisco?"

"To the bedroom. You smell too good," he replied with a grin, pulling her playfully along.

"You can't keep pulling this line every time."

She performed for him, as she had been doing ever since her return from Geneva. She straddled and rode him while he traced the contours of her breasts. Afterward, they lay side by side, both naked, both succumbing to the stifling heat of the country's humid climate. He reached out, intertwining his fingers with hers, and together they stretched their arms into the air, savoring the intimacy of the moment.

"You make me so happy."

"I'm glad I do," she said.

She was certain she loved him. She was supposed to be attracted to him, too. He hadn't changed; he was still her type. The same man she'd encountered four years ago at the São Tomé hospital during her gynecologist consultation. Handsome, perhaps too handsome for a doctor, some would say. Like many doctors in the country, he had returned from Cuba after twelve years of rigorous training, which had molded him into the exceptional doctor he was. Having been in the country for only four months, he still spoke with a soft Cuban accent that she found endearing. She enjoyed the way her name rolled off his tongue.

In a small country like theirs, their paths crossed repeatedly until the day he finally asked her out. Both Makeba and Angelina encouraged her to give it a try, treating it as an experiment. She agreed but was upfront with him about her lingering heartbreak and her uncertain readiness for a relationship. He assured her he could be patient, and he was. They remained friends for a year, during which time they also began working together when she invited him to join the first solidarity clinic on the main island. Then, tragedy struck when her mother passed away, and he stood by her side through it all. From that point on, their connection deepened, and the rest became history. Sometimes she wondered if her mother's passing hadn't occurred, would she be with him?

"I know I've asked this before, and you said you weren't ready, but maybe now is the moment. What do you think about us moving in together?" he asked.

"You mean in Príncipe?"

"Well, yeah. We've been living here for two years already. Do you think you're going to go back to living in São Tomé?"

"I don't know. I haven't thought about that."

"But we need to start thinking about these things. We could buy or build a house together either in Príncipe or São Tomé."

"You're still okay with me not wanting children, right?" she asked, her thoughts drifting back to a topic that had surfaced at the beginning of their relationship. She had been transparent about her lack of desire to have children. It wasn't that she was entirely opposed to the idea; rather, she simply couldn't envision herself as a mother. She would have children if she was a man, with lesser disruptions and greater autonomy. But she was a woman, and nature and society treated her differently. If it were only biological constraints, she could have made concessions. She could have sacrificed her body for nine months, or she could have adopted. But it was the social constraints of motherhood that gave her pause. In her country, women were often relegated to the role of primary parent, while men could easily opt out of parenthood, as they often did, without facing any consequences.

"Yeah. It's not like I have a choice. You sterilized yourself. And you don't want to adopt. But being with you is enough," he assured her, pulling her close in a comforting embrace.

She stayed silent, a thousand thoughts racing through her mind. She took a deep breath, bracing herself to deliver the news:

"O'Neil is the new monitor."

Her words hung in the air. Francis didn't react immediately, as if his brain struggled to process the implications of Rob's revelation.

"What do you mean O'Neil is the new monitor?" he finally asked, sitting down and fixing his gaze on her.

"Yeah, I don't know what to tell you. He's the monitor."

"You said you wouldn't see him again."

"I know what I said."

"So that's why you've been all affectionate? You've been preparing me for this?"

"What? I just learned it this morning. I had no idea. If I knew or if I had any say on the matter..."

"Then what are we going to do? What are you going to do? I know you like him; I know that, and I was okay with that because he wasn't going to be part of our lives anymore."

"I didn't choose this."

"Then we give the money back."

"What? You can't be serious."

"I don't know what to say. I don't know what to think. We made a pact."

"I know this isn't ideal. I didn't want this either."

"Are you sure? Are you sure you don't want to consummate whatever you started in Geneva?"

"You know I would never cheat on you. This much you must know about me. I'm not happy about this either and I don't know what to do. I can't control the fact that he is here, and I also can't control the thoughts in my head."

"Put yourself in my position. This guy wants you, and you still have feelings for him. What am I? I'm the villain in your story. I'm the obstacle that prevents you from being together."

"I don't want to be with him."

"Well, whatever you want, I won't be in your way anymore."

With those words, he turned away, signaling his resignation.

"You're being serious? This is not you."

"I'm tired, Rob. I don't know what to do. This guy was supposed to be out of our lives. I can't even be mad at you because technically you didn't do anything wrong. So I'm going to be mad at myself for being in this situation."

Rob scanned the room for her clothes, quickly gathering them up and dressing before wordlessly leaving Francis's house.

NICE TO MEET YOU!

The next morning, as was her routine, she rose early and headed to the gym. Her eyes darted around the gym in search of Francis. Not finding him there unsettled her, but she pressed on with her exercises, determined to harness the endorphins she so desperately needed. As she left the house later that morning, she still couldn't shake the disbelief that O'Neil was just a five-minute walk away. In those mere minutes, her heart would race, her body would betray her with a desire that would consume her thoughts. The fever of longing surged through her veins at the mere thought of him—his presence, his scent.

She pressed the intercom at the gate and waited. When he finally appeared, standing shirtless at the door in sweatpants that hung low on his hip bone, her body ignited with a heat she couldn't quench. His lean, muscular physique stirred sensations within her that defied description. Despite her efforts, she couldn't tear her gaze away from the enticing triangular shaped curve that contoured his lower abdomen.

"Hey, look up," he said, toothbrush in hand.

She quickly diverted her gaze, feigning nonchalance.

"Good morning!" she replied, though she sensed her eyes lingering where she wished they wouldn't.

"Come in."

"How did you sleep?"

"I was exhausted yesterday. Took a shower and crashed for twelve hours straight. Then I woke up around 4 a.m., reheated some food, and chowed down. Your bread is very light, by the way. But the stew? Amazing."

"Yeah, our wheat flour bread is not great. We do have some that are great. It's made with cassava flour or cornmeal. But our regular bread is not good. You'll miss French bread for sure."

"I want to try your good breads then."

"Noted."

"I also took a stroll, jogged on the beach. This place is paradise."

"I'm glad you're enjoying yourself."

"Can we drop the professional act? Your responses feel a bit... Off."

"I'm not sure what you're expecting, O'Neil. I never thought we'd cross paths again."

"That's why I'm here. I can't just let you go."

"You can't just walk back into my life and..."

"I spoke to my father. He said if I'm sure you still love me, I shouldn't give up on us."

"That's your mistake, you talked with your father. He's crazy."

"He's not crazy. He's my kind of insane ride or die. You said it yourself."

"O'Neil, I don't love you," she said firmly.

"I don't believe you," he replied.

"Even if I did, since when is love enough? You better than anyone else should know love is not enough. You said you loved me seven years ago. It still wasn't enough. Love is not enough. It wasn't enough then and it's not enough now," she said.

"I won't know unless I risk it all. I need to start honoring my name. Brave people, right? And not to brag, I see the way you look at me."

"What are you talking about?"

"You want me."

"I don't."

"Who are you trying to convince, me or you?"

"Are you guys up already? It's 7 a.m.," said Alice, emerging from her room, wrapped in a sheet.

"Life starts at seven in the morning. That's when stores open, school starts, administrative work, and also work at my organization," Rob said.

"My God, nobody told me the weather was so humid here. I'm all wet," Alice said.

As he left the room, O'Neil leaned close and whispered in Rob's ear: "And she's not the only one."

Goosebumps prickled her skin, and her body felt feverish to the touch. The scent of his sweaty body ignited sensations she had never experienced before. A primal desire, an insatiable hunger seized her, urging her to taste the salt of his skin. She longed to run her tongue over every millimeter of his body. But she couldn't. He was so close, yet she couldn't have him. She tried to speak, but the words refused to leave her lips.

"I'm just finishing brushing my teeth and I'm going to have a shower. I'll be ready in a minute," he said as he walked to the bathroom.

A minute that became two hours. They arrived at the organization around nine o'clock due to O'Neil and Alice being late.

"So, this is the organization's building. It's not too far from your house. Nothing here is far. I picked you up today. From tomorrow on, you can come on your own."

"The HQ is smaller than I thought," remarked O'Neil, scanning the place.

"We don't call it that, come on. And it's bigger than it looks from the outside. This used to be an old 2-bedroom house that we transformed into our office. It accommodates all of us just fine. We have seven employees and around twenty volunteers, who assist us with various projects across the island. They help manage the solidarity clinic, handle accounting, cleaning, procurement, payments, billing, and occasional punctual projects. Candjá also intervenes in non-health-related areas as needed. We donate to schools and families, provide books, school supplies, and even cover uniform costs for students. Currently, we're planning a provision distribution in April for two isolated communities," she explained, then turned her attention to O'Neil, who was holding a notebook and pen. "What are you doing?"

"I'm just jotting down some notes."

"All this information is available on our website," Rob pointed out.

"Yeah, but I prefer to have my own notes."

"You still do that!" Rob said, smiling.

"So, you two know each other? I sensed something," Alice remarked.

"We used to work together," Rob said.

"So that's why you didn't want me to mention your name to her," Alice said to O'Neil.

"Anyway, let's head inside," Rob suggested, leading the way.

SHE OBSERVED HIM, holding his notebook and pen, with a sense of nostalgia. It reminded her of the qualities she used to admire in him—his meticulousness and organization. Back when they worked together, he was always diligent about taking notes, creating brochures to keep himself and others informed. He was a planner, always thinking ahead and preparing for any potential setbacks with backup plans upon backup plans, a stark contrast to her own personality. Rob wasn't one to rely on notes or adhere to strict organizational routines.

She introduced them to Angelina first.

"This is Angelina's office," Rob announced, gesturing towards her. "You already know Angelina. She's the cornerstone of our operation, our bookkeeper, responsible not just for Príncipe but for overseeing the finances across all our offices. We have six offices in the six districts in São Tomé and this one in Príncipe. Dina recently joined to assist with our growing workload. You'll be working closely with them. Every penny, every digit, it all flows through them. Dina, Ange, this is Alice and O'Neil."

O'Neil waved, flashing a grin.

"So, I'm tasked with babysitting these two?" Angelina said in Forro, her expression skeptical.

"It's not like we have a choice. Please, be nice," Rob pleaded.

"With this one? Never," Angelina replied.

"Are you speaking Lunguyè?" O'Neil chimed in.

Angelina sighed, rolling her eyes.

"We don't speak Lunguyè," Rob said.

"But I thought in Príncipe, you guys speak Lunguyè," Alice joined the conversation.

"Yeah, but Dina, Angelina, and I are from São Tomé. We can't speak Lunguyè. But the rest of our team is from Príncipe. If you want to learn Lunguyè, just talk to them. I'll introduce you."

"So, you were speaking Forro?" O'Neil asked.

"Yes," Rob confirmed.

"And 'Candjá' is a Forro word?" Alice asked, their curiosity irking Angelina.

"Yes."

"Right, because I saw on your website that it means 'light' in your native tongue. But then you have four native tongues."

"Yeah, but I only speak Forro. Many people here speak at least two of our languages, but I only speak one," said Rob.

"You also speak the Cape Verdean crioulo," O'Neil said.

"Barely. I mostly understand it."

"You sing it too."

"Alright, are we done with this part?" she said, her annoyance palpable. They nodded, prompting her to lead them to meet the rest of the team.

In the afternoon, she took them to the solidarity clinic located further north on the island. O'Neil took precautions, covering his body with sunscreen, appearing paler than usual under its protective veil. They took advantage of the opportunity to ride along with Fehér, an employee of Candjá, who was scheduled to deliver medical supplies to the clinic later that afternoon. Midway, Rob's stomach began to churn, the onset of motion sickness making itself felt with increasing intensity. Despite the brevity of the ride, it was marred by the jolting movements caused by the rutted roads, riddled with potholes. Yet, it wasn't just the rough terrain that unsettled her stomach. The looming prospect of encountering Francis at the clinic weighed heavily on her mind. She wanted to see him, yet a cacophony of doubts clamored within her, suggesting that bringing O'Neil might not be wise. But she found herself without recourse; she was doing her job and part of it was to arm O'Neil with the necessary information to fulfill his role of monitoring their activities and reporting back on the utilization of funds provided by TUF.

Rob had made prior arrangements, requesting the staff to convene in the break room upon their arrival. She promised to compensate them for their time with coconut biscuits and fish patties. Upon entering the room, she introduced O'Neil and Alice to the assembled team, who shared in refreshments of cajamanga juice, coconut biscuits, and fish patties. Despite the full room, she couldn't help but notice that not everyone was there, including Francis. She broached the subject with caution, careful not to allude to her strained relationship with him.

"I notice a few faces missing. Where is Doctor Ana Bela?"

"She is currently in surgery with her team."

"And what about Francis? Is he here?" she inquired further.

"I think he's seeing a patient."

After mustering her courage, flanked by Alice and O'Neil, she rapped on Francis's office door.

"Come on in," came the response.

She pushed the door open. Francis was engrossed in conversation with a patient.

"Sorry to interrupt," she said apologetically.

"No worries. Ms. Carla was just leaving," Francis assured, escorting the very pregnant woman out before gesturing for them to enter.

"Francis, this is Alice and O'Neil. They're the monitors I mentioned to you," she introduced, as Francis extended his hands for a handshake with Alice and O'Neil.

"Nice to meet you two."

"Nice to meet you."

"Nice to meet you, too," O'Neil said. "Rob told me a lot about you."

"Right..."

"What is your specialty?" Alice asked.

"I'm an OB/GYN."

"Francis is the chief of the OB/GYN department."

"Rob is exaggerating."

"I'm not. He is amazing. He is my OB/GYN."

"That's great because I'll need one."

"We are two doctors in this mini department, there is Angela and me. You have the choice."

"I think I've made my choice," Alice said, smiling.

"Is Angela back? I thought she was still in São Tomé," Rob said.

"She'll be back tomorrow."

"Angela is Angelina's twin sister," Rob clarified.

"So what do you do, Alice?" Francis asked.

"I have a background in communication. I work at TUF as a liaison officer between the organizations across the world and TUF. My department is in charge of finding people doing great work and supporting them. I've been working there for only a year, so this is actually my first experience. But I've worked on the ground before, with UNICEF."

"That's very interesting. What about you? It's O'Neil, right?"

"Yes. I'm a lawyer. I work at HR."

"Strange! I wonder how a lawyer who works at HR got chosen for this monitoring position."

"What can I say? I excel in many areas."

"Right. Anyway, I won't be of much help for any of you, but my door is always open."

"Thank you, Francis."

As she turned to leave, he reached out and took her hand.

"Can I talk to you, Rob? Alone?" he asked.

"Could you please wait for me in the break room?" Rob instructed O'Neil and Alice. O'Neil left, clearly annoyed.

"I..." they both began simultaneously, cutting each other off.

"You first," she offered.

"I'm sorry about last night. I was stupid. That's it. I don't even have another excuse. I didn't mean it when I asked you to give up the money. God knows how much this money is going to help us. I was just jealous and I..." he trailed off.

She embraced him tightly, planting a kiss on his lips.

"I'm sorry. I swear to you, I didn't know he was going to be the monitor. I swear I didn't know."

"I know. Can we have dinner tonight?" he asked.

"Tonight's going to be a little complicated. I need to babysit the two of them. But tomorrow, I'm all yours."

"Promise?"

"I promise," she replied, sealing it with another kiss. "I've got to go now. I love you."

"I love you too."

She then headed to the waiting room to collect Alice and O'Neil.

"Are you and Dr. Francis a thing?" Alice asked.

"We've been together for three years," Rob said.

"I knew it. I told you, O'Neil."

"Enough about my life. We're going to work now. Angelina will give you all the information you need, including all the expenses we've made so far with TUF funds," Rob redirected the conversation.

Alice appeared eager, while O'Neil seemed less enthusiastic.

ISLANDERS

After various unforeseen challenges, technical glitches, and three days of the typical torrential rain so prevalent in the country, Sunday finally granted Rob the opportunity to ferry O'Neil to the island she had purchased for her women's clinic. The brief voyage aboard the small fishing boat spanned no more than twenty minutes. Ms. Candida dropped them off in the afternoon, promising to return to collect them in three hours. Given the islet's small size, three hours would be more than enough time.

Armed with the clinic's blueprint and several architectural sketches, Rob led the way, O'Neil trailing behind. They didn't have to trek far before encountering the skeletal framework of the site, some sections more developed than others. Rob elucidated the project, outlining what had been accomplished with the allocated funds and what remained unfinished. O'Neil captured images and posed inquiries for his monthly report.

After an hour, it started to rain. The rain, initially innocuous, intensified, compelling them to seek refuge in a storage area where construction materials and supplies were housed, along with the personal effects of the bricklayers and other workers.

Rob attempted to contact Francis multiple times without success, the already weak service on the islet deteriorating further with the rain.

"You're just wasting your time. They won't come. The fishing canoe wouldn't survive this storm. We're stuck here," O'Neil's voice echoed against the walls of the makeshift shelter, his figure sprawled atop stacked cement bags concealed beneath a tattered cloth.

"I can't. I can't be stuck here."

"Come here."

She hesitated, her resolve faltering momentarily before she reluctantly accepted his offer and settled into the space he had prepared.

The silence enveloped them like a suffocating blanket, their hearts heavy with unspoken words. She reclined on her back, mirroring his posture, her gaze fixed on the ceiling, maintaining a discreet distance between them. Occasionally, she fidgeted with her cellphone, attempting to call Omali.

"You'll run out of battery."

"Fuck... My luck, right?"

"There was a time we would laugh about stuff like this."

"Yeah, and there was a time you masturbated to KK's supposedly leaked video. Good thing we've changed."

"What? Wait... I was just, I was making conversation. How'd that turn into an attack? And I told you, I was fifteen. Fifteen when I did that. A stupid, horny fifteen, lacking understanding of consent."

"I will never not remind you of that."

"What about you? You used to drool over skinny guys, fantasizing about sitting on their faces."

"To be fair, I told you I only drooled over Stromae, not just any skinny guy."

"We talked so much shit without filters."

"30% of our conversations were flirty and sex. 30% were politics and ideas. 30% were us laughing at random things and making fun of people, especially our bosses. Gosh, do you remember Rebecca? She was such a bitch."

"She is German, what did you expect?"

"I'll never not love that white-on-white hatred."

"What was the remaining 10%?"

"Miscellaneous? I don't know."

She tried Omali's number again, but no luck.

"She'll be fine. You stress too much. If I fretted over Paule-Anne like you do over Omali, I'd have had two heart attacks by now."

"You and Paule-Anne only have a two-year gap. Omali and I have sixteen. It's not quite the same."

"Still."

"You wouldn't understand."

"Try me."

"She is doing better now, but she still has these moments, these… I don't know. I don't think she likes me very much. It's not her fault, I left her. I think she resents me. I try my best, but I don't think my best is enough."

"Where is your mom?"

"Oh… My mom passed away. I thought I told you."

"Oh my god, Rob, no you didn't tell me."

"Yeah, three years ago."

"Really?"

"Yeah."

"So that's why she's living with you."

"It's either me or her deadbeat father who didn't even bother to look after her. That man was suing my mother when she was alive, trying to get custody of Omali. But as soon as my mother died, he didn't want anything to do with her. He was only suing her out of spite because she had left him."

"I'm sorry. You never spoke a lot about her. I know you two weren't close, but the death of a parent is always heartbreaking."

"Not everyone has a picture-perfect relationship with their parents like you. Is your mom, okay?"

"Yeah, she's fine. Enjoying her retirement. Trying to get my dad to exercise."

"I'm glad. I'll tell her you've denied her more than Peter denied Jesus."

"She'd adore you."

"Of course you'd say that... What about your grandma?"

"She died."

"Oh, I'm sorry."

"It's alright. We knew it was going to happen. I think I told you about her cancer."

"Yeah, you did. I just... I hoped the treatments would work."

"No, she didn't make it."

"I know how much she meant to you."

"She was the first person I confided in about you. She was the one who made me realize I was in love with you because I couldn't shut up about you."

"You never told me this."

"Well, I didn't tell you many things. She thought I was going to marry you. She used to tease me by singing *"Nem As Paredes Confesso"* while we cooked, insisting I should tell you how I felt."

"Yeah, you told me she loved Fado."

"Now, every time I listen to Amélia Rodrigues, tears just flow. Even if I smile, they're there. Grief is strange."

"It is. But you two loved each other. She was happy, wasn't she?"

"We went to a Mariza concert a few months before she passed. Mariza covered *"Uma Casinha Portuguesa"*, her favorite song. She didn't see me getting married, but at least I gave her that moment. After she passed, I called off my engagement. I guess I was just forcing myself because I knew she wanted to see me get married."

The shift in his tone, the tremor in his vocal cords, and the shimmer of tears in his eyes conveyed the depth of his sadness. Rob reached out, tenderly brushing her foot with his own.

"I'm sorry."

"It's alright. She was happy. She led a full life, without regrets. That's more than most people can say. That's more than I can say."

"You're still young. Plenty of time to live a full life with few regrets."

"Can I say something else?"

"We're talking. You can say anything."

"I'm glad we're stuck here. I'm glad Alice is feeling sick. At least I have a chance to talk to you alone. These last two weeks have been torture," he said.

"I don't know what you expect from me."

"Look how far you are from me. You can't even lay near me."

"I can't. I'm in a relationship."

"Do you love me?"

"I told you; love is not enough."

"Do you love me, though?"

"It doesn't matter."

"It's a yes or no question."

"What if I loved you?"

"Do you?"

"Yes, I do. What does that change?" she said, her voice shaky.

He embraced her tightly, holding her close.

"Thank you. I needed to hear that from you. I needed to be sure."

"I still can't be with you," she said, her voice muffled in that hug, her heart heavy with unspoken words. The rain outside mirrored the storm in her heart, each drop adding to the turbulence within.

He gazed deeply into her eyes, the warmth of his breath sending shivers down her spine.

"I love you. And I'm not giving up."

"I can't be with you. I can't just erase everything I went through after you left. I can't accept it, I just can't. You're... Too close," she replied, her voice trembling with a mix of longing and apprehension.

"I want to kiss you," he whispered, his lips tantalizingly close to hers.

"We can't. I can't."

"Why not?" he pressed, his voice soft but insistent.

She opened her eyes, pulling back slightly, her cheeks flushed, her body ablaze.

"You say you love me," she began, her voice shaky yet resolute. "That means you love the person I am. Would you love a cheater? A disgusting, selfish person with no morals or empathy?" She paused, waiting for his response. Silence lingered between them. "Then don't try to make me one. I won't cheat on Francis. I'd rather stand in the rain than risk destroying everything I believe in, everything I am. You know how I feel about you. Please, don't use that against me, to push me into something I'll regret and resent both of us for."

As she spoke, she couldn't shake the feeling of guilt washing over her. The desire pulsating within her, the physical response to his nearness, her hardened nipples, the wetness in her cunt, the rush of emotions she felt for him—all of it made her feel like she was betraying Francis. With every beat of her heart, with every flicker of longing in her soul, she felt the weight of her infidelity. She knew, deep down, that she was straying from the commitment she had made. She was teetering on the edge of moral compromise, and there was no escaping that truth. All she could do was cling to the remnants of her integrity, striving to preserve what little remained.

"I'm sorry. You're right," he conceded, his voice tinged with remorse.

She parted from his side and retreated to the makeshift area she had arranged earlier. Despite her efforts, finding a comfortable position amidst the plastic and soiled fabric proved futile. To exacerbate matters, every movement seemed to disturb the makeshift bed, producing unwelcome noises.

"We can share this space. We're adults. We can control ourselves," he suggested, attempting to ease the tension.

She resettled onto the sacks of cement, widening the gap between them. They exchanged a knowing smile.

"We're idiots," she said.

"How did you fall for me? I just don't get it. You're so amazing, you deserve someone equally amazing. It makes sense for you to be with a doctor," he mused.

"A lawyer is also impressive. And it's even more amazing that you changed paths and worked in departments that have nothing to do with your academic background," she countered.

"I like it that you see something in me that I don't see in myself."

"Your wit and your kindness. That's what I fell for."

"When did you fall for me?"

"Why?" she evaded.

"I just want to know. I want to know how long it took me to figure it out."

"Actually, in Brest. And you approached me first, so you are also to blame. Actually, you are to blame in every possible way," she teased.

"Me? How?" he asked, amused in her playful accusation.

"You don't get to approach a girl and be funny and kind and insightful, and have similar values and ideas about the world, and discuss destroying capitalism and not expect her to fall in love. By the end of our first day together, I was fascinated, and I hadn't even seen your face," she recounted.

"Oh, that's true. The masks," he remembered.

"Yeah, covid was a weird time. So, by the end of day one, no matter what you looked like under that mask, I was already captivated."

"But you were pleasantly surprised, weren't you?" he prodded.

"Why are you fishing for compliments?"

"Just tell me I'm handsome."

"No matter what you looked like, for me, through my rose-colored glasses, you were the most handsome man that has ever lived."

"Yeah, but objectively, I'm handsome, right?"

"Fuck... Stop fishing for compliments," she said, playfully.

"Just say I'm handsome. I need validation from you."

"You're handsome. But I didn't think about that. I found you beautiful."

"So, you found me *bonita*?" he quipped.

"Very much so. And we kept on talking and texting. And one day I realized I was happy to go to work because of you. Seeing you there was enough to keep me going every day."

"I realized I loved you..." he began, but she interrupted, unwilling to delve into those emotions.

"I don't want to know it."

"Why?"

"Because... It doesn't matter. I don't want to create what if scenarios in my head."

They lapsed into silence; their gazes locked in a quiet exchange. A yawn escaped her, betraying the fatigue weighing heavily on her body.

"Come on, you're not gonna sleep, are you?"

"I'm exhausted. Work's been relentless. I barely slept last night."

"Why?"

"A legal setback. And my lawyer is not in the country right now. I can find another one, but it's too risky. She knows what we are doing, and she supports me."

"Where is she?"

"She went to Angola last Friday. She is visiting her sick sister.

She'll be back in a few weeks, which means everything will be shut for a few weeks more."

"What's the issue?"

"I can't even explain it. I've been poring over the documents over and over again, trying to make sense of it all."

"I could help."

"You studied European law. Can you do domestic law, especially from a country you know nothing about?"

"I don't know, but I bet I can understand more than a biologist," he quipped.

"Ouch."

"I've been doing my research on your country."

"Do you like what you've uncovered so far?"

"It made me realize how important your work is for your people. Rob, the work you're doing is amazing. You're amazing."

"Yeah, keep boosting my ego. I like that."

"I'm being serious though."

"We used to talk about these things, about change, minimizing harm, and confronting our complicity in the system. You shouldn't be that surprised. More than anyone, you knew how discontented I was at *Les Enfants de Demain*."

"I was discontented too, but I still didn't build anything. Talking is easy. Being intellectually engaged in change is easy. The hard part is doing the actual work."

"It got to a point where I was tired of having conversations. Of discussing things that could and should change, of discussing people who have the means but aren't doing anything. Discussing theories and engaging in debates became less of an exercise to find solutions and common ground to act and more an act of intellectual masturbation."

"Yeah, these are distractions."

"Exactly. We all can do something. My organization began with me visiting schools, distributing menstrual kits and educating kids on reproductive health and sexuality."

"I'm all talk then."

"We're all talk until we take action. I don't know. I'd wanted to do this for ages, but it took heartbreak and depression to push me because helping others made me feel better about myself. So, it wasn't entirely selfless."

"There's an argument to be made about people doing selfless things for selfish reasons."

"That's true. When I began, there were no selfish reasons. Finding personal fulfillment was just a side effect. But now, I don't know. This organization has given me access and influence. Power even. I know it's all fictitious and I'm still under others' thumbs… It's still more than I've ever had. You may not grasp it fully because your parents are well-off, and you haven't had to fight for the bare minimum. But for me, everything was a struggle, a fight. Now, my life is stressful and financially, I'm barely scraping by. I pay myself a small salary to survive. Yet, the position I hold matters. I matter. Maybe not in the grand scheme of things, and certainly not to most people, but within the microcosm of my existence, I do."

"I see the way your people look at you. They love you. And this might not mean much, but you've always mattered to me."

"Mtchiu," she sonoed him. "Stop playing," she laughed, slightly embarrassed.

"This thing you just did with your mouth. Tchip. What does it mean?"

"Oh, I sonoed you. We call it sono. It's a very weird Forro verb. It means so many things. Frustration, annoyance. Right now, it meant 'get out of here'. With friends, you can do it playfully. It can also be disrespectful, to show how little you care about someone or what they're saying. You never sono your parents unless you want to lose some teeth."

"So the meaning depends on the context."

"Mmhm. It can mean someone is vibing with you, like just

now, or someone doesn't care about you, but in a very disrespectful and nonchalant way."

"Sono."

"Yeah. I know people call it 'kissing teeth', but I don't get why. It involves the whole mouth movement and lips."

"Some people call it tsk-ing."

"I guess that's more accurate than tchip."

"Can you teach me?"

"Why would I teach you?"

"So, one day when we're old together and you tell me something I don't like, I can sono you."

She chuckled, brushing off his comment, though secretly she found it endearing.

"I don't know how to explain. I didn't learn it. I feel like I was born already knowing how to do it."

"Try me."

"Purse your lips like this."

"Like a duck?"

"Not quite. You know what? Try the duck, and then we'll see what happens."

She spent the rest of the afternoon attempting to teach him how to sono. They delved into conversations about the past and the future, discussing everything from movies and celebrities to life goals. It felt reminiscent of years ago, during their breaks, when they would talk and laugh so much that people mistook them for a couple. As evening fell and the rain persisted, by around seven p.m., they finally conceded that no one was coming. The intense darkness cloaked them, rendering even each other's faces invisible. After initially rebuffing the suggestion multiple times, as the small sounds of the night began to stir in the darkness, she relented and approached him.

"You're scared," he said.

"I'm not. I'm protecting you. If a white man dies on my island, in my company, my organization, my country, my people won't hear the end of it."

He touched her face, his fingers cold.

"You're very hot," he remarked. "Are you sick?"

"Let me be," she replied, feeling embarrassed by the fever of desire coursing through her body.

At least desire will keep me warm tonight.

* * *

THE NEXT MORNING, she awoke in a daze, momentarily startled as she faced him before recollecting the events of the previous night. O'Neil appeared serene in his slumber; his features so remarkably unspoiled that even the faint traces of his unibrow seemed endearing. His washed-out brown hair, suggesting a blonde childhood, invited her hands to travel between its strands. She caressed his face gently, mindful not to disturb his rest, but as she did so, her cell phone received a notification, rousing him from sleep.

"Hey!" he said, blinking his eyes open. His eyes bore a reddish tint, evidence of a night spent wearing contact lenses.

"Hey! You shouldn't sleep with your contact lenses" she said, her attention briefly diverted to her phone. "I'm getting notifications of messages and calls from yesterday."

"Is the service better now?"

"I think it's because the rain has stopped. I'm going to call Ms. Candida to come pick us up."

"I'm going outside."

After wrapping up her calls with Ms. Candida, Omali, and Francis, she joined O'Neil outside. He stood atop a scaffold, gazing out at the beach. With cautious steps, she ascended the scaffold and positioned herself beside him, sharing in the view of the tranquil shoreline.

"I came here to seduce you and then convince you to go back

to Switzerland with me. Or France I don't know. But now, I think I might stay here forever."

"I would never live in Europe again; you know that right? Feeling every single day of how I'm not welcome is not the way I want to spend the rest of my life. Besides, I like this. I like my country."

"I think I like your country too."

"You can stay here. Become an islander. We can be islanders together."

"And learn your weak-ass islander voodoo."

"Keep talking like this and your dick is gonna fall."

They shared a laugh.

"When am I going to visit São Tomé?"

"Next week. Angelina and I go to São Tomé every month and we try to visit the offices in at least three districts. It's completely random, without notice. It's so that we can control everything. I love my people, but I don't trust them. We have had a lot of cases of embezzlement. Don't write this on your report."

"I'm not sending any report without you reading and approving it first. I'm here for you, you know that right? In every sense."

As they waited for Ms. Candida, they indulged in the simple joys of exploring the islet and savoring the ripe star fruit from the bushes. Conversation flowed effortlessly between them, punctuated by bouts of laughter that echoed along the shoreline. She felt a pang of disappointment when she saw the canoe approaching. Reality began to infiltrate the happiness of those last moments. With a heavy heart, she realized it was time to be honest with Francis.

IT COULD ONLY BE YOU!

Francis stood on the dock, anxiously awaiting Rob's return. As she approached, he enveloped her in a tight embrace, the dampness of her clothes seeping into his. His lips found hers in a relieved kiss.

"I was so worried," he murmured against her skin.

"I'm okay."

"Let's go home," he said, gently taking her hand. She glanced back to see O'Neil watching her from a distance, longing evident in his gaze. She turned away, following Francis back home. Once there, she retreated to the shower, delaying the inevitable conversation that awaited her. Amidst the cascading water, she rehearsed the words she needed to say, anticipating Francis's questions and her responses. When the hot water ran out, she emerged, dressed in a T-shirt with a towel wrapped around her damp hair. She found Francis in the kitchen preparing breakfast.

"You didn't need to do that," she said.

"It's the least I can do," he replied, his gaze lingering on her.

Rob hesitated, grappling with the impending conversation that would irrevocably alter their lives. The prospect of the unknown filled her with trepidation.

"Can we talk?" she finally said, her voice trembling with uncertainty.

He regarded her with a puzzled expression, sensing the gravity of her request.

"Let me finish this first."

She settled onto the sofa in the living room, her pulse racing as though time itself were slipping away. Anguish gripped her soul tightly, knowing she was about to shatter someone's heart, and perhaps even her own. Minutes passed like eternities until he finally entered the room, wiping his hands on his apron. Though he wore a smile, she could sense the tension radiating from him. Francis, her dear Francis, was clearly on edge.

"Here I am," he quipped as he joined her on the sofa. "What's so urgent that it couldn't wait until after breakfast?" Rob drew in a steadying breath, her resolve faltering under his gaze. "Please don't look at me like that," he said, perhaps his intuition hinting at the imminent discussion.

"I love you, Francis. I really do."

"Are you breaking up with me?" His voice was steady, but there was a tremor beneath the surface, a hint of vulnerability that tugged at her heart.

"I didn't... I," Rob faltered, her carefully rehearsed speech crumbling in the face of his direct question. Her soliloquy under the shower had not prepared her for that. She met his gaze, searching for the right words, but they eluded her. "Yes," she finally managed to whisper, the weight of her admission hanging heavy in the air.

He brought his hands to his face, his expression a mixture of disbelief and resignation. For a moment, silence enveloped them as he grappled with the reality of her words. Then, with a heavy sigh, he turned to her.

"I've been making an effort, you know that, right? Ever since he came here, I've been upping my game. So none of that mattered."

Her heart ached at his words; at the pain she had caused him despite his efforts to bridge the gap between them.

"I'm so sorry. I wanted to be able to explain. Why didn't you ask me what happened yesterday?"

"Because I know what didn't happen. I know you didn't cheat on me."

"How do you know that?"

"Because I know you," he said, his gaze unwavering. "You're proud. You take a lot of satisfaction in the person you are and the things you've accomplished. And your image of yourself is the most important thing for you. You think of yourself as better than a cheater, so you would never be a cheater."

She received those words with surprise, struck by the realization that Francis truly saw her, knew her, in ways she hadn't fully comprehended. But this awareness only deepened her sense of guilt. Even if she hadn't acted on her feelings, the mere existence of her emotional betrayal weighed heavily on her conscience.

"You're right, I didn't sleep with him. I didn't kiss him. But deception doesn't have to be materialized. I'm deceiving you in many other ways. With my feelings," she admitted, her voice heavy with remorse.

"So you love him?" Francis asked, his tone strained.

"Yes," she replied, her voice barely above a whisper.

"Do you love me?"

"Yes."

"You love him, so what? It's going to pass."

"It's not that simple. It's not the same type of love. Besides, you are amazing, Francis. I'm not kidding, you are. I'm freeing you to find someone who will wholeheartedly love you. You deserve more than someone who thinks about someone else when they are with you."

"Don't make it sound like you're doing this for me. Like you're doing me a favor. You're not. You're doing this so you can be free to be with him," Francis countered, his frustration palpable.

"I don't want to be with him. I'm never going to be with him. I can't..." she began, her voice trembling as tears brimmed in her eyes. She quickly composed herself, stifling her emotions. After all, she was the one ending things. She didn't have the luxury of breaking down, especially when she anticipated Francis' response to her tears. She knew he would relent if he saw her cry, and that was not fair to him. "It's not about him, Francis. It's about me being honest with myself. I can't half love you. I can't kinda be with you. I can't be with you while being emotionally engaged with someone else."

He took a deep breath.

"Would you even be with me if your mom hadn't died? You were vulnerable, and I was there for you to lean on. It could've been anyone."

The realization that he also harbored such thoughts shattered her heart. All these years, he believed he was merely a convenient presence during her darkest hour, and that realization tore at her soul. She had pondered the same question herself at times, but to know he also wrestled with doubts saddened her deeply. How difficult it must have been for him to carry that burden, unsure of her love and genuine care for him?

"It could only be you, Francis," she replied, sidestepping the mention of her mother's passing. Although she too had wondered, she would never confess it. To do so would be too cruel, staining their memories with shadows of the past. It didn't matter how their relationship began. Their love was real. She loved him sincerely, and the circumstances of their start did not diminish that truth.

"Three years, Rob, three years. All for that man who had his chance with you and broke you." She remained silent, his words pressing down on her. "I hope it's worth it," he added, removing his apron. "I made you an omelet with micocó leaves, just the way you like it."

With that, he left. She stood there in silence for what felt like an eternity, unable to fully comprehend what had just transpired. Eventually, the tears came, streaming down her cheeks as she sank into the sofa in a fetal position. After some time, she mustered the strength to rise, wiping away her tears as she forced herself to eat the omelet he had prepared. Then, she turned to her work, burying herself in the tasks at hand to distract herself from the ache within.

THE UNIFORM OF DISCORD

As she busied herself in the kitchen, the sound of the door creaking open caught her attention. Omali attempted to slip into her room unnoticed, but Rob's sharp ears picked up the faint footsteps.

"Mali!" Rob called out.

"Yeah," came the hesitant reply.

"Come here. I'm in the kitchen."

"Let me change first."

Sensing the unease in Omali's tone, Rob approached and intercepted her before she could disappear into her room. Omali hurriedly attempted to conceal her school uniform, arranging her binder to shield her skirt.

"I didn't know you were going to be home," Omali muttered, her nerves palpable.

"Yeah, I worked from home today."

"Oh, okay. I…" she faltered, searching for words to fill the awkward silence while simultaneously attempting to unlock her bedroom door.

"I made dinner. Let me help you. Give me the binder," Rob

offered, taking the binder from her hands to assist her in opening the door.

"Thank you," Omali responded tersely, reclaiming the binder and quickly shutting herself inside her room. Confused by her abrupt behavior, Rob shrugged it off and returned to the kitchen. However, as she made her way back, the pieces of the puzzle began to fall into place. She knocked on Omali's door. When Omali finally opened the door, she was no longer wearing the skirt.

"Where is the skirt you wore to school today?" Rob asked, her tone firm.

"What the hell? You can't just barge in. I have rights, you know."

"Not when you're trying to hide your wrongs. Where is your skirt?" Rob pressed.

"What are you talking about? Are you crazy?" Omali shot back, attempting to deflect.

"Nice try. Accusing me of being crazy is getting old," Rob countered, her patience wearing thin.

"But you're acting crazy."

"No cellphone for a week then," Rob threatened, seizing Omali's cellphone from her bed.

"You can't do that!"

"Watch me," Rob said, determined to uphold her authority. As she turned to leave, she hoped Omali wouldn't call her bluff.

"Okay, okay… Here, take it," Omali relented, retrieving the hidden skirt from a nearby box and handing it over to Rob.

The skirt, a mandatory part of Omali's high school uniform, was a deep royal marine blue straight skirt supposed to reach her knees. But Omali's skirt was modified, almost leaving her cheeks exposed.

"What did you do to your uniform?

"It's very hot and humid right now," she replied defensively, her tone laced with irritation.

"You can't just change your school uniform. It's called a uniform for a reason," Rob admonished, trying to reason with her.

"So now you're also controlling my body. You know that these uniform rules are very misogynistic, right? Now you're going to say the teacher was right for saying that I'm asking for it. You're all the same."

"Sit down," Rob requested firmly, settling herself at the edge of Omali's bed. Omali hesitated, her defiance evident in her posture. Rob considered adding a polite 'please', but she knew it was crucial for Omali to recognize her as the authority figure in this situation. "Now!" she reiterated, her tone unwavering, silently praying that Omali would comply, unsure of what else to do.

Reluctantly, Omali pouted and finally sank down onto the bed.

"You don't need to tell me how the school has issues with misogyny. I know it very well myself. And no, you're not asking for anything. Your teacher is disgusting for saying that, and I want to know which one of them did it so I can have a word with them. Your clothes are never the instigator or a justification for anything. That's why I've never prohibited you from wearing whatever you wanted. But this is a uniform. It allows for a framework at school. You can wear whatever you want outside, and I'll never stop you, but in school, you need to respect the dress code," Rob explained, her tone firm but compassionate.

"These rules are applied in a very misogynistic way," Omali insisted, her voice trembling with frustration, employing the same word—misogynistic—, as if she had just learned it. "The guys can sag their pants, and no one says anything. Some of them even cut their pants into shorts, and no one bats an eye. But a girl from my class had her skirt a millimeter above her knees, and she was sent outside and given a three-day suspension. She wasn't trying to be a slut like the teacher said. She can't have a uniform made every year. Most students can't. She grew a bit taller. So all of us decided to do this to protest."

"Why didn't you tell me?"

"You have more important things going on. And it's not as if you actually care about what's going on in my life."

"Of course I care. There's nothing more important than you. You could've told me, and I would've helped. I'll talk to your school tomorrow."

"I was going to tell you later, but I got another suspension. Three days."

"I'll talk to them. You won't be missing any more school days. And I'm sorry you're going through this. But I'm proud of you for standing for what's right."

As Omali recounted her experiences at school, Rob couldn't shake the feeling that nothing had truly changed since her own school days. The institutional policies persisted in their deeply ingrained sexism, and perhaps unsurprisingly, given the pervasive influence of colonization's indoctrination in her country, racism too. Girls' behavior and attire were scrutinized relentlessly, while boys enjoyed far more freedom. The double standards were glaring—boys were mandated to keep their hair short, with braids and afros outright forbidden. However, exceptions were made for the few white students in the country, who could flaunt long hair regardless of gender. Mixed-race boys, too, were permitted curly locks, leaving only those with 'forro' hair subject to strict regulations. It was a system rife with bias that reminded everybody even unconsciously who got to be free and who did not. Despite her organization's efforts to intervene across various fronts, Rob couldn't shake the feeling of powerlessness in effecting real change. But if she couldn't change her country, at least when it came to Omali's situation, she could do something. She was going to have a word with the teacher as well as the director of the school.

As they sat down to dinner, Rob broached the difficult topic of her separation with Omali.

"Francis and I aren't together anymore," she said.

"Mmm..."

"Is that all you have to say?"

"Are you going to be with O'Neil now?" Omali asked.

"Why would you think that?"

"Because he loves you. And you love him."

"Who told you that?"

"I have eyes, you know that, right? I spent a week with you two in Geneva. Always smiling, always giggling, always touching each other. It was disgusting. Like, get a room or something. I never saw you this happy with Francis."

"I was happy with Francis."

"No, Francis is a good person, so you tried to make it work."

"You don't know what you're talking about. I love Francis."

"Like a person. Not like the person you want to spend your life with."

"Why do you know all these things?"

"Because I'm smart."

"I know you are."

"So you're going to be with O'Neil now?"

"No."

"Why?"

"You wouldn't understand."

"So you don't believe I'm smart."

Rob sighed in resignation. "We knew each other when I was working at *Les Enfants de Demain*."

"Yeah, I know."

"He hurt me back then."

"So you were in a relationship and he hurt you, like, he cheated or something?"

"No. It's complicated," Rob explained, sensing Omali's skepticism. "He ghosted me after our first kiss."

Omali couldn't contain her laughter. "You got ghosted. I can't believe that."

"Adults have their hearts broken too."

"But he came back, so what's the problem?"

"He didn't come back. We met by chance in Geneva."

"Tomato tomato."

"Not really."

"Since you broke up with Francis and O'Neil is out of question, Oliver will be very happy that you're single."

"Oliver? Oh, your classmate."

"I told you he has a crush on you."

"I have bras older than him."

They chuckled, falling into a brief silence until Omali broke it.

"But for real, like, I bet O'Neil came here for you."

"I can't go running back to him just because he sees that I matter now. I have to respect myself a little bit."

"Honoring your feelings is also a way of respecting yourself."

"Controlling your feelings too. I can't just... Do you remember when Amilcar cheated on aunt Zizza?"

"Yeah."

"Do you know why she didn't tell anyone she went back to him?"

"She said she was ashamed of being back with him."

"I would feel the same. I was very humiliated when it all happened. How could I face Makeba and Angelina?"

"I don't believe you."

"What?"

"Yeah, you might have felt humiliated, but like, Makeba, Angelina, and I are the only ones who know."

"O'Neil knows. Allowing him back into my life would imply that I'm okay with being treated poorly."

"I think your problem is that you can't forgive. Just like with mom."

"Don't bring mom into this."

"She tried to apologize many times."

"You don't know what happened between mom and I."

"And you don't know what happened between me and mom either because you completely cut us off."

"Ké kua, drop this! Let's enjoy dinner and not talk about mom, please."

"Of course. We can never talk about that," Omali said as she rose from her seat.

"Where are you going? Aren't you going to finish your meal?"

"No. I'm going to act like the stupid teenager you expect me to be."

"What does that even mean?"

"So much for caring about what happens in my life."

HOMEWRECKER

People often idealize life on the island, especially in a country as small as São Tomé and Príncipe. The beaches, the sunshine, the close-knit community where everyone knows each other and lends a helping hand. And to some extent, there's truth in those perceptions. But what's even truer? The fact that everyone knows everyone's business. It's a stark contrast to the anonymity Rob cherished during her time in Europe. In a country with a population of around two hundred thousand and residing on an island with just six thousand inhabitants, anonymity became a luxury she simply could not afford.

As Rob stepped into the office, she braced herself for the inevitable onslaught of inquiries. Gossip was the currency of that society, a currency she gladly traded in. But now, finding herself at its center, she loathed it more than ever.

Before Angelina could hunt her down for the scoop, Rob made a beeline for her office.

"Oh, so you're alive." Angelina greeted Rob with a raised eyebrow as she entered the office.

"I'm sorry I didn't answer your calls and texts. I've been busy."

"Mmm-hmm," Angelina responded, clearly unconvinced.

"You know me, I tend to disappear when things get crazy," Rob explained with a sheepish grin.

"And you know I would have gone to your house if I didn't have kids. I'm running on sugar and hope at this point," Angelina sighed, her fatigue evident in the dark circles under her eyes. "Ugh, kids… Don't ever have them, Rob."

"I told you; I don't plan to."

Angelina adored her children, there was no doubt about that. But she couldn't shake the feeling that motherhood wasn't the role she had envisioned for herself. Despite having a supportive partner, she often found herself longing for the freedom she had before becoming a mother. It wasn't that she regretted having children; it was just that she had hoped to start a family later in life, after pursuing her dreams.

She had plans to travel the world as a model. With her striking figure and a contract waiting for her at an Angolan agency, she was on the verge of living out her dream. But then, she found out she was pregnant with twins. While she staunchly supported abortion rights, she couldn't bring herself to terminate the pregnancy, especially considering the less-than-ideal conditions for such procedures in the country.

So, she embraced motherhood, loving her twins with all her heart. Yet, they also served as a constant reminder of the dreams she could not fulfill. But Angelina didn't resent her life or her body. Once tall and slender, the arrival of her twins transformed her into a zaftig woman. She was the poster child for miracles of pregnancy and childbirth.

"So you broke up with Francis."

"Yeah," Rob confirmed with a heavy sigh.

"Are you going to be with O'Neil now?"

"Of course not."

"Then what are you doing? You're spiraling, Rob. I'm worried. When you came back from Switzerland, you wanted to break up with him, and you guys talked, and worked it out. What happened now?"

"I wasn't honest with you. The reason why I wanted to break up when I came back is because I got emotionally involved with O'Neil in Switzerland. And I know, I know I'm stupid, I know it's my fault, but that's my burden and shame to carry. I told Francis everything and suggested we break up. He reasoned with me. He explained that I'm not going to see O'Neil anymore anyway, so whatever I felt was going to go away. But it didn't. And now, O'Neil is here and it's not okay to feel this way about another person when you are in a relationship. It's not."

Angelina looked at her, frustration evident on her face.

"Look, you know yourself more than I know you, so if you think that's the best decision, I'm not going to pretend I know better." She stopped and pondered. "But I do, though. I do know what's best for you."

They shared a laugh.

"I'm okay. Being honest was the best thing for both of us. I can't stand deception, you know that. I was deceiving him and there was no working on it."

"I just want you to be fine. I go to war for you. I don't care about any of these men. I care about you. So if you're fine, if you're not spiraling and took that decision with a clear mind, then that's all that matters."

"Thanks. You're being surprisingly reasonable today," Rob teased.

Angelina chuckled. "Look at my face, I didn't sleep. These kids are going to kill me."

"I know what I'm doing. You won't see me like that again, like seven years ago. I promise."

"How's Mali?"

"She's okay. She is Mali," Rob replied with a shrug.

"And you are you," Angelina added cryptically.

Rob raised an eyebrow. "What does that mean?"

"Nothing. Oh, by the way, there are all sorts of theories about you and Francis circulating. Some say he cheated; others say you did with O'Neil on the islet. People love their drama."

Rob sighed. "Do I deserve this?"

"Yeah, you kinda do," Angelina replied with a teasing grin. "Oh, and Makeba has been blowing up my phone because you didn't pick up her call yesterday, and I told her too. So she knows."

"Great," Rob muttered.

"Don't look at me like that."

"I wanted to tell her myself."

"Did you really think this would stay a secret until our next visit to São Tomé?"

"Yeah, you're right. Do we already have a date?"

"I bought tickets for Friday. And we get back the following Saturday. What do you think?"

"Okay. Did you buy tickets…" Rob started.

"Yes, for Alice and the homewrecker too," Angelina interrupted, provoking Rob with a playful grin. Rob shot her a look that said, 'come on, not you too.' "What? I'm just repeating what people have been saying. Toughening up your skin."

"Oh, what would I do without you?"

"Exactly! What would you do indeed. Oh, I might have to cut my trip short because of the twins."

"Yes, of course. I get it. If you want, I can take Dina."

"No, no… I want to go. I need to visit my mom. Do you already have in mind which offices we will visit?"

"After what happened in November, Mé-Zóchi for sure."

"Of course."

"And then what about Lembá and Lobata?"

"I was thinking we should go to Cantagalo instead of Lembá. There are some discrepancies in their reports that I want to check out."

"Yeah, okay. Mé-Zóchi, Lobata and Cantagalo."

"Noted."

"I need to buy motion sickness medication. Ugh, I hate going to São Tomé," Rob grumbled.

"Going home always sucks. Can't wait to hear my mom say that I'm too fat and that I'll never be a model again."

"She still does that?"

"I think she is going to do it until the end of her days. Or mine if she doesn't kill me first."

* * *

Before anyone could ask her anything, Rob took charge and addressed the room with a clear voice: "I'm sure you've all heard the rumors about Francis and me. It's true, we've split up. No drama, no cheating. Now, let's get back to work."

With that said, she retreated to her office, hoping for a moment of peace. However, her solitude was short-lived as O'Neil appeared at her door almost immediately. She rolled her eyes, already anticipating the predictable conversation ahead.

"So, you and Francis," O'Neil began, his smile barely contained.

"Mmm-hum," Rob responded.

"I'm sorry. It must have been..."

"Yeah, right. You're very sorry," Rob retorted, calling out his lack of honesty. "Don't think that means anything for us. I didn't do it for us. I did it for myself."

"I know," he said, taking a seat and fixing his gaze on her.

"What?" she asked, feeling a hint of embarrassment.

"I just like looking at you," he said, catching her off guard. Before she could even formulate a response, he changed the subject: "You didn't send me the legal papers."

"Oh, you were serious when you said you wanted to help me?"

"Of course I was. Then if I end up helping, you can hire me to be a part of your legal team and I can live here and learn low-quality islander witchcraft," he joked.

"You're going to keep insulting my country like this?" she teased.

"It's not an insult if it's true," he countered, managing to draw a genuine smile from her. It was remarkable how effortlessly he could brighten her day with the silliest of topics.

"Keep talking."

"What? My dick's gonna fall?" he quipped.

"When your thing stops working, I don't wanna hear any complaints."

"Is that a threat?"

"A threat? I would never. No, I'm just a friend giving advice."

"So we are friends now?" he asked mischievously.

"I take it back," she joked.

"Don't even try. We're friends."

"Don't go thinking things," she warned, though with a hint of amusement.

"I won't. I promise. Now, about your legal issue, what is it about?"

"Can I email you everything and then you tell me what's going on? I know there are two conflicts: the first one is about construction on the islet and the second is about the government's reach and control of my clinic."

"Yeah, send me everything."

"Thank you, really. You didn't have to."

"I don't know if I'll be able to help, so don't go thanking me yet."

"I know, but the fact that you are willing matters to me."

"I finished my first report. I'll send it to you. I already sent a first copy to Angelina, and she gave me the thumbs up, so now I only need you to approve it before I send it."

"I know you didn't come here with the right intentions, but I appreciate that it's you, and not someone else who would report certain things."

"I don't think you understood, Rob. I came here for you. My intention is you. So helping you, being by your side is exactly it."

She despised how casually he uttered those words, as if unaware of their impact. He had been like that before, careless with his expressions, professing sentiments he didn't genuinely feel, at least, she didn't think he did. She loathed even more how his words stirred diverging emotions within her—hurt and an unacknowledged happiness.

"We bought tickets for São Tomé. We'll be leaving on Friday."

"I can't wait. I'll send you the report. I need an answer by the end of the day. They are pressuring me."

"Okay, Mr. Thibault," she said, smiling involuntarily before catching herself using the same words and flirting tone they once shared. She quickly suppressed her smile. "Could you please close the door as you leave?" she added briskly, signaling for him to depart.

WELCOME TO SÃO TOMÉ!

O'Neil stepped off the plane with his camera in hand, discreetly capturing shots of Rob as she disembarked. Though she pretended not to notice, she felt his gaze upon her. As they descended the plane's stairs, he approached her, his voice a soft whisper in her ear.

"You look beautiful today."

His unexpected compliment left her momentarily stunned, her legs growing weak, her heart quickening its pace. Despite her efforts to deny it, a faint glimmer of happiness stirred within her.

"I look the same as always," she replied, avoiding his gaze.

"Yeah, but I couldn't say this before. You were in a relationship."

"Because you respected my relationship so much," she retorted, finally meeting his eyes.

"I did though."

"You said I was wet."

His brow furrowed as he struggled to recall the incident she mentioned. After a moment, realization dawned on his face.

"Oh, I remember now. I didn't mean it like that. I was referring to the weather. You're the one who keeps sexualizing me and everything I say. You want me so bad."

"How dare you put this on me? You are the one..." she began, only to be interrupted by his playful retort.

"Nu-huh... I never said anything about you being wet. But are you?"

Angelina and Alice shot them strange looks, hurrying away to avoid overhearing their rather inappropriate conversation.

"You're doing it again."

"But you're wet. You're sweating."

"Stop gaslighting me. On the islet, you tried to kiss me," Rob reminded him.

"As a friend."

"So you kiss your friends now?"

"It's part of my culture."

"Which culture is it again?"

"You wouldn't understand. We're friends, and the fact that you haven't kissed me yet means you don't respect my culture."

"I should kiss you then," Rob retorted sarcastically.

"Yes, you should."

"Are STIs also part of your culture?"

"About that... Yeah." O'Neil admitted, his expression a mixture of disgust and resignation.

"Then I won't be honoring your culture any time soon."

"But I only practice certain rituals with certain people, so you won't catch anything from me."

"Yeah, I'm not buying it."

"I promise."

"How many people have you practiced this tradition with?" Rob's question caught O'Neil off guard, leaving him momentarily speechless. "See? You don't even know how many people you have kissed," Rob continued.

"I actually don't know how many people have kissed me."

"Oh my gosh, you have herpes," Rob joked, feigning horror.

"I don't. I promise."

"Yeah, no. Practice your culture far away from me."

"Look at how a white man is treated in this world. No one respects my traditions."

"Oh, my poor white man, you came to the right place. Colonization did a number on us. Africans just adore white people."

"So you adore me."

"I was able to reverse my brainwashing since I was like, ten. I don't even like when you guys visit my country. You just take, take, and take."

"So you won't respect my culture, you don't want me in your country," he said, feigning offense.

"I would respect your culture if you could tell me how many people…" Rob began.

"But no one knows how many people they have kissed."

"I do."

"How many?"

"Four."

"Including me?" O'Neil asked, a hint of curiosity in his voice.

"Including you," she confirmed.

"Including high school?" he pressed further.

"Including high school."

"And uni?"

"Yeah, what is up with these questions?" she responded, slightly amused.

"Rob!" he exclaimed, surprised by her revelation.

"What?" she asked innocently.

"You haven't kissed anyone," he pointed out.

"I've kissed plenty of… Four people. Quality over quantity. Even though, my first kiss… Ugh, it was something," she said.

"Tell me," he urged.

"I can't."

"Tell me."

"You promise you'll tell me yours?"

"I promise."

"I was fifteen," Rob began, her smile widening as she delved into the memories of her youth. "May 25th is a holiday, it's Africa day. There are shows at school, and discotheques and all sorts of things and activities. I had a crush on this guy. He took me behind the school gym. It was my first kiss. He had been around. I didn't know what I was doing, but I had to act confident. No way I was going to tell him he was my first. I bit him so bad; I think he still has that scar. There was a lot of blood. Poor guy. I was mortified. Wanted to change country or simply die. I didn't want to confront him the next day. He told the whole school that I didn't know how to kiss, and everybody mocked me. That traumatized me."

Their laughter was contagious, filling the warm air with joy. O'Neil was red-faced from laughing so hard, clutching his belly as if to contain the laughter bursting from within. Rob couldn't help but adore his laughter. She was glad she was the one to make him laugh. After their break-up, she envied his ex who had then become his fiancée. She longed for the intimacy of sharing laughter, telling stories, and witnessing his unbridled joy as he struggled to contain his laughter behind his hand. She found herself envious of a woman she didn't even know. She wondered whether he laughed at her stories, whether he gazed at her with eyes brimming with love, as though she were the center of his universe.

"You know what's funny," he started, pausing for his laugh and then continuing, "the way you said it I thought the guy was the one who fucked up. You are the one who fucked up."

"I was a baby. I deserve more grace."

"You literally bit his lips off," O'Neil retorted, still chuckling at the story.

"I still bite lips, but intentionally now," she teased, flashing a flirtatious smile. His laughter halted abruptly as his gaze fixated on her lips.

"Now you're doing this on purpose," he remarked, his tone suddenly serious.

"What am I doing?" Rob feigned innocence as she continued walking, but he caught her hand.

"I want to kiss you," he said, his voice deepening.

"Stop kidding," she countered, trying to brush off the intensity of the moment. "This is never going to happen. Now tell me your first kiss story."

As O'Neil began recounting his first kiss, they were interrupted by Alice's call.

"Lovebirds, the car is here." Alice's words echoed, stirring memories of years prior when their colleagues had affectionately dubbed them lovebirds, long before they had confessed their feelings for each other.

They apologized upon seeing Angelina's annoyed expression and exchanged pleasantries with Rita, who had come to pick them up.

"Alice, O'Neil, meet Rita. She runs the office in São Tomé," Rob introduced them.

"São Tomé island or São Tomé city?" O'Neil inquired.

"São Tomé city," Rita clarified. "The island has six districts, each with its own main city. São Tomé is the city of the Água Grande district and serves as the capital of the country. São Tomé and Príncipe is the country, with São Tomé being the main island, and São Tomé city serving as both the capital and the city of the Agua Grande district."

Angelina intervened, "Rita, no one asked for a geography lesson."

"Sorry, former teacher," Rita apologized.

"No, Rita. Thank you. I like you. It's a nice change of pace," O'Neil said, shooting a subtle grimace at Angelina. Rob had observed their soft hatred relationship for some time. It amused her.

"Rita wasn't just a teacher; she was also a tour guide," Rob added.

"No one can survive on a teacher's salary alone... Anyway, I'll take you to the house now," Rita said.

"House? I thought we were staying at the pension," Rob said.

"Oh, the pension was full. Ms. Maria saved a double room for you and Angelina, but she didn't know about the monitors. So I contacted Ola to see if we could rent one of his properties for two nights, and he said you could use it for free."

"Ugh, tourists," Rob thought aloud. "You should've talked to me first."

"I'm sorry, I didn't think it would be an issue since we're used to partnering with him, and he has helped us a lot."

"Yeah..." Rob began, but then resigned. "It's not really a problem. It's just... It's okay. It's for two nights."

"I need to tell you something. You're not going to like it, but you might need to stay in São Tomé for a few more days."

"What is it this time?"

"Let me take you home so you can shower and refresh, and then we'll talk."

"Which one of his houses did he allow us to use?"

"The one in Oque-del-Rei. But first I need to go to the office. Only for two minutes."

"Okay."

As they arrived in the center of the capital, Rita, still wearing her tour guide's hat, said, "Welcome to São Tomé!"

O'Neil rolled down the pickup window, eager to capture every detail—every color, every sound, every smell. He closed his eyes as they rode along the Avenida Marginal, letting the sea breeze ruffle his hair and breathing in the coastal air. Then, he smiled.

"What?" Rob asked, brushing against him.

"I was just... When I met you, I thought you were Cape Verdean."

"Oh, the lesser island," she quipped.

He chuckled. "Yes, the lesser island. But then you told me you're Santomean and made it sound like meeting someone from your country was a rare privilege. You said there aren't many Santomeans in the world, implying I might never meet another. You even said I should be honored. I promised to meet your mother and family someday. You didn't take me seriously. But look at me now, surrounded by Santomeans."

"I'm not so special anymore."

He looked at her and smiled, intertwining his hand with hers as they turned their attention to the scenery.

* * *

AFTER A BRISK SHOWER that felt far too short for her liking, Rob and Angelina proceeded to the office, unexpectedly deciding to conduct a brief inspection of the work in the capital. Meanwhile, Alice and O'Neil leisurely wandered around the city. With their locations shared, they were unlikely to lose their way in such a small city.

As the evening approached, the trio—Alice, O'Neil, and Rob—participated in a beachside bonfire organized by the Progress Party. The atmosphere was vibrant with poetry readings, music, and dancing. Rob donned a loose, airy dress with a bikini underneath. After introducing them to the gathering, she retreated to a secluded corner of the beach. Moments later, O'Neil quietly joined her, taking a seat on the sand beside her as they both savored the serene ambiance of the beach.

"Where's Angelina?" he finally broke the silence.

"You miss her, don't you?" she teased.

"God, no."

"I caught you once in her office. You two were giggling, and then your demeanor quickly changed when you saw me."

"That never happened."

"It did. I like your soft-hatred relationship."

"Oh, is that what we're calling it, huh?" he chuckled.

"Yeah. She's warming up to you. She doesn't call you a motherfucker anymore, so I'd say that's progress."

"She even reminded me to take Malarone. She said my death would be inconvenient."

"Or maybe she doesn't want paludism to kill you before she does," Rob said, chuckling.

"I don't think she likes me. Actually, I don't think she likes anyone."

"Oh, no… Angelina has a capacity for love greater than anyone I know. She just lacks a filter and says whatever comes to mind first."

"Why isn't she here?"

"She's with her family."

"This is nice," he said, gazing at the people dancing around the flames. "I like Artur and Sonia."

"Oh, they're amazing, aren't they? So young and inspiring. Officially, I don't have political affiliations or publicly support a party, given my position. But I'm with the Progress Party. I back their ideas, their vision. Hopefully, they'll shake things up in the upcoming election," she confided.

"What's on your mind?"

"Nothing much. I just like being alone sometimes."

"I know you do. Do you want me to go?"

"I like being alone with you too, so don't leave."

They sat in comfortable silence for a while.

"I initially planned to stay for just two days to let you two explore São Tomé a bit before heading to Cantagalo. But now, I might have to extend my stay here," she explained.

"How much longer?"

"I don't think I'll make it to the other offices. So Angelina is going to handle the visits this time. She'll head to Cantagalo Sunday morning. You'll go with her. You'll love it; Cantagalo is stunning. Then, you'll head to Lobata and Mé-Zóchi," she outlined.

"I'm staying with you."

"No. I have matters to attend to. Politics," she sighed, rolling her eyes.

"I don't care. Alice can accompany Angelina and report back to me. I'm staying with you. Unless you'd rather I didn't."

She brushed against him and smiled.

"If you want to stay, you can stay."

"Or you could just say you want me to," he teased.

"You know what, I changed my mind..."

"No, you didn't," he interjected, brushing up against her.

"Are you sure you want to stay? You're passing up the chance to explore these amazing places."

"You said you come to São Tomé about once a month, right?"

"More like once every six weeks, but yeah."

"Well, I guess that means I'll have the chance to explore these places in about six weeks. Besides, when you marry me and I become officially an islander, I'll have all the time in the world to explore. I can't just leave you all by yourself, especially considering you can't even drive," O'Neil teased.

"Right. I don't know how I managed all this time without you."

"Luck, I suppose. But now I'm here."

"I can never tell when you're joking or not."

"That's on me, I guess."

She reached for his hands. As their fingers intertwined, O'Neil remarked, "Your fingers are cold."

"Well, good thing yours aren't," Rob countered playfully.

"I told my mom about you."

Rob's eyes widened in surprise. "You didn't," she challenged, her curiosity piqued.

"Well, my father ratted me out, so I had to come clean."

"What did you tell her?"

"That I ventured to this unknown country in search of her future daughter-in-law."

"You've got some nerve."

"You'll just have to prove me wrong," O'Neil challenged.

"O'Neil, I know you see what I do for other people, and you might think I'm a good person. I'm not."

"Why are you telling me this?"

"I feel like you're attached to this idealized version of me, the one I presented when we worked together years ago. But I'm not that person anymore. Heck, even back then, I wasn't entirely the person I portrayed. I was trying to seduce you, so I hid many of my flaws. And it still didn't work, God damn it!" She chuckled. "I don't want to hide anything anymore."

"Then don't. I fell for you because of how you see the world. Because you're intelligent, kind, and compassionate. But I know you have flaws. You're judgmental and can be a bit self-righteous."

She placed her hand dramatically over her heart. "Me?"

"Yes, you."

"Am I self-righteous, or am I always right? I think it's the ladder," she said half-jokingly, half-serious. "But more often than not, what you hear in my voice is not moral authority or superiority, it's anger."

"Not suffering, but fury. Audre Lorde."

"Oh, you know it?"

"Yes, I read it a while back."

"Did you like it?"

"Of course. I like how she is so similar and at the same time so different from bell hooks for example. Especially when it comes to accountability. I wouldn't say bell hooks doesn't hold people, men, accountable, but it's easier to use her writings to justify our behaviors and escape accountability."

"Huh, that's interesting. I never saw it this way."

"It's just my impression, but bell hooks almost demands

compassion for men, and I struggle with the idea of asking the oppressed to show compassion for their oppressors. I prefer Lorde's approach. She doesn't say women shouldn't have compassion for men, but she makes it clear that women don't owe us compassion, and we haven't earned that compassion and trust. Her partner was a white woman, and she extended the same principles to white people. It's not the job of Black people to be kind, compassionate, or to educate white people. Our self-actualization is our responsibility, and your mistrust and sometimes dislike of us is more than justified. I would hate people who oppress and kill me too."

She had never wanted to kiss him so much. The way he understood her—how she didn't have to translate her innermost thoughts—deepened her love for him. As she gazed at him in silence, a warm, sweet feeling enveloped her, until he finally spoke: "Anyway, that's why you can't just read one author. You need different perspectives and approaches. I like bell hooks, but Audre Lorde opened my eyes to so many things."

"Me too. Anyway, let's get back to you thinking I'm judgmental."

"Just a bit," he said, holding his fingers close together.

"I guess I can be a bit judgmental… I caught myself internally judging you when you were raving about Euphoria."

"Not just internally. You made fun of me."

"I only make fun of people I love."

"But you also watched weird shit, like all those MacFarlane's animation series."

"Yeah, but I never hyped it up like it was great."

"Fair enough."

"Did we cover all my flaws?"

"Humm…" he pondered. "You also like it when I hate the same things you hate."

"Guilty," she said with a shy smile. "Ugh, I didn't like it when you started warming up to Peter from work. I liked that we didn't like him together, and then you betrayed me."

"I know. I was always observing you, catching every subtle expression on your face. You can be angry and funny. Hopeful and nihilistic."

"I agree with all of that, except funny."

"You are funny. At least for me, you are. I think..." he paused, as if searching for the right words. "There's something about you that inspires me to be the person I want to be. All those ideas, all those conversations we had so often, you make them real for me. You inspire me to be the person I want to believe I am. I don't have these conversations with anyone else, and when I left *Les Enfants de Demain,* Paris..."

"Me. When you left me."

"Yeah, when I left you, I turned away from everything. I felt guilty, but with time, I simply got used to being like everybody else. You're amazing," he said, a smile playing at the corners of his lips. "And having great legs does help."

"You're such a pervert. You couldn't keep your eyes off my legs."

"Your fishnet tights had me in a chokehold."

"I know. I saw how you looked at me."

"No."

"Yeah. I saw. You didn't hide it very well. Or how you used to stare at my boobs. You're a pervert."

"I thought I was slick."

"I loved seeing you struggle not to look but still looking."

"You're evil."

"You're doing it now."

"I'm not," he protested, turning his face away momentarily before returning his gaze to her. "I can't help that they are there."

She chuckled softly. "Sometimes, I miss those moments. They were, in some ways, simpler times. Now, it feels like I'm trapped in a web, and I fool myself into thinking it's my own creation, that I'm the spider weaving it. But I'm not. I have zero control. I'm still dancing to everyone else's tune," she sighed. "Sometimes, I wish I could disappear. I thought that desire would fade once I had this organization, but it's still here. I fantasize about vanishing, living in the heart of the forest with just a dog, a cat, and maybe even a mouse—I'd call them Spike, Tom, and Jerry."

"When you decide to leave, to escape society, take me with you," he said earnestly.

"You're just saying that now."

"I'm not, but tell me what's going on. I want to help," he insisted.

"Same old shit. Every time I try to create something, there's always someone or something standing in my way. People just..." She paused, taking a deep breath. "People can be real assholes."

"They really can."

"The construction work on the islet is halted until I resolve the legal issue. The tricky part is, I'm still on the hook for paying the construction company because of the contract, and it's not their fault. They've diverted all their resources to my clinic, putting their other projects on hold. Money just runs out so quickly; you don't even realize it. Now, in the capital, I secured authorization last year to kickstart a solar farm. The land was granted to me by the prime minister in exchange for attending numerous events, posing for photos with him and his cabinet members, and giving the impression that I support his politics. Which I don't, by the way. Also, my organization won't have full ownership of the plant. The government will hold shares, along with the prime minister himself. But now, the authorization seems to be in jeopardy. It hasn't been officially revoked yet, but Rita informed me that the Prime Minister's nephew, who happens to be the president of the district council, paid us a visit and issued a warning. I'm sure they tried to contact me too, but I probably overlooked it."

"Why are they pulling the plug on the authorization?"

"Because it's an election year. They want to use me as a pawn, parading me around. They're worried about the Progress Party gaining traction. They expect me to attend their events, speak on their behalf. The people trust me, and if they see me cozying up to them, they might be swayed to vote for them again."

"This is disgusting."

"You don't even know half of it. We only have one hospital in the entire country, and it's located in the capital. Last year, we experienced a widespread power outage that lasted for over three days and affected the hospital as well. Don't get me wrong, the hospital faces these issues frequently, but nothing like this. People died. And those who were already dead began to decompose because the mortuary couldn't keep the bodies preserved. You could smell the dead bodies without setting foot on the hospital ground. That's why I began the solar grid project. But for these people, everything is just a game. They're so fixated on money and power. I despise them with every fiber of my being. I hate having to put on a fake smile, I hate allowing these men to touch my bare shoulders for photos. I hate that I have to compromise my integrity just to get a single project approved. It feels like an endless battle. Remember how much I hated going along to get along back in France, just ignoring or pretending I didn't hear things to keep the peace outside? I'm doing the same thing here. The only difference is that I convince myself it's for the greater good. Sometimes, I just want to scream 'fuck off, go to hell.' I even fantasize about killing them. But at the end of the day, all I can do is play their game."

"Come here, lay your head on my lap," he offered.

She hesitated, casting a wary glance around to ensure nobody was paying them any mind. Satisfied that everyone was engrossed in the festivities around the bonfire, she curled up and nestled her head on his lap. With gentle hands, he began to massage her head, each stroke easing the tension in her mind. At that moment, she couldn't help but reminisce about the second night of their mission in Brest. It was then that she had found solace in resting her head on his lap, closing her eyes as if seeking refuge from the chaos around them. In his presence, everything felt like it was going to be okay.

"So that's why you need to stay in São Tomé."

"Yeah. I'll meet them on Monday and try to work things out."

"I thought you're not supposed to have any party affiliations in your position."

"It's not that I'm not supposed to. It's my decision. It's a rule I imposed on myself, not only to maintain my integrity but also to safeguard my work. I attend events without speaking or endorsing any party. I take pictures and that's it. But perception is reality. And that's also why I can't support the Progress Party. Until I'm certain of their success, I can't risk aligning with them. The current establishment would halt everything I've worked for."

"Your country is so small, but so complicated."

"It's frustrating, really. Despite our size, corruption is everywhere. We have no excuses for our underdevelopment; it's just corruption. It's a vicious cycle that seems impossible to break. Even people I went to school with, who once opposed it now do the same thing. I feel so powerless, like I'm applying band-aids to a crumbling dam. Fuck, what's worse is that in a century or so, our island might even be underwater, because of the rise of the sea level. Other countries pollute and destroy, and we bear the burden."

"I would give anything to put your mind at ease."

"I'm going to be okay. I'm just feeling drained right now, and this situation with the prime minister has really thrown me off. But tomorrow is a new day, and I'll find my footing again. I'm just venting, not giving up—I can't give up." She sighed deeply. "I can't give up," she said, as though trying to reinforce her own resolve.

"When the time comes, just say the word. We can find a plot

of land in the middle of nowhere, build a cozy house, and live with our own versions of Spike, Tom, and Jerry."

She turned to him, her head still resting on his lap.

"That would be a dream."

"Do you want to get into the water?" he asked minutes later.

"Okay. But I don't go far. I can't swim."

"No way!"

"I told you that," she reminded him, her voice carrying a hint of annoyance.

"Yeah, years ago."

"Well, someone broke my heart. I was going through a rough patch. Didn't have the energy to learn how to swim," she said, her tone defensive.

"But you had the energy to create this massive organization," O'Neil pointed out, a teasing edge to his voice.

"Don't judge me. Let me perpetuate the black stereotype in peace," she quipped.

"You don't have an excuse. You live on an island. Water everywhere. I see children swimming every day in Príncipe. Even babies."

"Okay… What's this? Why do I feel like you're judging me?"

"Because I am. Come on. Strip down," he insisted, a grin playing on his lips.

"You just want to see me in a bikini, you pervert," she teased, feigning indignation.

"This pervert at least won't drown if the boat sinks. You need the boat to get to the islet."

"Yeah, we use boats to travel between islets."

"Don't you see the risk? You can't swim, and those fishing boats don't have life jackets. You could have drowned," he pointed out, his concern evident.

"I'm not dead, am I?" she retorted, rolling her eyes at his exaggeration.

"Because of luck. But luck eventually runs out. Come on, I'll teach you," he offered, extending a hand to her.

"I'm not learning how to swim tonight," she protested, feeling overwhelmed by the suggestion.

"Yes, you are. At least the basics," he insisted, determination evident in his voice.

After a few minutes of negotiation, she finally gave in. The goal was to at least teach her how to float, yet the lesson proved as challenging as she had anticipated. Trusting him and herself was a struggle. Amidst her self-deprecating remarks likening herself to a sinking rock and his encouragements to believe in herself, small arguments erupted. The notion that belief alone could enable success seemed absurd to her. However, against her doubts, she succeeded. When she managed to stay afloat for a minute, he hugged her, lifting her out of the water.

"You did it. You did it!"

"I did it. Fuck, I did it!"

As realization dawned upon her of their closeness, she pulled away.

"Didn't I say you could do it?" he said.

"I'm freezing. Let's go home."

They reached out to Alice, who hesitated but eventually acquiesced to the end of the evening. She said goodbye to the guy she had been kissing and ten minutes later, they arrived home. After taking a quick shower, Rob dressed and wrapped a towel around her head before heading to the kitchen to prepare some tea. She brewed two cups and carried them to O'Neil's room, where she knocked gently on the door. He answered, surprised.

"Hey."

"Oh, hey. I thought it was Alice. She's always borrowing my night creams."

"No, it's just me. I made you tea," she said, offering him a cup.

"Thank you."

As she stood there, she hoped he might invite her in, but the invitation never came.

“Thank you for tonight. I’m not as preoccupied anymore. You took my mind off these things,” she said.

“That was all part of my genius plan,” he teased lightly.

“Really, thank you.”

“If you ever feel this way again, try floating. Let the water calm you down.”

“I sure will.”

They lapsed into silence once more.

“Well, good night, Mr. Thibault,” she said, breaking the silence.

“Good night, Ms. Frades. Our lesson isn’t over yet. You still have a lot to learn.”

“I can’t wait,” she replied with a smile, before heading back to her room.

EASY TO DRAW

Rob heard the distant sound of a door slamming in the realm of her unconscious. She ignored the first few knocks, attributing them to the whims of her dreaming mind. However, the persistent tapping eventually penetrated her slumber, prompting her to awaken.

"Who is it?" she grumbled; her tone tinged with irritation. Disrupting someone's sleep was a cardinal sin in her book. Her steadfast rule dictated that unless it was a matter of life and death, and even then, unless her wakefulness could yield a beneficial result, she was not to be disturbed.

"It's me," he whispered.

She emerged from her bed, annoyance evident in her movements, and reluctantly opened the door for him. Shielding her eyes from the harsh hallway light with her arm, she squinted at O'Neil's broad smile, noting the notepad in one hand and the computer in the other.

"What?" she asked.

"I found it. The solution for the clinic on the islet. A solution to both problems," he said eagerly, his words tumbling out in a rapid stream.

Still groggy from sleep, she motioned for him to enter. "Come in," she muttered.

He launched into his explanation, his speech fast paced and his eyes wide with excitement.

"Are you on drugs?" she asked, taken aback by his frenetic energy.

"I'm just excited," he said, his enthusiasm undeterred. "And I might have had a can or two of energy drink."

"Please, calm down. You're buzzing with energy. I'm not."

With a visible effort, he managed to control his excitement. "Fine, fine."

"Sit down. Let me go wash my face so I can wake up."

Rob splashed water on her face, attempting to shake off the remnants of sleep. After a moment, she reached for her phone.

"It's 4 a.m., O'Neil," she muttered, peering at the glowing screen. O'Neil remained undeterred, his excitement palpable. "Okay, show me," she relented, resigned to indulging him in his early morning discovery.

"The problem with this is that we were looking at the law to find a solution that would be applicable to our situation. But laws are general texts, often abstract. That's why we needed..." he explained, pausing expectantly for her response.

The silence lingered.

"Are you expecting me to complete?"

"Jurisprudence. We needed jurisprudence," he explained. "I reviewed jurisprudences since your country's independence in 1975. Not everything has been digitalized, but I found old papers hinting at some relevant cases. Some are related to the nationalization of plantations, while others from the nineties address the use of private property, including properties along the littoral. Guess what? This includes a property on Cabras Islet. To date, there has been no reversal of these case laws, and no new legislation has overturned these decisions. So, we can deduce that they still apply. I'll request copies of these rulings at the courthouse on Monday."

"Could you explain again, but slower this time? I'm having trouble following," Rob requested, her voice heavy with fatigue.

"I'll show you, scoot over," O'Neil replied, sliding into her bed and pulling the covers around himself. Despite her weariness, Rob attempted to focus on his explanations, her eyes following his computer's cursor. However, as he continued, her eyelids grew heavier.

To Rob's surprise, the energetic O'Neil eventually drifted off to sleep in her bed. She covered him with the sheet and lay beside him, her mind drifting in the hazy borderland between sleep and wakefulness. Hours later, a noise at the gate stirred her from her drowsiness. Assuming it was Angelina returning from her mother's, Rob paid it little mind, choosing to remain in bed and watch O'Neil as he slept peacefully beside her. She played with his hair that had not been cut since he had arrived in her country, finding comfort in his presence.

Suddenly, the sound of frantic knocking followed by a scream shattered the tranquility of the moment. O'Neil remained undisturbed by the commotion. Rob left the room and rushed toward the source of the disturbance. It was Alice, engaged in a heated confrontation with Ola.

"What's going on here?" Rob's voice cut through the tension in the air.

"This... Man attacked me. He came to my room," Alice said.

"I didn't attack her. I knocked, she opened the door, and then she screamed. I apologized and tried to explain..."

"Explain what? What are you doing in my room?"

"This is his house, Alice. He was kind enough to let us stay here for free," Rob clarified.

"But... But..." Alice stuttered.

"I'm sorry, Ola. Alice didn't know," Rob said, diffusing the tension.

"Yeah, if she just had listened to me," Ola added, frustration evident in his voice.

Alice retreated to her room, closing the door behind her, while Rob gestured for Ola to follow her to the kitchen, where they could talk in private.

"I didn't know you were coming here today. You could've texted."

"I wanted to surprise you," Ola said.

"You know I don't like surprises," she said, as she busied herself making tea.

"I told Kacha that this one was your room."

"We arrived late; Kacha wasn't here anymore. Besides, it doesn't matter. The room I'm in is also great," she assured him.

"But the one I arranged for you has a balcony, a better view, and a hot tub."

"It's okay. I'm used to the view. Alice chose it. Let her have it for two days. Oh, I meant to ask you, can I stay here for the whole week?"

"Of course," Ola readily agreed.

"Thank you," she replied with a grateful smile.

"I heard about you and Francisco," Ola said, a hint of curiosity in his tone.

"Yeah. How's your father?"

"The old man is fine. He is still at the hospital, but he is being well taken care of," Ola responded.

"I'm glad. Do you want milk in your tea?"

"Yeah," he accepted, and she handed him his cup. "I don't want to rush anything, but I want to invite you to my house in Lagos."

"We've talked about this. I don't..." she began to decline.

"That was before. You're not in a relationship anymore," he interjected.

"I'm not going to sleep with you, Ola."

"You island girls. Why una dey so untrusting? I told you; I want to marry you."

"Right, the same way you wanted to marry the six girls you got pregnant, right?"

"I never told them I wanted to marry them. Never invited them to visit my house in Lagos. Never introduced them to my father," Ola countered.

"You've lived in this country long enough to know that marriage is not our thing. I don't want to marry you."

"It can be marriage, or we can just be together."

Just then, O'Neil emerged in the kitchen, his appearance suggesting he had just roused from sleep.

"Sorry Rob, I ended up sleeping in your bed," he said in a sleepy voice, before registering Ola's presence.

"O'Neil, this is Ola. He is the owner of this house," Rob introduced.

O'Neil squinted, his vision impaired because Rob had insisted he remove his contact lenses before sleeping. He stepped closer to Ola, adjusting his position to get a clearer view of his face, and then reached out his hands to greet him.

"Oh, I remember you from the organization's social media posts," O'Neil recalled, his memory stirred by Ola's familiar face.

"Yeah, Ola is one of our main donors and he also provided the funding for the purchase of the islet," Rob explained.

"So you two are sleeping together?" Ola asked bluntly, his tone serious. Rob felt a wave of surprise and irritation wash over her at the audacity of the question. She had a plethora of retorts at her disposal, but instead, she chose to placate him, as usual. Still dancing to other people's tunes. Still biting bullets and swallowing toads, still going along to get along.

"O'Neil is actually here as a monitor for TUF, reporting on the use of the funds they've allocated," she clarified, keeping her tone composed.

"Now you share your bed with colleagues? I've donated money to your organization, bought you an islet, volunteered... Technically, we've been colleagues in many instances. You never allowed me to share your bed," Ola's voice carried a tinge of accusation.

"Hey, buddy, you're crossing a line," O'Neil interjected, his tone firm.

"Buddy? You're under my roof, buddy. You're sleeping with my girl under my roof."

"I'm not your girl, and I'm not sleeping with anyone. What the fuck is wrong with you?

"What's wrong with me? What's wrong with you?" Ola shot back, his voice escalating.

"You don't speak to her like that," O'Neil intervened, reaching for Ola's arm.

"Don't touch me," Ola warned, pulling away.

"You need to leave, now!" O'Neil said.

"I'm in my own house."

"I don't care. You're leaving or I'll make you."

"Please, Ola. Please. I'll leave your house," Rob pleaded.

Eventually, Ola calmed down and left. Though Rob tried to appear composed, inwardly, she was upset, her heart racing, and her hands trembling slightly.

"That's a lot of audacity coming from a guy who looks like he'd be easy to draw," O'Neil quipped, eliciting a burst of laughter from her.

"You…" she began, pausing to laugh before continuing, "You say the most out-of-pocket things."

"I mean, I'm no artist, but I could probably sketch him," O'Neil added with a smirk.

Her laughter erupted again, so hearty that the tears of anger transformed into tears of mirth.

"Thank you," she managed to say between giggles. She wasn't sure if O'Neil's comment was intended to be funny or not, but she appreciated the moment of levity.

Once their laughter subsided and they both found themselves sitting on the floor, exhausted from their bout of laughter, O'Neil posed the question:

"What are we going to do?"

"I don't know," she said. "But I'll figure something out."

* * *

After initially resisting Angelina's suggestion, Rob eventually relented. She made her way to her mother's house, a place she hadn't set foot in for years. Not even during her mother's funeral had she entered its doors; she had only visited the cemetery. Armed with a copy of the key from her aunt, who still tended to the house once a week, she approached the familiar threshold.

Upon opening the door, a rush of nostalgia enveloped her. The scent of the house transported her back fifteen years, to when she was just seventeen and had left for the last time. Inside, the house stood as a testament to the passage of time, with its six bedrooms untouched by her absence. Rob didn't bother allocating rooms; instead, she left the keys on the table for each person to choose their own.

She took her old bedroom key and made her way to her room, a place that held both fond and painful memories. As she entered, she was struck by the familiarity of it all. Determined not to dwell too much on the past, she busied herself with making her bed and preparing for the night ahead.

Despite her best efforts, sleep eluded her. Memories flooded her mind, each one a vivid recollection of days gone by. Unable to find solace in the quiet of the night, she reached for her phone and dialed Omali's number, seeking comfort in the familiar voice of her sister.

"Hey Mali!"

"Oh, it's you."

"How are you? Not doing anything weird?"

"You don't have to check on me. I've always been responsible."

"Right. How's Irina?"

"She is fine. She is cooking or something."

"Tell her I say hi."

"Irina, Rob says hi," Omali yelled. "She said hi back."

"Guess what? I'm at mom's," Rob said, a heaviness in her tone. A silence settled between them.

"I can't believe it."

"Yeah, neither can I."

"Mom said you would go back one day. She never let me go inside your room."

"I… I've got to go. Take care. Don't do anything weird."

As she tossed and turned on the bed, someone knocked on her door.

"Come in."

"Oh, I was not expecting this," O'Neil said as he entered the room, eyeing the posters on the wall. "Who are these people?"

She sat up, a spark of excitement igniting within her as she prepared to share these memories with him.

"This is Loony Johnson. He's a Cape Verdean singer. I had a huge crush on him when I was growing up. And this is Noite&Dia. She's brilliant, an Angolan singer."

"What about this one? Is it you?" he inquired, pointing to a particular poster.

"Yes, that's me with Mika Mendes. I went to his concert when I was a teen and took this picture backstage with him. This is my cousin, and here's my brother, Regi."

"You have two brothers, right?" O'Neil asked.

"Yeah, Regi and Rashid. Oh, fun fact, Mike Mendes' song 'Mágico' is my favorite kizomba song ever."

"That's not exactly fun, but it's a fact," O'Neil teased.

"Quit mocking me," she replied with a playful grin.

"Did you know Alice is learning kizomba?"

"Yeah, she told me."

"I think it's just a way for her to meet men. She says she is learning kizomba and asks for them to teach her. She brought some guys home."

"Oh my gosh, really?"

"Yeah."

"But, guys, like, plural? Príncipe is not that big."

"I've seen three different guys naked in the kitchen in the morning. I'm sure there are more."

"At least she is getting the full experience of the country."

They laughed. He settled onto her bed, and she reclined, contemplating the roof.

"I know you didn't want to come here. Why didn't you let me pay for hotel rooms for us?"

"You're already helping me a lot. I don't want you to help me with your money."

"I don't mind."

"I know."

"Why did you resist coming here?" he asked.

She debated whether to answer, weighing her thoughts.

"The last time I stepped foot in this place, I was seventeen. I swore I'd never return," she finally responded.

"It's fine if you don't want to talk about it."

"No, it's okay. I know plenty about your family. From your grandmother who didn't know who your mother's father was to your uncle and his children who are jealous of your father's success, your family drama is enough to fill a novel. You won't find mine any more scandalous."

He chuckled. "See? United by messed up families."

"The father of my siblings is a terrible man. He makes my own father look like an angel in comparison, because at least my father left and didn't traumatize us."

"What do you mean, he left?"

"Well, he lives in the country. I know where he is, but after getting my mother pregnant, he just stopped caring. It's pretty common, actually. I used to see him almost every day, driving by as I walked to school."

"And child support?"

"That doesn't exist here. Most women raise their children alone. Men might 'help' if they still have access to the woman's body, but if she leaves him or if he finds another woman and loses interest, the child is forgotten. Men in my country aren't fathers, even though they have many children. My father must have at least twenty with several women."

"Wait, wait, wait... You have twenty siblings plus the three others from your mother's side?"

"It could be more."

"But how do you live like this? You don't have any contact with them? And what about your father? How does this work?"

"I don't know all of them, and the ones I do know, we aren't close. We don't see each other as siblings. It's like we were conceived from the same sperm donor." O'Neil's face contorted in horror at this unknown reality. "Don't look at me like that. It's normal. There are very few exceptions, but this is how it is here."

"What about your father?"

"He tried to reach out. They all do when their child becomes successful. There's even a song about this phenomenon. I've managed to ignore him so far, and I don't often come to São Tomé, so I'm good. Anyway, this isn't supposed to be about my father."

"But Rob..."

"It is what it is, O'Neil. Don't try to understand it. Anyway, getting back to my story, my siblings' father treated my mother and me poorly. Remember when I mentioned the celebrations on May 25th, Africa day?"

"Yeah, the day you butchered a poor boy's lips."

"You can mock me all you want, but that kiss was the most unforgettable moment of his life," they laughed together. "Anyway, this is two years later. Not the same year I butchered... The lip incident happened. I had a curfew—home by 8 o'clock. Meanwhile, my brothers, who were two years younger, had the freedom to stay out all night. So, there I was, hanging out with friends at the beach, eating and talking shit, and before I knew it, I lost track of time. It was around 10 p.m. when I finally made it home. But as soon as I walked through the door, he slapped me. Then he stripped me naked and left me to sleep outside. 'If you're going to behave like a slut, you should start living their lifestyle', he said. My mother didn't say anything. She had never defended me, but this... I expected her to step up. That man was under her roof, it was her house that she built herself, still, she let him mistreat me and she never defended me. I slept outside that night, and in the morning, I left, naked. I remember her at the window with Omali in her arms, silently watching me leave. She stood there, by that man, and watched me leave." As she recounted the story, a wave of pain surged within her, reopening wounds she thought had long healed. Tears welled in her eyes, betraying the depth of her lingering anguish. "Angelina was living in the capital by herself. She was supporting herself with her model career. She took me in. And her father helped me find a scholarship. I never spoke to my mother again. She tried to reach, to apologize, but I couldn't forgive her. I can't forgive her. The thing is, I'm completely indifferent to my father. For me, he doesn't exist. Maybe because if you're absent, you don't cause pain. Maybe because only those close to us can hurt us. Maybe because it's easier to blame the person who stayed, it's easier to blame the woman, but fuck... Why couldn't she do anything?"

"I'm sorry, Rob," he said, reaching for her hand.

She dabbed her tears away. "You see now. I'm a shitty person who let an old woman die without forgiveness."

"There are worse things, like biting off half of a boy's lips," he joked.

She chuckled amidst her tears. "It wasn't half. Oh my God, I shouldn't have told you."

“I’m terrified. It could’ve been me.”

“I kissed you so gently, what are you talking about?”

“I don’t know. Maybe you developed a thirst for blood, an appetite for soft lips of young boys.”

“You’re not a boy.”

“I’m two years younger. Almost a boy.”

“Now I feel like biting your lips.”

“God no. I don’t want to be disfigured.”

“So you don’t want to kiss me again, Mr. Thibault?”

“I don’t know, Ms. Frades. Only if you promise not to devour me.”

THE TEACHER'S BOYFRIEND

The week passed swiftly in some respects yet dragged on in others. By Saturday, the four of them boarded a plane back to Príncipe. While Rob hadn't managed to visit the other offices as planned, she found solace in the fact that her presence at events and discussions with the prime minister had reignited momentum for her project. She was also happy that O'Neil had found a solution for the construction on the islet. All in all, things were looking up. Upon their return, Rob immediately resumed her duties at the organization. In addition to her regular tasks, she was asked to fill in as a biology teacher during a maternity leave. Having previously substituted at the high school, she gladly accepted the opportunity once again.

Two weeks later, Angelina and O'Neil had to return to São Tomé after an incident in Caué. Discrepancies in the health fund's books in Caué necessitated an investigation, which uncovered a much deeper case of corruption and embezzlement, taking almost a month to unravel. Rob remained in Príncipe to closely monitor the construction on the islet. On a Wednesday morning, O'Neil and Angelina returned from São Tomé. She briefly caught sight of them and promised to meet for dinner to discuss the situation. While she was teaching, one of her students said:

"Ma'am, there's a man at the window," pointing to someone waving outside.

Rob turned to the window and was surprised to see O'Neil standing there, peering into the classroom. She quickly masked her astonishment before addressing her students.

"Everyone, please continue reading up to page 27. When I return, we'll be discussing angiosperms."

"Sperms!" a student quipped, eliciting laughter from the class. Rob couldn't help but wonder at what age such jokes would lose their humor.

She left the classroom, and she made her way to the hallway to meet O'Neil.

"What are you doing here?" she asked.

"I'm here to see you. I missed you," he replied with a smile.

"You can't just come here… This is a school."

"I know."

"Don't you see that it may not be well perceived, a foreign white man without children wandering through the corridors of a school?"

"Ohhh…" he said, realization dawning. "I look like a pedo."

"Yep, that's pedo behavior. And there are a lot of precedents."

They shared a laugh. She felt the urge to hug him. Despite talking every day, it had been a whole month since they had last seen each other. She missed him, deeply, but voicing it was out of the question. Acknowledging it to herself was hard enough.

"Seriously, what are you doing here?" she pressed.

"I was looking for you and couldn't find you anywhere. So I asked Dina. She told me where you were," he explained.

"What do you want? I'm teaching."

"I just wanted to see you. And to give you this," he said, handing her a file.

"What's this?"

They noticed the children peering at them through the window. She took his hand and guided him into the garden, away from the curious eyes of her class. They settled onto a nearby bench, and she opened the file he handed her.

"I did an STI screening. I'm clear. No herpes, no nothing. You can now honor my culture," he said, eliciting a laugh from her.

"I can't believe you did that," she chuckled.

"I did the test since I came back from our trip to São Tomé, but only now I could go pick up the results."

"You could've just texted me. We're meeting for dinner later anyway."

"I wanted to see you in action, teaching with my own eyes. I think I'm becoming Santomean," he joked.

"It's not a big deal. I'm just subbing for a teacher on maternity leave," she explained.

"But you've always said you didn't have the patience for teaching."

"I still don't like it."

"Oh, but I was there looking at you for a while. You seemed to enjoy it."

"No, I don't."

"You do."

"I don't. I just... Gotta put that master's degree to use, somehow."

"Yeah, but teaching?"

"When I came back from France, after everything... I was living with Ange. I quickly felt guilty because I wasn't contributing to anything. Stalking you full time wasn't paying my bills. Shame drove me to take action. I started working as a teacher. I hated it at first, but over time, it grew on me. I can't say I like it, but I don't hate it anymore. Dealing with kids and teenagers is overwhelming, but they have something... Hope, I guess. They still harbor hope for life and the world. Being around them inspired me to start my organization."

"That's beautiful. You're amazing."

"Don't do that."

"What?"

"Don't say that I'm amazing with those big eyes of yours."

"It's true."

"You used to say that a lot when we worked together."

"How is it wrong for me to admire you??"

Rob didn't mind his admiration for her; it was the implications that came with it that she despised. In the past, that admiration had created a distance between them, blurring his perception of her as a mere person, as human. Instead, she was elevated to the status of a role model, an inspiration. And nobody wants to fuck their inspiration. She couldn't say that, though. Admitting this would mean acknowledging she wanted him to fuck her.

Not anymore, she thought.

Back in her classroom, her students were relentless in their inquiries about O'Neil. She attempted to divert their attention, shifting the discussion to archaefructus liaoningensis, but to no avail. Their persistence disappointed her. Despite her feigned indifference towards teaching, there remained a part of her that found joy in it. She recalled her own fascination with evolution and the gratitude she felt towards her teachers for imparting such knowledge. Instilling that same wonder in her students brought her a sense of fulfillment. And perhaps, buried deep within her, was a yearning to be loved in return. Maybe not then, but certainly after her heartbreak, when she first began teaching. The students' curiosity about O'Neil persisted, prompting her to make a promise: he would visit the following week, allowing them to pose all their questions directly to him and enabling her to return to the task at hand.

The following week arrived, and true to her word, O'Neil was present.

"Alright, everyone," Rob addressed her eager students. "You've been anticipating O'Neil's visit, and here he is. I asked you to prepare your questions in advance. While each of you has the right to ask one question, with our class size of 47, we may not have time for everyone to ask. However, if your question has already been asked and answered by a classmate, please pass when it's your turn to ask, understood?"

"Yes, ma'am," they chorused enthusiastically, ready to engage with their special guest.

"Let's begin with Abigail. What's your question?" Rob prompted.

"Where are you from?" Abigail asked.

"That's an easy one. I'm from France," O'Neil replied.

"Ohh, so you came to destroy the rest of our cocoa production?" someone jeered from the back of the room.

"What? What do you mean?" O'Neil asked.

"He works at my organization," Rob interjected.

"What does that mean?" O'Neil whispered to her.

"I'll explain later," Rob whispered back.

"Let me clarify. My mother is French, but I consider myself more Norwegian, from my father's side," O'Neil addressed the class.

"Just like Peter denied Jesus," Rob whispered to him, sharing a chuckle. "Alright, next question, Akita, it's your turn."

"Are you the teacher's boyfriend?" Akita asked bravely, breaking the silence that enveloped the class. Rob's heart skipped a beat as she awaited O'Neil's response, unsure of what he would say.

He glanced at her, a mischievous grin playing on his lips, before turning back to the class. "Not yet. I'm working on it. If you all could pitch in, I'd appreciate the support," he replied with playful charm.

The class erupted into laughter. "The teacher has a boyfriend!"

Rob's cheeks flushed with embarrassment. "I don't have a

boyfriend," she protested, attempting to regain control of the situation.

"But you're going to have one soon," another student chimed in.

"I'm not going to have anything. Let's stick to your questions, no more comments," Rob asserted firmly.

"I can handle it. You can trust me," O'Neil reassured her, his smile unwavering.

She retreated to her desk, allowing him to take charge of the class. As she watched him engage with the students, she couldn't help but smile. His animated gestures, the warmth in his smile, and the genuine interest he showed in the children's questions were all charming to her. Despite her efforts to maintain composure, a silly grin crept onto her face. She attempted to shake it off, but soon found herself succumbing to it once more.

At the end of the class, they strolled together toward her home but paused at an ice cream stand and indulged in two large cones.

"You're sure?" she asked, mindful of his lactose intolerance.

"I'll suffer the consequences later," he replied with a grin.

Seated near the beach, they savored their ice cream and engaged in conversation.

"This is so fucking good. What flavor is it?" he asked.

"Safu. It's the best. Right up there with Bulgarian yogurt," she answered.

The rapidly melting ice cream dripped onto their hands, faces, and even their clothes, leaving sticky trails behind. They rinsed their hands at a nearby tap. She kicked off her shoes and strolled near the shoreline, feeling the cool waves drenching her feet. He followed suit, enjoying the refreshing sensation of the water on his bare feet.

"What did they mean by me destroying the cocoa production?" O'Neil asked, still puzzled.

"The kid must have heard the story from their parents. I don't know everything, but I heard it from my grandmother. The French convinced us to accept a project they promised would boost our cocoa production. They introduced genetically modified beans, but instead, those beans ended up destroying many of our local varieties."

"Fuck…"

"Yeah."

"So I'm hated everywhere."

"After all the chaos your people caused and are still causing around the world, I guess you are." O'Neil feigned sadness. "Oh, the oppression of my poor white French man," she joked.

"Norwegian."

She gasped playfully. "If your mother heard you now."

They walked side by side until they reached her place.

"Come in," she invited him. "Mali is going to spend the night at Irina's."

He took off his shoes and stepped inside.

"Are you going to cook me dinner?" he asked.

"I don't know, Mr. Thibault. What do you want to eat?"

"Can I be honest?"

"You're going to say some crazy shit, so no, you can't."

After dinner, they settled on the sofa to watch a movie on television.

"Why isn't there ever anything new on your national TV?" he asked.

"Are you criticizing my country?"

"Just your movie choices."

"It was worse when I was growing up. They would play the same movies over and over. I grew up on a repeated diet of American and Asian movies. Mostly Asian though. I watched them so many times I could recite the lines in Mandarin."

"Not Korean?"

"Actually no. China, Hong Kong, Taiwan."

"Let me guess. A lot of Jackie Chan movies."

"I loved the 'Police Story' franchise so much. The last two, *New Police Story* and *Lockdown,* are my favorites. Oh, and the animated series is gold. I also watched a bunch of Jet Li movies," she said. "I had a huge crush on Jet Li after *Romeo Must Die,*" she whispered. "And on Aaliyah."

"I think I know this one."

"It's really good. God, I had so many crushes. *So Close* made me fall in love with Shu Qi."

"I used to like Maggie Q," he said.

"I don't like her because of *Naked weapon.* I loved that movie. My friends and I would cover our backs afraid that someone would dislocate our vertebrae. My generation is one marked with trauma of getting a massage."

He took out his phone and looked up the movie. Then, he played the trailer.

"This is inappropriate for a child."

"You have no idea. But there weren't these types of filters when I was growing up. I watched everything. Sex, violence, they didn't give a fuck.

"Oh, I see. Maggie Q is in it."

She rolled her eyes. "Every time she appears in a movie, I'm like, 'You should've died, Katherine should've lived.' Or at least, they could've fallen in love and ended up together. But no, she chose to fuck a man while Katherine was dying. I hated her so much in that movie that it colored all her subsequent work for me."

"Kind like how people still to this day crucify Kate Winslet for not sharing the door."

"Right? *Titanic* is another movie that I must've watched thousands of times. Poor Rose."

"Kate Winslet is my mother's favorite actress."

"I was a huge fan of hers, but after *Ammonite,* I became a whole air conditioner."

He laughed. "You need to come to my place. I'll cook something for us and then we'll watch a movie."

"We can watch a movie here."

"The TV in my place is four times bigger than yours."

"Okay… Excuse me, sir," she retorted, playful defiance in her tone.

They sat in a heavy silence, his fingers tracing patterns on her legs as they rested on his lap.

"Why aren't we together, Rob?" His question hung in the air. Rob shifted uncomfortably, avoiding his gaze. "You love me. I know it. I love you; you know it. Why are we still doing this? Why do I have to pretend I don't want to hold you and kiss you?"

"I don't know what to tell you," Rob said, her voice barely above a whisper.

"Angelina told me that I'm wasting my time. Am I wasting my time?" His voice wavered with uncertainty, seeking reassurance in her response.

"I… I told you. I can't be with you."

"Is it because I left you? I'm sorry. I'm sorry I left you. I was stupid. I'm sorry you suffered so much after I left you. You didn't deserve that. I wish I could take it all back, but I can't change the past. All I have are my apologies, and I know it's not enough. But we have a second chance. Please, give me a second chance."

"Can we talk about this tomorrow?"

"Why not now?"

"I don't know what to tell you now. Please, tomorrow. At Fehér's birthday party. Please," she implored.

"I…" he hesitated, uncertainty flickering in his eyes. "I'm going home now."

She reached out, her fingers curling around his hand, a silent plea for him to stay.

"You don't have to go. We can finish watching the movie."

"Another day," he replied with a bittersweet smile.

UNFAIR

That evening, after slipping into her Benfica uniform, Rob made her way to the party, arriving later than she had anticipated. She exchanged pleasantries with the birthday boy, mingled with the guests, and discreetly inquired about O'Neil's whereabouts.

"He's not feeling well, so he decided not to come," Alice informed her.

Rob attempted to distract herself, sipping cocktails, engaging in conversations, and even hitting the dance floor. Yet, despite her efforts, her thoughts remained consumed by O'Neil. As the evening progressed, even before the chorus of 'Happy Birthday', she excused herself, feigning a sudden bout of illness, and quietly slipped away.

She walked briskly towards his house, her mind racing with uncertainty. Should she knock? Should she simply walk in? What would she even say? All she knew was that she needed to see him, to confront the unresolved tension between them.

She stood at his doorstep and hesitated, her heart pounding with anticipation. She hadn't formulated her words yet, but she knew she had to take the plunge. With a deep breath, she knocked on the door, signaling the end of her internal deliberation.

The door swung open, revealing O'Neil standing shirtless, clad only in sweatpants.

"Oh, hi!" she said, making a conscious effort to avert her gaze from his bare torso.

"I thought you were at Fehér's birthday party."

"Alice said you weren't feeling well."

"I'm fine. I just didn't feel like celebrating. And the theme is football. I don't have any..."

Before he could finish his sentence, she cut him off. "Yeah, I'm gonna kiss you now," she said, rising onto her tiptoes and reaching up to his face.

"Wh..."

Before he could finish his sentence, she closed the gap between them, pressing her lips against his. In that moment, time might as well have stopped. Never before had they experienced such urgency, such an overwhelming need. It felt as if just a minute later, they would both die of thirst for each other's lips. Rob's teeth grazed against O'Neil's lips, yet he ignored the pain and reciprocated the kiss with equal fervor. With his body pressed against hers, the heat of his body consumed her as his tongue wandered inside her mouth. In that moment, the world made sense, every unspoken longing finding solace in that embrace. As he lifted her up, she wrapped her legs around him.

"We're not together," she uttered between kisses as he carried her into the bedroom.

"We are not."

"This isn't a thing."

"It isn't."

He tossed her onto the bed, his hands moving swiftly to undress her. Heat surged through her veins, her lips yearning for his, her body hungry for his touch. She became aware of a pulsating hollowness between her legs that desperately needed to be filled with him. As she attempted to remove his pants, he stopped her, his gaze filled with restraint.

"Not yet," he murmured, placing her back against the bed.

As if magnetized, his lips were drawn to her nipples. The soft, delicate moans that escaped her lips only served to intensify his desire. As he sucked on her breasts, he pulled down her Benfica shorts. His hands caressed her crotch over her panties, teasing her, eliciting more alluring sounds. He slid his hands inside her underwear, his fingers exploring the whole area, teasing and caressing different parts of her crotch. He ran his hands between her cunt and licked his fingers, enjoying the liquid of her body.

"Fuck me! Please O'Neil," Rob begged, her breaths coming in short, eager pants.

"Not yet."

As he sucked her voluptuous breasts, his hand found its way down to her crotch again. This time, he didn't tease. He didn't explore. He went straight to her clitoris and began stroking it with his two fingers in a circular motion, her moans growing louder and louder. She was at his mercy, having lost all control over her own body.

"O'Neil," amid the moaning, she called his name. "O'Neil." Her breathing grew more and more panting until she reached orgasm. He licked her liquid off his fingers again and kissed her. As she lay there, her body spasming and writhing with pleasure, she pondered the unfairness of it all. How unfair was it to her past lovers that her body responded in such a way for O'Neil? He didn't need to try; he didn't need to put her in the mood. His mere presence, his scent, his voice, were enough to arouse every atom in her body. How unfair was it that her body made things so easy for him?

"I'm going to clean you now," he whispered in her ear, reawakening a desire she thought had died. He began kissing her from the chest down, playing with her nipples, and then her belly and teasing every part of her crotch. Her throbbing clitoris became swollen again. He kissed her clit, played with it and then kept going down to clean the wetness in her cunt and between her cheeks. She closed her eyes, feeling his tongue, moaning and calling his name. He then moved up again and put his mouth on her clit. He bit it, softly, and then his well-trained tongue muscle stroke it.

"Wh… O'Neil… O'Neil…" she said, stuttering her words with pleasure.

She gripped the sheets tightly as her body reveled in the pleasure he bestowed upon her. Then, he whispered into her ear:

"I'm going to put my cock inside you now."

Those words sent a shiver down Rob's spine. The hollow ache between her legs, yearning to be filled, was on the verge of finding completion.

"Please, put it inside me."

"You want it?" he teased.

"Yeah," she gasped, her breath heavy and warm.

She grabbed his hard and sinewy cock in between her legs, that simple act making him moan for her. With a satisfied smile, she pulled him closer and kissed him as she massaged her clit with his cock and played with it at the entrance to her vagina.

"Say my name again," she demanded.

"Rob," he said.

"Again."

"Rob."

"Do you love me?" she asked.

"Yeah, yeah, I love you."

"Do you adore me?"

"Yeah. Yeah, I adore you. I adore you so much. You smell so good. You feel so good."

"Would you do anything for me?"

"I would do anything for you."

She pushed his cock inside her. Their moans blended together in harmony. A solitary tear trickled down her cheek.

"Fuck Rob, you feel so fucking good. Fuck," he said as he thrusted inside her. She opened her legs more, all the way up, giving him range and allowing all his length and girth to penetrate her.

In that moment, he possessed her entirely, both physically and spiritually. She surrendered completely, her mind a blank canvas devoid of thought, consumed only by sensation. She existed solely in the realm of feeling. Every aspect of him enveloped her —his cock moving inside of her, the warmth of his body, the flex of his muscles against her, his breath mingling with hers, the fragrance of coconut shampoo that clung to him, the salt of his sweat on her lips—a culmination of desire seven years in the making. And in that instance, she wished fervently for time to stand still, to prolong the ecstasy of their connection.

He collapsed onto her, his breath heavy, his body finally at ease. For long, quiet minutes, they simply reveled in the tranquility of the moment, as if time itself had paused to accommodate their peace. Eventually, he shifted to lie beside her, his fingers tenderly tracing the contours of her face, her neck and breasts. Their gazes met, and a smile danced across their lips, soon followed by the infectious warmth of laughter.

"Seven years," he murmured.

"Seven years," she echoed, a soft chuckle escaping her lips.

"Actually, eight years. I've been wanting to do this since we first met."

"You're a pervert."

"You're perfect. I mean, seriously, how can someone be so perfect?"

"Can I tell you something super shallow about me?"

"Of course," he replied.

"If I ever get plastic surgery, it'll be for a boob lift. It's my biggest appearance-related fear—that one day they'll sag."

"They're still perky. And even if they do sag, it'll be a long time from now."

"But I don't want them to sag. I'm fine with getting older, with wrinkles and gray hair. It's just... Not my boobs."

"Until the sagness kicks in, I have about thirty years to enjoy these delicious boobs and this delicious ass," he said, touching her, sending a ticklish sensation through her body.

"You're going to pay for my boob lift."

"Or I'm just going to love your saggy boobs."

"Never."

At some point, they ambled into the kitchen, where he made pain perdu to satisfy her sweet craving. As the night wore on, she contemplated returning home, yet weariness gradually overtook her, leading her to surrender to sleep in his bed.

The next morning, she was startled awake by sounds emanating from the kitchen. As her senses sharpened, she discovered O'Neil sleeping beside her, his hands resting lightly on her back. Hastily, she rose, using the light from her cellphone to locate her scattered clothes. The commotion stirred him from his deep sleep.

"What are you doing?" he asked, his voice thick with sleep.

She hushed him, pressing a finger to her lips. "Where is my underwear?" she whispered.

"I don't know. It's too early. Come back to bed."

"I need to go home."

He fumbled for his phone. "It's 4 a.m."

"I shouldn't have slept here. Scoot over," she requested, attempting to search for her underwear amidst the covers. Finally, she found it crumpled beneath his body.

"Why are you in such a hurry?"

"Because... Just go to sleep, O'Neil. We'll talk later."

She hastily dressed and tiptoed her way towards the door. Just as she approached it, the light flicked on, revealing Alice, who had just gotten home and was munching on bobo frito in the dimly lit room.

"Rob? What are you doing here?" Alice's voice held a mixture of surprise and curiosity.

Rob attempted to improvise. "Heyyyyy, Alice. What are you doing here?"

"I live here."

"Yes, of course. I mean, what are you doing here in the middle of the night?"

"After Fehér's party, I hung with some friends. I just got home and was starving. What are *you* doing here?"

"I'm… I'm," Rob struggled to come up with a convincing excuse.

At that moment, O'Neil emerged. "Rob, you forgot a foot of your sock."

"Ohhhhh..." Alice's realization dawned as she caught on to what was happening. "Finally. I won the bet."

"What are you talking about?" Rob's heart raced.

"You two," Alice clarified with a knowing smirk.

"Alice, please, don't tell anyone. I'm… I'm not…" Rob pleaded, her panic evident.

O'Neil's brow furrowed in confusion as he observed the distress on Rob's face.

"Don't worry. I won't," Alice assured, flashing a wide grin.

"Thank you so much."

Rob retrieved her sock from O'Neil and left in a hurry.

RATTRAPAGES

Rob knew it was impossible to make up for seven years of fucking in a month, but did she try. Every day, several times a day if possible. She couldn't get enough of him. O'Neil eventually stopped pushing her to reveal their relationship, finding at times a certain thrill in their secret rendezvous. While Rob felt uneasy about deceiving others, including Angelina, Makeba, and her sister—even though Omali couldn't care less, she couldn't bring herself to confess the truth.

That week, they left for São Tomé together, just the two of them. Angelina couldn't join them due to her sick children, and Dina had to stay behind to handle organizational matters. At O'Neil's request, Alice feigned illness, opting out of the trip. This left Rob and O'Neil alone, a rare occurrence that offered them a degree of freedom they couldn't enjoy in Príncipe. Stepping off the plane, O'Neil reached for her hands eagerly.

"Not yet," she murmured, hesitant about drawing attention from anyone who might recognize her in the capital.

After completing their rounds at the various offices, they made their way to an isolated area in Santa Catarina to visit Makeba. Makeba had withdrawn from society following the tragic loss of her partner in an accident. Her trauma had rendered her unable to venture beyond the boundaries of her residence. Merely stepping outside the gate triggered debilitating panic attacks—she would freeze, tremble, and struggle to speak or move, sometimes even experiencing bouts of vomiting. Over time, she had fashioned her home into a sanctuary, a haven where she could escape the judgment and misunderstanding of society. As they arrived at the gate, Makeba embraced Rob warmly.

"Rob! It's been too long!" Makeba said as they held each other tightly for several minutes. Despite the years that had passed, she hadn't changed at all. If someone compared her to a photo from ten years ago, she'd look exactly the same. Every time Rob visited —which was three times a year, though not as often as she should —she felt as if Makeba was frozen in time. Perhaps in some ways, she was. Her hair was still in the same locks, she wore the same boubou dresses, and time seemed to have no effect on her dark skin.

"Makeba, this is O'Neil," Rob said.

"So you're O'Neil. It's nice to meet you," Makeba said, surprising O'Neil with her kind embrace.

She led them to their rooms, where they would be staying for the next couple of days. The afternoon was spent assisting Makeba with her vegetable garden and tending to the animals. Makeba had created a self-sustaining sanctuary within her residence, complete with solar-powered electricity and a natural spring for drinking water. She raised animals and cultivated her own food. That night, she made quizacá, one of Rob's favorite dishes. They shared a delightful dinner, accompanied by a bottle of wine that Rob had brought as a gift.

As the night settled in and the surroundings grew quiet, Rob found herself making her way to O'Neil's room. To her surprise, she encountered him already tiptoeing towards hers. With a silent understanding, they retreated back to her room together.

Before any words could be exchanged, he leaned in and kissed her.

"I couldn't touch you all day," he whispered as they undressed each other.

"Makeba doesn't sleep. We need to be quick, okay?" she reminded him, urgency in her tone.

He moved to toss her onto the bed, but she halted him. "The bed creaks."

She removed her top and turned around, pressing her hands against the wall for support. He slipped her panties aside and grabbed her from behind, pounding hard on her ass.

She relished in the way her body stirred such strong reactions from him, causing him to utter her name despite her plea for silence. She enjoyed the feeling of being worshiped, revered, adored. And she enjoyed even more the power she had over him, how she could command his attention and affection. His calling her name only fueled her desire, intensifying her yearning with each utterance.

As they settled onto the bed together, he broke the silence.

"I like Makeba."

"Yeah, she's amazing."

"So, do you think that'll be us one day? Living in seclusion like this?"

"The funny thing is, Makeba wasn't always like this. She used to be very outgoing. Did you notice the photos of the woman on the wall?" she asked.

"Yeah, they're hard to miss."

"That's Sara. She was Makeba's partner. After Sara passed away, Makeba… Changed. I guess she developed agoraphobia, but there was never an official diagnosis. People just labeled her as 'crazy'. So she invested all her savings into this house. She's a writer for a foreign paper, so she manages to support herself well enough."

"That's incredibly sad. She seems like such a good person."

"Yeah, life can be cruel. It gives you people you love deeply, only to take them away," she replied.

They lapsed into silence.

"Rob… I love you," he said.

"I know."

"You know, you can just say it back, right?"

She looked at him, surprised by the sudden turn in the conversation.

"What's this about?"

"Are you ashamed of me? Of us?" he asked, his words revealing a depth of emotion that caught her off guard, hinting at a conversation he'd been holding onto for some time.

"Don't you like this, us? Fuck… We just had great sex. Aren't we happy? Aren't you happy?"

"It's not about the sex. It's about more. I want to be able to hold your hand in public, to kiss you freely. I want slow mornings with you, where we can take our time together, not just rushed moments with you running off."

"Why do you want to ruin this?"

"How is it ruining? I just want to be open about us."

"It's too convenient now, isn't it? For you to want these things. It's too easy."

"What do you mean?"

"I don't expect you to understand."

"No, tell me. I want to understand."

"I don't want to talk about it."

"You never want to have serious conversations about us. Do you even take our relationship seriously? I feel like you're just using me for sex."

She scoffed, taken aback by his accusation. "So, you're saying you don't enjoy sex with me?"

"You know what I mean. Every time we're alone, we have sex, and that's it."

"We talk; we're talking right now."

"Not as much as before. Ever since we started having sex, you've been hesitant, afraid people will catch on."

"So, you don't want this anymore?"

"See? You… I'm trying to find a solution, a compromise, and you're already thinking about ending things. Why can't we just be together?" She fell silent.

"I don't know what you want me to tell you."

"Just tell me why."

"I want you to leave."

"I don't want to leave. You promised we'd sleep together during this whole trip."

"I'm serious."

"Rob…"

She didn't answer, turning her face away from him, signaling her desire for him to leave. He hesitated, searching her expression for any hint of a change in her decision. Eventually, realizing her resolve, he turned to leave, hoping for some indication that she might reconsider.

The next morning, they crossed paths in the bathroom. He had just finished his shower and was leaving as she was about to step in. Without a word exchanged, their eyes traced each other's figures draped in towels.

After her shower, she dressed and stayed in her room, called Omali while waiting for him. She anticipated the sound of his knock on her door, but it never came. Swallowing her pride, she mustered the courage to knock on his door.

"Come in," he said, his voice deep with tension.

He was in bed, clad in shorts and a casual t-shirt, engrossed in the screen of his phone, his attention scarcely registering her presence. Undeterred, she sat on his bed, her fingers tentatively tracing the contours of his feet before gradually ascending to his thighs and then to his crotch. The bulge was evident beneath her touch. She continued her massage, feeling him grow increasingly aroused under her hand. She traced her lips and tongue over the fabric, tenderly teasing and caressing. She sensed his struggle to stifle his moans, but eventually, he succumbed to the pleasure. He set aside his phone and shut his eyes as she removed his shorts and boxers. She grabbed his cock, feeling it pulsating in her hand. Years prior, she had made a conscious effort not to idealize his cock, fearing disappointment, but disappointed she was not. The sight of it ignited a deep yearning within her. She yearned for the sensation of him inside her, filling the hollowness in between her legs. She teased him, tracing her tongue over the tip and kissing it here and there, and then she engulfed it all with her mouth. Her lips enveloped his cock as she began moving slowly up and down from the tip to the base. She increased the pace, sucking it faster, maintaining eye contact with him. At this point, he couldn't restrain the moans he had previously fought so hard to suppress. She kept going, licking, kissing and sucking, reveled in the pleasure his face expressed. He grasped her hair, synchronizing his movements with the motion of her head, praising the acrobatics her tongue performed and the skills of her hand.

"Your lips, Rob… Your mouth… You're amazing," he barely could formulate a sentence. "Please don't stop," he begged, as she teased him. She loved it when he begged. Then she put it all in her mouth again.

She continued, alternating between slow and fast movements, her tongue twirling inside her full mouth, attuned to his breathless moans until he came in her mouth as he called her name. She swallowed it all, before kissing him tenderly and nestling beside him in quiet intimacy, while he appeared spent. After a moment, he turned towards her, his lips meeting hers in a lingering kiss, his tongue exploring every contour of her mouth.

"Are you hungry?" she asked, her face caressed by his touch.

"I love you so much."

"I love you, too," she said. "Makeba wakes up late, so come. I'll prepare you something."

As she moved to leave the bed, he caught her hand, his eyes filled with longing.

"I want to be with you, Rob."

She smiled. "You are with me."

WHILE THEY WERE COOKING, stealing kisses between chopping vegetables and stirring pots, Makeba entered the kitchen. Rob's heart skipped a beat, and she instinctively pushed O'Neil away, her eyes wide with apprehension. Makeba didn't utter a word, her expression inscrutable. Rob spent the rest of the day in a state of uncertainty, pondering whether Makeba had noticed their intimacy and was choosing to ignore it, or if she remained blissfully unaware, having just awoken from sleep. As evening descended, they gathered around a crackling fire, enveloped in the soothing sounds of the night. When O'Neil retired to bed, leaving Rob and Makeba alone, Rob finally summoned the courage to broach the subject.

"This morning..." Rob hesitated, struggling to find the right words.

"Mmmm..."

"When you came to the kitchen this morning, I... I need to tell you something."

"Mmmm..."

"I've been sleeping with O'Neil. There. You have it."

Makeba chuckled. "I was wondering when you'd finally come clean."

Rob felt a pang of surprise. "You knew?" Makeba nodded. "I've spent the day unsure... It's been eating away at me."

"I'm not talking about today."

"Then what are you talking about?"

"You're very observant, but don't forget that we can see you too. Or in my case, hear you too. For a month now, I've sensed a change in your voice, your demeanor. You seemed genuinely happy, not just putting on a show. I asked Angelina if anything special had happened to make you so happy, but she was clueless. She said it might be because things were going well lately at work, but I knew there was more to it. And when I saw you two together, the way you smile, the way you look at him, it was obvious. You're not fooling anyone."

"I guess I let my guard down when we came to São Tomé. We're more cautious in Príncipe."

"You need to tell Angelina. If she finds out and then discovers I already know, I don't want to be in the middle of it."

"I can't tell her. I can't tell anyone. I... Fuck... I don't know."

"You're still doing that?"

"What?"

"Standing in the way of your own happiness."

"It's not that simple."

"It can be, if you allow it to be. Life is short, Rob. We're not immortal. Losing Sara taught me that. I regret all the time we wasted being angry at each other. Don't make the same mistake."

"I understand what you're saying, but it's not easy for me. I wish I had your kind heart. Or even Angelina's boundless kindness. But I don't."

"You'll find your way. Just don't waste a lot of time. You'll only regret it in the end."

Rob took a deep breath, and shook her body, attempting to dispel the emotions coursing through her.

"What about you? You mentioned having something to tell me, but you refused to discuss it over the phone."

"I just needed a reason for you to visit."

"I'm sorry I don't come as often anymore."

"I know you're busy. I do have something to share."

"Go on..."

"I've been talking to someone." Rob squealed with happiness, reminiscent of a teenager. "Take it easy. It's not official yet."

"How long have you two been talking?"

"For about four months now."

"Oh my gosh."

"Come on now, you're making me blush."

"Can I see a picture?"

Makeba pulled out her phone and showed a photo.

"She's hot!"

"Isn't she? God…"

"Is she in São Tomé?"

"No. She moved to Portugal ten years ago, but she's planning to return."

"Show me the picture again…" Rob requested. "Damn… Look at that ass!"

"Stop!" Makeba chuckled, covering her face with her hands.

"Does she know about your condition?"

"I haven't had the courage to tell her yet. But I will. I just…" Makeba's voice trailed off.

"You're afraid. You like her."

"I do. I never imagined I'd feel this way about someone else after Sara. I almost feel like I'm betraying her memory."

"I'll tell you what you'd tell me in this situation. You deserve happiness. You loved Sara deeply, and that doesn't change…"

"I still do…" Makeba interjected. "Do we stop loving people when they die? It feels odd to speak of love in the past tense when the person dies. I never stopped loving her."

"I'm sorry. Yeah. I know you love her. But she's not here anymore. You deserve happiness and companionship. She would have wanted that for you. It's the best way to honor her memory."

Makeba took a deep breath, processing Rob's words.

"Don't tell Angelina yet. I don't want to go around and tell people, especially if things don't work out..."

"Don't worry. I won't tell anyone. So, what's her name? What does she do? And when is she planning to visit?"

"Her name is Luisa. She is originally from Uba Budo. She's a graphic designer. She's hoping to come during Gravana to see me."

"Oh my gosh... Look at you. You're in love."

"You're in love too, we're in love," Makeba said. "She's a bit older."

"How much older?"

"Eleven years. She'll be turning forty-eight in May. May 10th, actually. She's a Taurus with Scorpio rising," Makeba explained. Rob didn't find much interest in astrology, but she knew it was a passion of Makeba's, so she always tried to engage in the conversation.

"Are Taurus and Cancers compatible?"

"They're an ideal match. In romance, friendship, and well... You know, intimacy," Makeba whispered the last part suggestively.

"Is she out?"

"Yes, thankfully. She even wants to get married."

"That's a relief. At least you won't have to hide. But marriage? Do you want that?"

"I don't care for marriage. But after everything with Sara, I don't know. I don't want to go through that again. And why not marriage? Lucas and Alfie celebrated their ten-year anniversary last year and it's going great for them."

"I haven't talked to them in ages."

"They live nearby so they visit me often. Things are going great."

Sara and Makeba had always kept their relationship private, despite living together. They were content with people assuming they were simply close friends. Makeba didn't like the idea at first, but for Sara's sake, she accepted living in ambiguity. She would vent to Rob, however, about how hard it was not to love her partner publicly. But Sara was too afraid to lose her parents' approval. When Sara passed away, Makeba found herself unable to assert her grief in any meaningful way. She couldn't even have a say in the funeral arrangements because she was just seen as a friend. Makeba had to dim her deep pain, which seemed excessive to others. She wasn't permitted to express how much she missed Sara or to mourn openly.

That night, they talked by the fire until it died down, finding solace in each other's company. Afterwards, Rob sought comfort in O'Neil's room, holding him close as he slept.

"Hey, hey... Slow down. We don't want Makeba to hear us," he said, bit groggy from sleep.

"It's fine. She knows," she reassured him. His face, previously worn with sleep, suddenly brightened.

"You're serious? You told her?"

"Yeah."

"Rob," he said, smiling, as he leaned in to kiss her.

She straddled him. "Now I want to fuck you."

"The noise. The bed might creak."

"We can make it work," she whispered.

MAN ENOUGH

Back in Príncipe, they fell back into their clandestine routine, always meeting in haste. O'Neil grew weary of the secrecy, longing for a more open relationship, but he patiently waited for her to be ready. However, it seemed like her readiness would never come. Despite his attempts to broach the subject, she always evaded the conversation. That evening, after finishing work, she met him at the deserted beach. She brought two metal rat tail combs, and they sat on the sand as he helped her undo her braids.

"Can I ask you something?" she asked.

"Nine. It was ten two minutes ago, and now there are nine braids left," he quipped, eliciting a chuckle from her.

"I wasn't going to ask that," she replied.

"Right..."

"I'm serious."

"Then what were you going to ask?"

"I... Do you know what... Of course you know."

"What do I know?"

"I'm just going to go ahead and say it, okay?"

"Fine, just stop moving your head."

"I've been thinking about this for some time now. I... I..."

"Just say it."

"I want to peg you," she blurted out quickly. He took a few seconds to process the information before chuckling.

"What?"

"I want to peg you."

"I got that part. I just... Where does this come from?" he asked, still surprised by her revelation.

"I don't know. I've been interested in that for a very long time."

"So that's why you tried to put your finger in..."

"I asked you first."

"Well, you asked as you were trying to."

"And you said no, and I stopped."

"If I said no to a finger, what makes you think I'll say yes to a dildo?"

"I don't know. I just wanted to tell you."

"Is this a deal breaker? Are you not satisfied with our sex life?" he asked, his tone tinged with concern.

"No, our sex is great. I just... It's not like I need it. It's just something I'm into. But if you don't like it or don't have interest in experimenting, that's okay."

"Promise?" he inquired, seeking confirmation that all was well.

"Yeah, I promise."

After they finished undoing the braids and spent some leisurely time at the beach together, he walked her home. During their stroll, the earlier conversation seemingly still weighed on his mind, prompting him to broach the subject.

"So if you're into pegging, does that mean you've done it before?"

"No, I haven't. I just... I find it hot. Like I find you hot."

"So you haven't done that with any of your previous... Partners?"

"No. But I've researched it extensively, so I'm confident I'd be skilled," she said, smiling suggestively as she brushed against him. Her playful expression hinted at a lightheartedness that contrasted with his stoic demeanor, a contrast that had escaped her notice.

"Of course," he replied, his tone firm.

"What?"

"Of course you haven't done it with any of your previous partners. They were black. And I'm white, so you don't see me as masculine, as man enough."

"What?" she said, taken aback by his sudden accusation. "What does your skin color have to do with any of this?"

"You haven't pegged anyone else you've been with," he pointed out.

"And I haven't pegged you either."

"But you asked," he persisted, his tone challenging.

"Yeah, I asked. I've been with two men before you. Two. It's not like I've been with a bunch of black guys and suddenly you're my first white guy, and the first one I want to peg. I didn't target your white ass to fulfill some kink. Besides, I did ask my first boyfriend if he was into it, but he wasn't. And Francis, well, I never felt comfortable enough with him to even bring it up. So, no, it's not just you. And I don't give a fuck that you're white." He remained silent. "I… This is so disappointing. I never thought I'd hear this from you. How would pegging take away your masculinity? I thought either you'd say no, and we'd laugh about it, or you'd say yes, and we'd laugh about it. It's not like I need it. It's just something I'm curious about. It's not that deep. And yeah, I heard myself."

She stood there, waiting for him to break the silence, but not a single word escaped his lips. Disappointment etched across her face; she shook her head incredulously before turning to leave. He followed, a silent shadow trailing behind her.

"Please, don't follow me," she said, but he remained resolute, matching her steps stride for stride. Eventually, resigned to his insistence on ensuring her safety, she ceased her efforts to dissuade him. As she reached her doorstep and closed the door behind her, he left.

For the next three days, she didn't see him. She even tried to catch the sight of him running at the beach early in the morning like he usually did, but he was not there.

On Saturday, as Omali braided Rob's hair on the porch, O'Neil made an unexpected appearance.

"Hey, Mali!" he greeted cheerfully.

"I'm still recovering from that terrible movie you recommended," Omali complained.

"Come on, was it really that bad?" he asked.

"What movie was it?" Rob asked.

"Breakfast Club. You have the worst taste in movies," Omali said.

"Not just in movies," Rob murmured.

Ignoring Rob's comment, O'Neil turned his attention to Omali.

"Can I steal your sister for a moment?"

"Hmm... If she gets up, I'm not touching her hair again, and she'll have to rock half-done braids. And these are braids for a braid out for a meeting she'll have, so extra important."

"Please," O'Neil begged.

"We can negotiate."

"What do you want?"

"You know what I want."

"I already bought you two games by Hideo Kojima," O'Neil reminded her.

"I've finished them already. I need something new. Plus, I want to expand my collection. You know how much I love Kojima."

"Fine. Which one?" O'Neil relented.

"I think you meant which ones."

"Okay, let's pause it. You can't keep buying her these things," Rob intervened.

"So you're going to pay me for these braids I do for free?" Omali countered.

"Okay, go on, ignore me," Rob conceded.

"I have a list." Omali pulled up her phone. "Metal Gear 2014, 2015, and 2018, and Death Stranding 2025… I rented Death Stranding years ago, but I don't have it in my collection. My stingy sister never buys me anything when she goes to Europe."

"You know my salary is awful. And converting dobra to euro, the price of your games is almost my entire paycheck," Rob defended herself.

"But you have…" Omali started.

"I can't use the organization's money. That's theft," Rob interjected.

"I can't do four games. How about three?" O'Neil suggested.

"Look at him, he has spent too much time going to the market with you, and now he's haggling with me," Omali teased.

"Three games," O'Neil reiterated.

"Four," Omali persisted.

"I can talk to your sister any other time."

"Come on, you're well-off. You can buy me four games."

"I can't give you everything you want now. What if I need something from you in the future?" O'Neil reasoned.

"I'll always want something."

"Three or nothing," O'Neil insisted.

"Fine… Forget about Metal Gear 2018. It wasn't developed by Kojima anyway," Omali compromised.

"Deal," he held out his hands to seal the pact.

"Deal," she said with a grin.

Omali took off at a brisk pace, leaving them alone on the balcony. Rob grimaced as O'Neil approached to sit near her.

"You bribed her so that you could talk to me. But who told you I want to talk to you?" Rob challenged.

"No one. But I'm a man. If I have anything, it's audacity," he replied with a faint smile.

She chuckled. "Trying to make me laugh won't cut it."

"I know. So let me start by saying I'm sorry. I really am, Rob. I was an asshole about this whole pegging thing. No pun intended. I just... I did some introspection these last few days. I think I was just insecure. I thought I was immune to these messages, to these things we hear... But..." he sighed, searching for the right words. "When we worked together, I told a coworker that I liked you and he said I don't have enough dick for you. I laughed it off and obviously didn't take it seriously. I just ignored him and never talked to him again. But these things... They stay with us. And they come out in the silliest and most hurtful ways. I'm sorry. You didn't deserve that."

"You know what made me fall in love with you? Truly? I didn't have to make an effort to be understood. You just got me, somehow. We come from different worlds, completely, opposite realities. Still, you simply understood me. We finished each other's sentences, completed each other's thoughts. I've never experienced that with anyone else. I thought we were soulmates, connected on a deeper level. But the person I thought you were, that I want to believe you are, wouldn't react this way, O'Neil. I understand we all have insecurities, including me, but I don't project them onto you. They are not your responsibility."

"You're right. You're absolutely right. I crossed a line. That reaction... I didn't even recognize myself."

"Okay," she said.

"Okay?"

"Yeah, okay."

"Can I kiss you?"

"I don't know, can you?"

He leaned in for a kiss.

"Are you out of your mind? We're out in the open."

"So, I'll see you tonight?"

"Yeah."

He gently stroked her legs, his gaze darting around to ensure they were alone.

"I think your sister knows about us," he said.

"Don't say that."

"You know she's very smart, right?"

"I know."

"I'm fighting with all my strength not to kiss you."

"Who said you don't have enough dick for me?"

"Léo."

"Seriously? You listened to that guy?"

He chuckled. "That little shit."

"I missed you," she confessed. "I missed our conversations. It's tough not being able to gossip with you. Please, don't ever shut me out like that again. Especially when I have gossip."

"Do tell."

"Fehér told me that Alice and Dina are seeing the same guy."

"No?"

"Yeah."

"But Alice isn't exclusive with anyone. She said she's just living life, so maybe they all have an agreement."

"I don't think so. Maybe? But that's not all. The guy used to date Dina's sister. And apparently, she started dating him while he was still with her sister."

"How you get them is how you lose them," he said, smiling wryly.

"Right? That's what I thought. He must have a magic dick though, because he drives a moto taxi, and all these highly accomplished women are willing to fuck up their lives for him. Alice even gives him money."

"They say island girls are something else… Maybe island guys too?"

"So am I something else?"

"You sure are," he said, mischief in his voice.

"Do you think we should tell them? The guy already has four kids with different women in São Tomé."

"Is there anyone innocent in this story? Alice knows what she is doing. Dina backstabbed her own sister for that guy. They won't hear us."

"I love that we have this," she said, taking his hands in hers. "I love you."

"I love you, too," he said, his eyes lingering on her lips. "Damn it, I want to kiss you."

"Tonight, I promise."

"Alice won't be home. We can have the whole place to ourselves. By the way, she mentioned that Ola was in Príncipe two days ago?"

"Yeah, he came to apologize. Said he'd continue supporting the organization."

"I didn't expect that from him."

"He is a good person. But it's so tiresome sometimes."

"What?"

"Men messing up and then apologizing. One day, I won't need you, so I won't need to accept your apologies."

"So, you need me?"

"Not you. Only the cock that's attached to you."

"God... I feel violated now."

"Do you?"

"Stop looking at me like this."

"How?"

"Stop."

Their laughter filled the air on that rainy day. Later that evening, he prepared a meal for her: his own version of *Magret de canard,* using the ingredients available on the island. It was delicious, though different from the French original. The ducks on the island were leaner, but he managed to create something wonderful, perhaps even inventing a whole new dish. As the meal concluded, she led him to the bedroom.

"Is it going to always be like this?" he asked as they lay naked in bed, spent.

"What?"

"This sweaty? I feel like I've just run a marathon every time we have sex."

"What can I say? Blame the humid climate."

"I've been thinking about your question the other day."

"What question?"

"You said you want to peg me."

Rob's attention piqued; her curiosity evident in the way her ears seemed to perk up at that moment.

"Go on," she said.

"I think I'm okay with giving it a try."

She sat on the bed, needing a moment to process his revelation.

"I don't want you to do it just because of me," she began, her tone earnest. "Sure, it's kind of because of me, but I don't want you to feel pressured. I'm happy with our sex life just the way it is."

"Oh, I know you are," he replied, his words laced with a teasing tone.

"What do you mean by that?" she asked, arching an eyebrow.

"I like how you get more and more turned on when I praise you and call your name," he continued, his voice growing huskier. "And when I moan in your ears, you come immediately. You're so easy."

She couldn't help but smile at his audacity. "The disrespect," she said, a hint of amusement in her voice.

"I'm serious though."

"What made you change your mind?"

"Because of your sister actually."

"You're saying very weird things tonight, O'Neil."

"No, no, no, listen to me," he continued. "You want something, and I want something."

"Oh, so you're bargaining. What do you want?"

"I want dates. Real dates. I want to go out with you. Restaurants, cinema, karaoke, trips, the whole thing," he explained.

"There is no cinema in Príncipe. We have eaten in the two restaurants here and we have had street food," Rob pointed out.

"Yeah, but it wasn't a date. I want to be able to touch you and kiss you."

Rob started to feel annoyed. "I don't want to have to explain myself to people."

"You're an adult, Rob. You don't have to explain anything to anyone. What do you have to explain anyway?"

"I can't do this," Rob said, feeling overwhelmed.

"Last time, you said it's too easy now. What is too easy now? Please talk to me."

"You don't get to ask me this. It's... I don't want to fight," Rob responded, her frustration evident.

"We're not fighting. We're talking."

"How many dates?" she asked, trying to change the subject.

"You're trying to haggle with me?" he teased.

"One date a month. In São Tomé," Rob suggested.

"Two dates a month. In São Tomé but in the Capital. Other districts don't have nearly as many activities."

"Deal," she agreed.

"Deal," he confirmed. "Now, about the pegging part."

"Before you say anything, get dressed, I have something to show you."

"I don't have energy."

"I promise you'll like it. Or at least you'll laugh. And I have safu ice cream at home. And tamarind juice."

After getting dressed, they made their way to her place. Omali was in her room with Irina, engrossed in a video game. Rob motioned for O'Neil to follow her quietly to her room. Carefully closing the door behind them to avoid any noise, she went to her closet and retrieved a box hidden beneath piles of clothing. She opened the box, revealing its contents to O'Neil. He couldn't conceal his surprise as he beheld strap-on dildos, a bullet vibrator, vibrating cock rings, and a cleaning enema kit neatly arranged inside.

"Rob..." he said, his smile a mix of surprise and curiosity. "What? Where did you get this?"

"I picked it when we were in São Tomé," she replied, her own excitement evident. "Remember that morning you went for a run while we were in the capital? Well, I went to the post office to pick up some things I had ordered from Lisbon."

"What even is this?" he asked, picking up the cock ring from the box.

"I'll teach you," she said, a naughty glint in her eye.

"You know too much about this for someone without experience," he said.

"I've been fantasizing about this for ten plus years. You know when I grab you by your waist to push you inside me, I imagine gripping your waist from behind. You have such a cute waist. I love it so much."

"Why do you sound horny?" She kissed him. "No, no, let's... Let's take a step back. This is too big. This is not going inside me," he said, holding up a twenty-five-centimeter dildo.

"We can start with this one, which is only ten centimeters, and then we'll work our way up."

"I don't know about that, Rob. You seem too excited. And I barely have an ass. How do you expect any of this to fit?"

"Oh, it will fit alright," she assured him with a mischievous grin.

"We need to establish some ground rules."

"Okay, what rules do you have in mind?"

"I'm not entirely sure how this works, I researched, but... I don't want to assume what you want to do to me."

"To you? You make it sound like I'm going to torture you. You're going to like it. I'll be gentle, very gentle."

"See? It's the way you're talking."

She chuckled and then quickly covered her mouth to stifle the sound, wary of Omali overhearing.

"Let's make a deal, okay? I'll give you one date. A day just for us. You can plan it however you like, and we'll do whatever you want. In return, you'll give yourself fully to me afterward. I promise not to use the twenty-five-centimeter dildo. And if you want us to stop at any stage, you just have to say it. If you genuinely don't enjoy it, just tell me, and we'll never have to do it again. We'll still have our dates twice a month in São Tomé. Deal?"

"You're awfully confident that I'm going to like it."

"What can I say? Give a girl a strap-on, and she gains the confidence of a mediocre man," she quipped with a grin.

BACK TO TÜRKIYE

Time couldn't seem to move quickly enough. O'Neil departed a week before, heading out alone to organize the date and to sidestep any suspicions. Rob's departure didn't come until next Friday. Given it wasn't a business trip, O'Neil arranged and paid for a hotel entirely on his own. He greeted her at the airport, driving a car he'd rented for the occasion.

"I missed you," he said as he leaned in to kiss her. Her initial instinct was to dodge the kiss, but she quickly reminded herself of their agreement.

"I missed you too," she replied, attempting to conceal her unease.

He escorted her to the hotel, encouraging her to unwind and rest in preparation for the carefully planned date on Saturday.

On Saturday morning, she was greeted with her favorite breakfast. They indulged in a leisurely morning in bed, a rare luxury for her due to her demanding work schedule. Afterwards, they headed to the hotel pool where they spent a relaxing time, and she practiced her swimming skills. In the afternoon, they pampered themselves at the spa, indulging in massages, manicures, pedicures, face masks, and sauna sessions. As the evening approached, he whisked her away to a beachside restaurant where they could dine with the waves gently lapping at their feet. He made sure the restaurant had her favorite fish on the menu, and he had thoughtfully arranged for her favorite wine to accompany their meal.

After dinner, they wandered along the beachfront until they reached a karaoke bar. They took to the stage together, launching into a spirited and horrible rendition of Abba's *Dancing Queen*. That was the most fun she had had in a very long time.

After returning to the hotel, they didn't head straight to their rooms. Instead, they ventured to the hotel bar. Tourist men attempted to strike up conversations with her, offering to buy her drinks, assuming she was an escort due to her being a local woman accompanied by a white man in an upscale hotel. For most people in the country, staying at such a luxurious hotel was out of reach, including for her. It was a place by foreigners, for foreigners. Even stepping foot in such a posh place felt like a transgression. She accepted the drinks and shared them with O'Neil.

"Is it common for men to assume you're a sex worker?" he asked.

"Did you see this place? Look around. Do you see any other Santomeans here? They either think I'm a sex worker or a naïve local girl hoping for a visa to escape poverty—easy to exploit."

"Gosh, I can only imagine what these service workers go through. White men are the worst," he said as she poured him a glass of wine gifted by one of the men.

"Yes, you are. But it's not just white men. Men with power and influence. Nigerians and Lebanese have lots of businesses here and can be just as bad. Although, for us, Lebanese are white too."

"How come?"

"Our perspective on race is different. For us, Asian people are white. Race is determined by skin color, not facial features. If your skin is white, you're considered white, unless you're a black ocosso," she explained.

"Don't you think that's tricky?" he said, taking a sip of the wine.

"But they are white. Like, East Asians for example are white."

"But they don't look white."

"But whiteness isn't just one 'look' for us," she countered. "Consider the San people. They're black, with the same facial features we associate with East Asians. Are the San people not black? Different ethnicities in Africa have different features. Still, all black. And as for darker-skinned white people, sure, a Portuguese or an Italian may not be as white as a Norwegian. But they're still white. Just like I'm not as dark as Makeba, but not as light as Angelina. I'm still black."

She paused briefly before continuing, "If we accept that black people come in all shades and features, we need to accept that white people also come in different shades and features."

"So, in your understanding, there are only black and white people?" he queried, his brow furrowing with curiosity.

She shook her head. "No, it's more nuanced than that. We have white and black. Within black, we have categories like bobo. I would be considered bobo. We are not light, but we are not dark skinned either, even though, depending on the context, we could be considered dark skinned. Then there are mulattos like Angelina, even though neither of her parents is white. We just call mulatto every light skinned person. We also have ocossos for albinos, and so on. And for those we don't have specific labels for, we simply associate them with the country they're from, like Indians."

"What if an Indian is light skinned?" he asked.

"Then it's a white Indian. It's not that complicated. We're not categorizing people to oppress them. We're just describing them."

"That's very bizarre," he remarked, finishing his glass.

"Not really. You guys created the concept of race, but race is not a fixed concept based in an objective reality, so it's interpreted following different realities. In South Africa, someone like Angelina wouldn't be considered black. She would be considered colored. But in Europe, she would be seen as a light skinned black person or mixed race. Which designation is more legitimate?" she said, refilling his glass with wine.

"There is not one legitimate interpretation of race."

"Exactly."

"But, with colorism for example and the appropriation of black spaces by non-black people... Don't you think this idea is dangerous?"

"In what way?"

"You said once that Mariah Carey isn't black. But if all interpretations of race are legitimate, then she is black. So, people like her, Halsey or even Zendeya deserve to be in safe spaces actual black people have created for themselves."

"I think the one drop rule was never a thing. If you pass, you are. Not always, but more often than not, especially nowadays. At the end of the day, race exists because of racism. Race matters because of racism, so there is still legitimacy because of the context even if there is no one legitimate interpretation. Is Mariah Carey being subject to racism as actual black women? Of course she isn't. We think Chinese people are white in here, but in the US, they are discriminated against. So, there is legitimacy in them not seeing themselves as white. The same way the Irish didn't see themselves as white because they weren't treated as such even though that's what they are. Race is messed up. Every system that tries to put people in a box is messed up. But it is what it is, and there are real consequences depending on where you fall on the spectrum of race. That's why we need to be careful not to ignore the reality of race and not to call a dove a crow. But then the dove might say it's mixed because its great grandfather was a crow, while having the privileges of the dove or proximity to the dove. How light skinned a person can be until they are simply white?"

"I always found it interesting how complex this is. I've seen people as white as me saying they're not white, they're Latino or mixed."

"All while benefiting from whiteness. It's crazy, isn't it? As if culture was race. And what would black Latinos say? They don't get to say they are not black because they are treated as such, second-class citizens even in their own countries. There is also the other side, people who say they aren't black, which most of them aren't anyway, they are mixed or black adjacent in some way, but they will still benefit from being in black spaces while being protected by their proximity to whiteness."

"Race is a lot," he said as she poured him some wine. "It's hard to navigate it because it's different depending on the country, the region, the person..."

"Yeah, but there are still universal truths. White people are privileged everywhere in the world. Proximity to whiteness is a privilege anywhere. Antiblackness and colorism are a problem everywhere. It just manifests in different ways."

"I just don't get how a black country can be antiblack. I mean, what do you gain by perpetuating the same messed up systems created to dominate you?"

"It's not easy to erase centuries of brainwashing. Especially here because it all started here, in São Tomé, with Portuguese men raping Kongo women for mixed babies who were given the Portuguese nationality, education and privileges, so they participated in the oppression of the real black people, even their own mothers."

"I didn't know that."

"Yeah. My country was a major and one of the first actors in slave trade, in hierarchization of skin color. But now, in the context of race, unlike you still do, we don't use race to oppress, we use it only to identify or describe people. Race isn't really important here. Well, it is but it isn't. Proximity to whiteness is. Having Angelina's skin color comes with privileges. And being white, either French like you—"

He cleared his throat. "Norwegian," he said under his breath.

"I'm sorry, Mr. Thibault," she said jokingly. "Either Norwegian like you or Lebanese have a lot of advantages. In the collective imagination of Santomeans, white people are seen as better. That's why we treat you so well when you visit our country."

Another man approached their table and engaged O'Neil in conversation, attempting to ascertain Rob's 'price' and obtain her contact information.

"She is my woman," O'Neil said with heartfelt pride. It was the first time he had asserted such a claim, the first time he had been allowed to.

"Sure she is, buddy," the man replied, patting O'Neil on the shoulders in a gesture of camaraderie. He left his card on the table before leaving.

"They aren't usually this straightforward. I think this beach dress doesn't help. It's light with cleavage," she remarked.

"You look beautiful," he said as she poured more wine into his glass. "I think you're trying to get me drunk."

"Me?" she replied, feigning shock at his accusation.

"Yes, you. You haven't finished your cocktail yet but keep pouring wine into my glass. And you keep talking so that I wouldn't notice that you aren't drinking."

"I want you to be tipsy. I remember how you used to call me tipsy, telling me that you can't stop thinking about me."

"Why do you want to see me tipsy?"

"I want you to be relaxed," she said, as he drank again.

"Why do you want me to be relaxed?"

She pulled out her phone and sent him a picture. He reached for his own phone, his eyes widening as he viewed the image. Swiftly, he concealed the screen against his chest and glanced around, wary of prying eyes.

"Rob… What was that?" He cautiously unblocked his screen and adjusted the brightness, ensuring no wandering eyes caught sight of the picture. She stood naked in the image, adorned solely in a white underwear and a strap-on harness holding the largest black dildo he had ever seen.

"This one wasn't in your box, right?"

"No, and don't worry, we won't be using it tonight."

He remained transfixed by the picture, zooming in and daring to increase the brightness to scrutinize all the details.

"I don't know if it's the wine talking, but you look so hot in this," he said, mesmerized.

"Yeah? You think I'm hot?"

"I would do anything for you."

"Yeah?"

"Yeah."

"You'll let me take advantage of you?"

"I'll let you do anything you want."

"I'm going to drill you," she whispered in his ears as she took him by his arms. "Let's go to the room."

As they entered the room, he headed straight for the shower.

"I'm sweaty," he said.

"Okay. I'll wait," she replied.

"Just a minute," he said, planting a kiss on her lips before disappearing into the bathroom.

She sensed he might be stalling, but she granted him his time. While he was in the shower, she took the opportunity to freshen up and change. Among her options were two lace lingerie sets, one in red and the other in white. Unsure of which to choose, she tried both on. In the hotel room's lighting, the white set seemed to enhance her skin's natural allure. Carefully, she slipped the dildo into the harness, adjusting it until it felt secure. She scrutinized herself before the mirror. Excitement and anxiety shared the same visage, leaving her body unsure of how to discern between the two. She applied a coat of red lipstick and carefully glossed it twice, a touch of boldness contrasting with her nerves. As he emerged from the bathroom, a towel wrapped around his waist and another in his hands drying his hair, she stood poised, ready for him. As his gaze met hers, she saw desire flickering in his eyes. He stood there, momentarily awestruck, his gaze fixed on her body.

"Fuck, Rob..."

"Close your mouth, you're salivating."

"I need to have you in my mouth."

"Oh no..." she said, her mischievous smile revealing her intentions. "I'm going to fuck you now. Don't worry, I'll be gentle."

She kissed him as she removed his towel, her lips trailing down his bare chest to his cock.

"Rob, it's going to hurt."

"It's not going to hurt, I promise," she said between kisses. "Now get on all fours," she commanded him, and he obediently complied, fueling her arousal even further. The knowledge of his willingness to bend to her desires, to do anything for her, and the power she held over him only heightened her excitement.

"I used the cleaning kit this morning and now."

"You even shaved for me," she whispered the words against his skin as she kissed his back, her hands trailing down his body until they reached his ass.

"This is very uncomfortable," he said.

"Yeah, and yet, you're all hard," she said as she massaged his cock. He began to moan, pleasure and embarrassment mingling in the sound.

"Arch your back for me," she ordered, and he complied. She spread his cheeks and slipped the tip of her finger into his tight hole, tracing small circles. Then, she pressed her face between his cheeks and began to lick his hole. His restrained moans erupted into loud, panting cries of pleasure, his knees buckling under the intensity of sensation. He called her name between gasps as he surrendered to the overwhelming ecstasy coursing through him. She inserted first one finger, then two, applying lubricant for smoother penetration. His impassioned cries reverberated in the room, each one sending shivers down her spine as she marveled at the profound effect his pleasure had on her.

"Is it good?" she asked.

"Yes," he uttered, his voice trembling.

"Am I good?"

"You're so good… Rob. You're amazing."

"Am I?"

"You are."

"Do you love me?"

"I love you… I adore you."

As he lay on the bed, she straddled him, ensuring the dildo attached to her strap-on nestled between his cheeks. She teased him, tracing the tip of the dildo in circular motions around his puckered entrance.

"Do want me to put it in?" she asked.

"Yes."

"Yes, who?"

"Yes, Rob."

"Are you going to obey me?"

"Yes, Rob."

"Are you going to do anything for me?"

"Yes, Rob."

She coated him once more with lubricant before easing the dildo inside him. He groaned in pleasure as the shaft filled his ass. She allowed him to adjust to the sensation before beginning to move slowly, thrusting in and out.

"Look how your tiny ass is taking it all. Do you like my cock?"

"Yes, Rob. You're amazing."

"Am I the only one you'll let peg you?"

"You're the only one."

"Say it louder."

"You're... The only one."

"Am I the only one you love?"

"You're the only one. I'll do anything for you."

"Anything?"

"Anything."

She intensified the pounding, her thrusts growing harder and faster, his skin reddening as her cock plunged back and forth, stimulating his prostate.

"I love you," she whispered in his ear, feeling his body tense and writhe beneath her.

"Rob, you're too good... I'm... Coming...," he gasped.

She continued to thrust more gently as he reached climax. Once his spasms subsided, she straddled his face.

"Now you're going to eat this ass," she said.

"I thought you'd never as..." as he was answering, she clasped his head firmly between her thighs, gripping his hair tightly as she guided his head closer to her. Her juices flowed into his mouth, trickling over his face and drenching her thighs in the process. She moaned as his tongue explored every intimate crevice. As she reached climax, she kept pulling his head closer, gripping his hair tighter and tighter until she burst on his face.

She collapsed next to him, both panting. He tenderly caressed her and toyed with her plastic cock, making playful noises. Then, amidst their sweaty and sticky selves, laughter erupted. It began slowly, building into loud, joyful peals as they relished the silliness of the moment.

"If you keep pulling my hair like this, I'm going to have to go back to Türkiye."

"If you keep eating me good like that, I don't think you'll have a choice."

WHY DID YOU LEAVE?

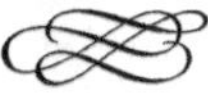

As the sun set on that Wednesday, concluding a full day of overseeing construction work on the islet, Rob and O'Neil returned to Príncipe.

"Come home with me tonight," O'Neil suggested. "Alice is going out. We'll have the house all to ourselves."

"Mmm... Tempting. But I need to go home," Rob replied. "I promised Mali I would be home for dinner. She's leaving for São Tomé tomorrow morning on a school trip, so I want to have this dinner with her."

"I could eat."

"No. I want to be alone with her. Besides, we've eaten dinner together four days in a row."

"Rob..."

"What about I meet you later? After dinner?"

"Alright."

"Hey..." she touched his face. "Is everything okay?"

"It will be."

"Go see Fehér. He'll give you a haircut."

After dinner, she knocked on his door. He opened it, and she immediately jumped in his arms, kissing him passionately.

"You look so hot," she murmured between kisses, admiring his freshly cut hair. "I can't stay for long," she added, her hands already working to undress him.

"Hey, hey... I want to talk."

"Yeah, and I want to fuck," she replied, her hand moving down to his crotch. "And by the looks of it, you want it too."

He took a step back, trying to regain control of the situation.

"Where did you put the, hm, harness?" she asked.

"Not today."

"What?"

"I just want to fuck you."

"You can fuck me after. You always do."

"Yeah, but today, I only want that."

He pushed her to bed, kissing her passionately. He kissed her breasts, sucking on it for long minutes while his fingers teased inside her underwear. She moaned as he started going down on her. As she was about to climax, he put her in all four and slid his cock inside her thrusting it hard and slow until they came together.

They remained in silence, lying on his bed, basking in the pleasure and relief their bodies had provided each other.

"Have you heard about Angelina's and Angela's surprise party?" she asked.

"Yeah," he replied, his voice lacking its usual enthusiasm.

"It's going to be fun, to prepare the party for them."

"Yeah."

"Okay, tell me... What's going on?"

"In six weeks, my monitor position ends. The day after Angelina's birthday, I'll leave." She stayed silent, unsure of what to say. "Alice bought the tickets this morning."

"You'll get to enjoy a bit of the summer in Geneva, I see," she said, awkwardly, as her heart raced in her chest. She knew what he wanted to hear, but she also knew she wouldn't be able to tell him.

"I can't do this," he said, rising from the bed to dress himself.

"What?"

"I don't know what we are. Is there even a 'we'? Do you ever intend to come clean for us to have a relationship?"

"You can't expect that from me. I never promised you anything. How do you think I feel having to hide this?"

"I don't know. You seem fine."

"You're being unfair. I don't expect you to understand how hard it is to be me. I told my friends everything you did, and they saw how much that affected me. How can I just go back to the person who was responsible for that? I have some shame. How would I face Angelina?"

"You only told Angelina and Makeba. Makeba gave us her blessing. And I talked to Angelina."

"You did what?" She got up off the bed.

"Yeah. I talked to her. I asked her what I could ever do to deserve you again. Do you know what she said? It's up to you. She said it's up to you."

"I never said it wasn't up to me."

"I'm sorry, I am. I'll be sorry my whole life for doing what I did to you. Just tell me what I need to do to make up for it. I'll do anything. Anything."

"Why can't we just be like this?"

"This is not sustainable, Rob."

She sat on the edge of the bed, grappling with the tumult of thoughts swirling in her mind. He reached out, his touch gentle upon her shoulder.

"Talk to me," he asked.

She remained silent and he remained patient, waiting for a word from her, something, anything that would alter the course of their relationship.

She gazed at him, her eyes reflecting a mix of pain and frustration. "Why did you leave, O'Neil? I know you still had feelings for your ex, but I also know you loved me."

"I did. I did love you."

"Then why?"

"I know you want a clear answer. I don't have it. I would like to say something to ease your hurt, but I don't know what to say for the man I was. I can only speak for the man I am now. And this man wants to make you the happiest woman alive."

"The problem is not that you don't know why. The problem is that I do," she said, her gaze shifting to the scattered clothes on the floor.

"Then tell me."

"I can't be doing this. Giving you everything, telling you everything," she said as she began to dress herself. Afterwards, she left, leaving him to grapple with their unresolved past.

The next day, she worked from home to avoid crossing O'Neil. The prospect of facing Angelina was equally daunting, but she knew she couldn't hide forever. The power was out. She was in her room, using the last minutes of her computer's battery to watch a YouTube video with her headphones on. Suddenly, she felt a hand on her shoulder, causing her to jump in fright and let out a piercing scream.

"Fuck, Ange! Don't do that."

"I've been calling your name for who knows how long."

"You nearly gave me a heart attack."

"Yeah? Better that than being actually… I don't know, killed? You can't just leave your door open and blast music through your headphones. That's dangerous. Anyone could sneak in and…"

"There's nothing worth stealing here."

"You know there are worse things that could happen to a woman. Don't play with these things."

"I'm sorry."

"So, you're trying to avoid me?"

"Me?" She dramatically feigned innocence.

"Yes, you. You didn't answer any of my calls or texts."

"I…"

"So, he told you that he told me, right?"

"Yeah," she replied, avoiding Angelina's gaze, too ashamed to meet her eyes. "I'm sorry."

"Why are you sorry?"

"I don't know. For being stupid."

Angelina moved closer to sit on Rob's bed.

"Huhum, not with your outside clothes. Come to the sofa. Are you hungry?" Rob said as she grabbed the candle lamp from her nightstand.

"Do you have tamarind juice?"

"You're in luck. I have it."

"I know you do. O'Neil loves it."

"He's quite childlike, isn't he? Gets excited about things in a way that only a child would."

"Well, I'm not the one fucking the childlike man, so."

"I don't mean it like that. Forget it."

"For how long you two have been fucking?"

"Why do you have to say it like that?"

"You also say fuck."

"It sounds different coming from you."

"For how long you two have been exchanging fluids, touching parts, poking holes…"

"Okay, okay, okay. Stop. We started on Fehér's birthday party."

"That explains a lot."

"Makeba knew it right away. You're too oblivious."

"You told her, and you didn't tell me."

"I didn't have to tell her. She just knew."

"You know I don't see things. If you don't tell me, I can't know."

"I know. Are you too disappointed? Do you feel like kicking my ass?"

"How many times have I told you to stop assuming things and just talk to me? I need words. I don't work with cues."

"What are you talking about? You said plenty of times."

"Yeah, but that was before I got to meet him. We've been working for almost five months. It would be weird if I hadn't changed my mind about him. Besides, he's crazy about you, always talking about you, saying how great you are, trying to get me to talk about you, wanting to hear stories about when we were growing up. I always told him to not even think about it and to forget you. But this whole time, you were exchanging fluids. Who looks stupid now?"

"Stop saying exchanging fluids."

"What can I say then?"

"I don't know. I'm sorry I didn't tell you before. I was afraid you would judge me."

"Of course I would judge you. And maybe beat you up. But I would still be here."

"Please don't beat me."

"I won't. I don't hate him anymore. He cares about you. He loves you. I don't know what you see in him. He's weird, but you love him too. He told me that he regrets what happened. He thanked me for taking care of you when he dumped you and asked for my blessing."

"He didn't dump me."

"He ghosted you. It's worse."

"How can I forgive that?"

"You don't have to. That's what connected us in the first place. We don't adhere to forgiveness. I haven't forgiven Yuri for many things. If you're ashamed, I'm going to share something with you, so you have something on me too. When I got pregnant, Yuri threatened to leave me. He was working on getting a visa to go to Portugal and me being pregnant was the last thing he wanted."

"You told me that. He panicked. People do stupid things when they panic. He could've done what 90% of men of this country do. He could've left you alone to take care of the kids."

"Yeah, he panicked. And he wanted a way out so bad that he

asked me if I was sure he was the father. That broke me. I cried so much. I didn't tell you because I was ashamed. I still am. Didn't he think I wanted out too? It's so easy for him to sully my character just to not take accountability. But Linda's death traumatized me too much for me to get an abortion, so I knew I was going to have these children. So, I went back to him, not because I was in love, but because I didn't think I could do this alone. I know women in our country often do it alone, but I'm not as strong. We needed to make that work. But I fell in love with him again. He apologized many times. I still hold it against him. But I can't imagine my life without him."

"I don't mind being alone. I really don't."

"I know you wouldn't if you hadn't met O'Neil and if you two weren't given this second chance. But you know him. You fell for him again. Now being alone will feel like settling. And you will mind it."

"Why are you on his side?"

"I'm on the side of your happiness. And I've never seen you this happy. I guess it makes sense that you were suicidal after him, because when someone brings so much happiness into your life and then leave… I can't even imagine."

"You keep saying I was suicidal. I was depressed, that's what the doctors said."

"You don't remember, do you? You once stepped in front of a car and then you got scared and retreated. You told me you wouldn't do anything to harm yourself, but you wouldn't mind dying in your sleep. This is suicidal behavior."

"I must have been kidding."

"You don't 'kid' with these things. And you were not kidding."

"So now you want me to be with the person who put me through that?"

"Heartbreak is part of life. You didn't have the tools to deal with it back then. Your life was empty, and he was the only thing…"

"You make me sound miserable back then."

"You kinda were. But now you have this organization, you do important work... A heartbreak won't break you as much. But I also don't think he's the same man who ghosted you. I guess what I'm saying is you two are different people now."

"I wish it was that simple."

"I cannot make the choice for you. I wish I could. You would make fewer mistakes." They shared a laugh. "But love is a rare thing, isn't it? Two people loving each other at the same moment in time. More often than not, love is unrequited or there are obstacles. Millions would love to be in your shoes now, don't forget that."

"I won't."

"I have to go home now."

"Don't you want to spend the night here?"

"Don't offer me heaven when you know I can't accept. I can't wait for our next visit to São Tomé. Being away from these kids is my time off."

"O'Neil took me to a hotel in São Tomé, it was so fun. Beach, massages, jacuzzi, spa. I'll take you there for one day. I'm paying."

"I make more than you and I can't pay for these things. How will you be paying?"

"I'll figure it out."

"Okay then, it's a promise."

"It's a promise."

As she prepared to leave, she approached Rob and enveloped her in a hug. Hugging wasn't her usual style, but she had an uncanny ability to know when Rob needed it most.

"Talk to him."

"I will."

THAT NIGHT, after Angelina left, Rob summoned the courage to call O'Neil. She invited him over to her place, a departure from their usual routine. Typically, he would suggest she come to his, after all, he had a generator. But on that particular night, she needed the dimness, the anonymity the darkness provided. It allowed her to confront the impending conversation with a sense of liberation. In less than ten minutes, he arrived at her doorstep. As he entered, he removed his shoes, his demeanor subdued. She led him to the living room, and they settled onto the sofa, a weighty silence enveloping them.

"I don't..."

"Please, don't say anything. Not yet. I'm trying to gather courage to say what I'm about to say," she interrupted him, her voice trembling slightly. They fell back into silence. She searched for the right words but found none that seemed adequate. Instead, she focused her gaze on the flickering candle, its soft glow casting shadows across the room.

"O'Neil..."

"Yeah..."

"What do you want with me, from me?"

"I just want a relationship. A normal relationship. I don't want to hide this anymore. I want, when you feel ready, to take you to meet my family, my friends. I told everybody in my life that we're together. They keep asking to meet you, to say hi. I know you didn't promise me anything, but I also know you don't do casual, so are we or are we not in a relationship? I want you to be part of my life. I want to make plans with you. My mom is planning Christmas trip this year. She asked if I'll bring you. I can't say anything. I can't make plans. I can't love you the way I want to, the way you deserve to be loved because as soon as we have sex, you run away. We have good moments. But I want more of them. More of you."

"This is a very valid ask. You deserve to be fully loved and appreciated and have a real relationship. I'm a relationship person so I get it. I've never had sex outside of a relationship. You're always my exception."

"You wouldn't have sex with me if you didn't love me, so I know you love me. Then why can't we be in a relationship? We are already in one in my eyes."

"I talked to Angelina. I think she might like you now. I don't know if I should be happy or pissed that you're able to charm your way into everybody's heart."

"The only person whose heart I wish to charm is yours."

"It's harder for me now to justify why we can't be together…"

"Rob…"

"Please, let me finish. This is taking everything in me. The shame from having told Makeba and Angelina, especially Angelina because she saw me going through it, was huge. I was sick, skin and bones, without life. It was embarrassing to be honest. I know you're sorry, but you don't need to apologize anymore. You broke my heart by disappearing, but I can't blame you for my mental health issues. You're very powerful, but not that powerful," she said, smiling softly. "I guess I could say that if you had talked to me instead of just disappearing without saying a word, I would've been better. But I had issues and loving you was my source of happiness. When this source disappeared, the issues just took over. I'm afraid if you had stayed, sooner or later, we would have to deal with my depression, and it wouldn't be fair to you." She stopped, looked at him, his face dreading her words. "And as much as I'm a proud person, I think I still would accept to be in a relationship with you, especially after Angelina's blessing. But it wasn't just that. It wasn't just that you disappeared. It was why you did it."

"I was stupid…"

"Yeah, no, you weren't, O'Neil. You were not stupid. You were very lucid when you made that decision even if you didn't realize it yourself. You don't… You want to have a relationship now. You didn't want it back then. And you know I don't do casual. That's why when we kissed, it got too real, and you disappeared. The anguish you felt at that time was fear of this, of us together. I actually thank you for that. Because you could've just lied and tricked me into sleeping with you and then disappeared. That's why I do know you loved me. And you have integrity. But you couldn't be with someone like me."

"What do you mean by someone like you?"

"You know what I mean."

"I don't."

"I'm black, O'Neil. I'm not kinda black, not ambiguous, not exotic, not anything. I'm just plain black. And you didn't find the prospect of being in a relationship with me validating, good enough."

He rose from his seat, his expression a mix of confusion and uneasiness.

"What are you talking about? I've never… I've… I'm not… My ex is Chinese for God's sake."

"Don't do that. Don't." She maintained her composure, mustering all the strength within her to articulate her thoughts. "You know very well it's not the same thing. You know it and one of the reasons I love you is because I don't have to explain these things to you. You know it, the world knows it. I won't be gaslighted. I won't." He remained silent, looking at her. "That's why I can't have these conversations with white people. The first reaction is always defensiveness. I have no use for your defensiveness."

He settled back into his seat, his demeanor shifting noticeably. "I'm sorry. I know it's not the same. I heard myself just now. Huh… So that's how it feels. You're right. I'm sorry. But Rob, I never thought about that. I promise you; it never crossed my mind. Not once."

"You might not have thought about it consciously, but you did. And just hear me out. I know this is hard because I'm telling you how you feel. That's why I wanted you to figure it out yourself. I didn't want to have to tell you this. I don't like talking about these things. I know white people think we enjoy talking about race, but we don't. It's anxiety inducing. Having to choose the right words to not feel like an attack or accusation, having to walk on eggshells, having to care for your feelings on top of carrying the emotional burden of the experience of being who I am… I don't like it. It's too much. But that's the reality. And believe me, it hurts me much more than it will ever hurt you. I felt it, I saw it. You never said it and I can't pinpoint one instance to show you what I mean. It was the whole time, small moments, small things here and there. You couldn't be with someone like me."

"I still don't get it. You're beautiful and intelligent. You're one of the most intelligent people I know."

"You might think I'm beautiful, but the world doesn't. You might think I'm smart but that's not something concrete you can show off. The world's opinion matters, doesn't it? Even though you pretend it doesn't. And I'm not anyone's ideal companion. But now it's easy because I'm not just a black woman anymore. I'm black and something more. I'm a black woman with the biggest nonprofit in PALOP, that has been recognized by many important people around the world. Now I have something to compensate for my blackness. I can make up for it with the things I've built. So now it's easy for you to want to be in a relationship with me."

"So, you think you need to be great for me to love you?"

"I don't think so, O'Neil. I know. Maybe not for you to love me. But for you to want me. If I was just working at a nonprofit in a small position, you wouldn't be here today. If I were rich, you wouldn't have left seven years ago. We like to pretend that the world or the systems have no influence on our lives, our romantic choices, but they do."

"Rob, I don't say this often, but I'm rich. My family is rich. You're poor."

"You didn't have to say it like this."

"No, I do because I don't…"

"I don't have to be rich; I have status. You're still a product of your environment. I might not have money, but I have the appearance of money, the appearance of success. Having status, having money, being great..."

"But you were great. You were always great for me."

"Yeah, but not for society. Not for your friends. Not for other people. For men, having a desirable woman by their side is viewed as a benchmark of their success. Being with me would be a reflection of your success. And me being black doesn't reflect well enough, does it? Even if I'm beautiful, even if I'm smart. So, I needed to have something tangible to compensate for it. Now I have."

He took a deep breath. "You think I'm racist and you still slept with me."

"I don't think you're racist, O'Neil. But we all carry antiblackness because that's the world we live in. Centuries of dehumanization, of stereotyping, of creating standards that exclude black women or put us at the opposite end of beauty, of grace, of intelligence, of anything good or desirable... These things leave a mark on us. We aren't raised in a vacuum. We all need to constantly check ourselves. Including me. I know my position in the world. I don't let it be an obstacle even though I can't control when it is, but I'm aware of it, of how I'm seen, how I'm perceived. If it makes you feel better, most people are like this. Not in the same way because the context isn't the same, but in order to see me as a person, as equal, as worth it, to give me the benefit of the doubt, I always have to make up for being black, either by being very smart, or very kind or very something. And I get it, this is the game, and I play it in order to get to where I need to be. But I don't want to play any games at home. I just want to be a person. A woman."

"And I just want you to be a person. My person. My woman."

"I just don't know how or if I can get past that. I want to. I know you love me. But..."

"Even if I was that person back then. I'm not that person today. When I saw you in Geneva, you could've been a server, a whatever. I just didn't realize how much I had missed you until I saw you. I regretted every choice I made seven years ago. I regretted losing… Leaving you."

"I know. I know." She drew in a deep breath. "Fuck, this is hard. These conversations are hard. I won't sleep tonight."

"I feel even worse now that… I'm sorry."

"I don't need your guilt. And I accept your apologies. I do. I just don't know how to move forward."

"It would be disingenuous of me to say anything now. I think I need to sit with this for a while."

"Okay."

As he stood to leave, she stood with him, enveloping him in a wordless hug. Neither could find the right words, nor did they know if words were needed at all. As she had predicted, she did not sleep that night. The relief she had anticipated did not come with that conversation. Instead, her heart was just heavy with anguish.

NEVER MIND

The following day, after wrapping up her work, as she strolled home, she sensed a weight bearing down on her shoulders, pressing against her body, urging her downward. She veered across the street and made her way toward the beach. As she walked, she shed her clothes, casting them aside until she stood bare before the water. Despite the warning he had given her about floating alone in the ocean, rationality held little sway in that moment. She remained suspended in the water, eyes closed, until a voice from the shore pierced the solitude.

"Rob!"

Reluctantly, she opened her eyes, and there he was. She swam back to the shore.

"I told you; you can't float all alone by yourself."

"I didn't die." He offered her the shirt he wore over his t-shirt. "Thanks." She put on the shirt.

"Can we talk?" he asked.

"Yes, we can."

They settled onto the sand.

"Do you remember our mission in Paris?"

"I remember you; I remember the risotto we ate. It was the

best I've had. I remember seeing you for the first time in casual clothing. I fell in love with you in suits, so it was weird. I remember you watching Euphoria very wary that someone would catch you watching soft porn."

"Oh my god, your face when you saw me watching it. You're so judgmental."

"I am. I thought better of you."

They shared a laugh.

"During dinner, Julie was talking about consent and how women are taught not to say no even if they want to because being polite is more important than safety. And then Guillaume, very eagerly jumped into the conversation and said he doesn't believe that because he never saw anyone telling women anything like that."

"Ugh, Guillaume was such an asshole. You were the first one to notice it."

"He gave me weird vibes from the beginning. And then all that thing with Mita happened. Anyway... We were eating and talking and barely paying attention to their conversation, but then, you interfered. You talked about how you never felt the need to shave your legs before going to France and how you had never done it before even though you're fairly hairy. You went to France during the fall, so you hadn't realized something had changed inside you, but then, summer came. You wanted to wear shorts and skirts, but you didn't feel comfortable wearing them without shaving, so for the first time, you shaved your legs. No one in France ever told you that hair on legs is bad, that you should shave or that you look ugly without shaving. It's just social conditioning. No one had to teach you. Society just taught you that, conditioned you through its messages, images, through cues and media and its people, through the reality of it."

"And even though I'm aware of this social conditioning, I still can't bring myself to not shave my legs anymore. Awareness isn't enough."

"Yes, awareness isn't enough. There must be a conscious effort to dismantle certain notions, get out of the comfort zone and the conformity zone and be willing to be or do different. What you told me yesterday was hard to hear. I felt attacked, but I also felt like you were being unfair."

"How dare I?"

"Right, how dare you call me racist..."

"I didn't call you racist."

"But it felt like it. How dare you call me racist when I'm not." They laughed together at his exaggerated imitation of himself in his feelings. "But I had to sit with it and see that it's not about me and much less about my appearance of being non-racist or whatever. I called some of my friends."

"No, you didn't."

"I didn't ask them if I was racist. They're mostly white, come on. I asked if they remember when I was in love years ago. Maryline told me that she thought I would marry you. And they said I was so happy. But they don't know you. They have no idea how you look. I never told them you're from Africa or that you're black. I never sent them a picture of you. Of us. Which is very unlike me. They said they had asked, but I always found an excuse. At the time they said I was being mysterious. I'm the furthest thing from mysterious. I always send pictures and brag about how beautiful they are."

"They? So, you've done that a lot, huh?"

"No, I'm talking about my ex."

"Right..."

"I'm serious. I don't fall in love often."

"Right..."

"She is the only one I've introduced to my friends and family. I've been with her since I was a teen."

"And after her, you haven't seen anyone?"

"I was seeing this girl when I left Germany, but it didn't work. I've been single for over a year."

"Single single or single with company?"

"Single single."

"Right..." she said skeptically.

"I'm serious."

"Okay, enough about your sex life. So you sent pictures of your ex to your friends."

"Yeah, always. That's when it hit me. Why didn't I send a picture of you? I think you're beautiful, I couldn't take my eyes off you, but I still, I didn't... But now, I've sent the link to your organization website to everybody I know so that they can donate. I'm always bragging about you. I sent pictures of you. Of us."

"Of us, huh?" she said, brushing against him.

"Stop, not those pictures," he said, smiling. "Rob, I don't know what changed in the meantime. Maybe it is because of your career, or maybe it's because I changed. I care less about what people think. Care less about society or even what my parents think. I'm thirty, so yeah, maybe that's it. But whatever it is, that's still something I need to work on. I'm not asking for your help. I can work on my biases by myself. I don't need you to and it's not your job to help me with that. But I need you in my life. I really do."

They remained silent, the cool breeze of the afternoon hinting at the approaching Gravana.

"Please say something," he asked.

"Why can't we just continue the way we are?"

"I'll leave in a month."

"Six weeks."

"Six weeks is not enough time."

"Why do we have to think about the future now? Let's just enjoy what we have."

"I want a future with you, that's why I'm thinking about the future."

"I don't want to stop what we have. I'm happy with this. I love you so much... And I love this so much," she said suggestively, running her hand along his crotch over his pants. That didn't have the effect she expected.

"I don't want that."

She looked around to ensure they were alone before attempting to kiss him. He rejected her advance. "I know you want me," she whispered in his ear, confident in her allure. After all, how could he resist her?

"I want to have a relationship with you. You want... I don't know what you want. I guess we can't give each other what each other wants. It's better for us to just stop," he said as he got up and shook the sand out of his pants.

"Are you... Are you breaking up with me?"

"Breaking up what, Rob? I'm just making things easier for me. I can't be near you and expect not to be attached even more. I'm going to leave now."

Rob felt her throat tightening, a sharp pain stabbing at her, and tears threatening to spill. She fought hard to maintain her composure. He wouldn't witness her tears. She rose to her feet, attempting to appear unaffected, as she began removing his shirt.

"It's alright. You can keep it. Or give it to me another day."

As he left in slow, hesitant steps, perhaps harboring a hope that she might change her mind, a million thoughts raced through her mind. She struggled to contain her tears.

"O'Neil..." The sound of his name escaped her lips, ringing out louder than she had anticipated. He paused, acknowledging her call.

"Yes?" His response was measured, expectant.

"Never mind. See you tomorrow."

He didn't answer. He turned around and left.

REBEL

Throughout the week, Rob and O'Neil maintained a facade of civility, exchanging nothing more than pleasantries. Rob had to pretend she was okay. And she did it as best as she could.

On the first day, she brushed off O'Neil's demeanor, convincing herself that he was merely kidding and even if he was serious, it was only temporary. After all, he couldn't resist her. Eventually, he would yield and go to her. By the third day, however, her confidence waned. She was less sure of her irresistibility. Or surer of his character. By the seventh day, certainty settled in. He didn't want her. He wouldn't yield. She went home and she cried. She would've cried in the shower, but the power was out. She just sat on her bed and cried until her head hurt.

THE NEXT DAY, as she was getting ready for work, her phone rang. It was Irina.

"Hey Irina!" she answered, trying to masquerade the sadness in her voice. "What did my sister do this time?"

"Ms Robinson, Mali is being taken to your clinic. She was found unconscious this morning."

"What?"

"I don't know much more. The clinic is sending a car to pick her up. She isn't waking up."

"Is she breathing?"

"I don't know..."

"Irina, please. Calm down. It's all okay. Is she breathing?"

"Yes. Yes, I can feel air coming from her nose."

"Okay..." Rob said, her eyes brimming with tears. "Okay. Thank you, Irina. I'll be there soon."

After ending the call with Irina, Rob wasted no time. She immediately dialed the clinic director in Mé-Zóchi, ensuring everything was prepared for her sister's arrival. With no flights available until Friday, she set aside any concerns about her pride and reached out to Ola, asking to use his helicopter. He agreed to come in the afternoon as the helicopter wasn't ready for immediate use. She took a moment to compose herself, wiped her tears and headed straight to work, making her way directly to Angelina's office.

"Dina, where is Ange?"

"She is buying condensed milk for tea. Do you need something urgent?"

"I just want to talk to her."

"She'll be back soon."

"Tell her to come see me as soon as she comes."

She went to her office. Only a few minutes later, someone knocked on the door.

"Who is it?" she asked.

"It's me," O'Neil said.

"I'm busy, O'Neil. I can't talk now."

Despite her dismissal, O'Neil entered her office, shutting the door behind him.

"I told you I'm busy."

"I saw you coming. You don't look well. What happened?"

"I'm okay..."

"Don't say you're okay."

"It's Mali. She was found unconscious. She is being taken to the clinic in Mé-Zóchi."

"What happened?"

"I don't know. Irina called me."

"I'm so sorry." He moved to hug her, but she turned away, avoiding his attempt at physical contact. "What can I do?"

"Nothing. I'm waiting for Ola to send his helicopter so I can go see her."

"Can I go with you?"

"I don't..." she paused. "Why?"

"Because I care about Mali. And I don't want to see you going through this alone."

"Okay. I was hoping Ange would..." Rob's sentence trailed off as Angelina opened the door, stepping into the room at that exact moment.

"What happened? Dina sounded like someone died."

"Omali..."

"No, no, no..." Angelina started, fearing the worst.

"She didn't die. She is at the hospital."

"You could've started with that. What happened to her?"

"She was found unconscious."

"Found where? How was she unconscious?"

"I'll know more when I get there."

"There are no planes today."

"Yeah, I asked Ola if he could come pick me. I was wondering if you could come with me, but I don't think you can."

"Yuri is in São Tomé so I'm alone with the kids. I can't. But O'Neil is free, isn't he?" Angelina suggested, turning to O'Neil.

"I am."

"Okay then. Thank you, O'Neil," Rob said.

Rob arrived at the clinic around 4 p.m., her heart pounding

with apprehension. She hurried to the reception desk, where the staff guided her to Omali's room. As she approached the room, she found the clinic director waiting for her, a look of concern on her face as she greeted her.

"How is she?"

"Rob, calm down. She is doing well. She is fine. She is awake."

"Can I see her?"

"Yes, of course."

She entered the room. She was struck by how pale and frail Omali looked, her usually vibrant energy replaced by a sense of vulnerability. Rob embraced her sister tightly, tears welling up in her eyes.

"Don't ever do this to me again."

"Ai ai ai. You're hurting me," Omali responded weakly.

Rob then turned to Irina and hugged her.

"Thank you so much for taking care of her, Irina."

After taking a moment to absorb the overwhelming relief of seeing her sister alive and well, Rob's mind filled with questions, and she began to seek answers.

"How is she, Cintia?" she asked the director.

"She is doing well. She suffered a head injury, so we'll be keeping her under observation in case of a concussion."

"Where was she? What happened?"

Irina ducked her head.

"Can I talk to you outside for a minute?" the director asked. Rob followed her out of the room, a knot of worry forming in her stomach.

"What is it?" Rob asked.

The director took a deep breath. "She was very intoxicated, wearing a dress that... Well, it was quite revealing. We checked for signs of sexual assault and found none, but I still think something might have happened."

"No, no! How did this happen? She was traveling with her school. Where were her teachers? Who let this happen?"

"I don't know, Rob. Just tread carefully. She might not remember everything. I tried to talk to her, but she wouldn't open up."

"Thank you."

"Don't mention it. I'll leave you alone. If you need anything, just call."

Back in the room, Rob's demeanor had changed. Omali glanced at her with a hint of fear in her eyes, as if sensing that Rob was aware of what had happened.

"Irina, O'Neil, could you leave us alone?" Rob asked.

"They can stay," Omali said.

"I'm not going to eat you, Mali. I just want to talk to you."

"And they can stay."

"Okay then," Rob said, a tinge of frustration in her voice.

"You're sure?" O'Neil asked.

"Yes. If my sister doesn't want to be alone with me, she must have her reasons," Rob said, and then turned her attention to Omali. "What happened?"

Omali pointed at her bandaged head. "Head injury, remember? I don't remember anything."

Rob turned to Irina. "What happened?" Irina looked at Omali, trying to get approval to speak. "Don't look at her, Irina, look at me. What happened?"

"So… Some of the g… There was a party at Sami's place."

"Which Sami?" Rob asked.

"Sami Husseini. He is… He is older. Goes to university."

"Son of Ali?"

"Yes."

"But how did you go to his party? You are not peers."

"I… I didn't go."

Omali scoffed at Irina. "Of course you didn't."

"We weren't allowed to leave the pension. But some people snuck out in the middle of the night," Irina proceeded.

"And Omali is some people," Rob said.

"But... She wasn't the only one," Irina tried to defend Omali.

"It doesn't matter."

"This morning, I went to look for her and the people she went to the party with said she stayed there. So I went to Ali's mansion. And I found her there."

"Why were you drunk? And wearing almost nothing. You could've gotten raped... You could have gotten killed."

"None of that happened."

"But it could have. All because you cannot listen. You don't respect anyone."

"So, you're saying it would be my fault if I had been raped or killed? You're all witnessing this, right? My sister is victim-blaming me."

"You..." Rob struggled to contain her frustration, her emotions bubbling beneath the surface, evident in the tightness of her jaw and the tension in her shoulders.

"Come Rob," O'Neil took her by her arms. She followed him outside.

"Am I a bad person? A bad sister? What am I doing wrong?"

"It's not about you."

"What do you mean it's not about me? She hates me. I've been nothing but patient. I've been doing my best. Since our mother died, I've been present, I've provided food and comfort. I even pay for therapy for her because I know things aren't easy. But her life isn't the only thing that has changed. Mine too. I'm not her mother, and I'm not trying to be. For fuck's sake, I don't even want to be a mother. I just... I'm tired. Can you imagine what could have happened? I don't..."

He hugged her. At first, she resisted, but eventually, she surrendered, burying her face into his chest. They remained like that, in a wordless communion, clinging to the fleeting sanctuary of the moment. She didn't want to leave the comfort of his embrace. She didn't want to face reality. Eventually, he pulled back.

"Maybe she doesn't need me. Maybe…"

"Mali is a child. She needs you. She needs your guidance. And you need to listen to her."

"She likes you more than she likes me."

"That's not true. She likes us both equally," he said.

She chuckled and brushed against him.

"Stop making me laugh when I'm upset," she said as she wiped her tears.

"See? You're going to be just fine."

"Thank you."

Omali spent the night under observation at the clinic and was discharged the following morning. On Saturday, they boarded the plane back to Príncipe, with O'Neil accompanying them home. As Omali and O'Neil walked ahead, laughing and chatting, Rob couldn't shake the feeling of jealousy gnawing at her. What exactly was she envious of? She couldn't pinpoint it. Perhaps it was the ease with which people gravitated towards O'Neil, his effortless charm that seemed to make him welcome anywhere. Before leaving, he offered her a hug which she accepted.

"Thank you for these last few days," she said.

"I told you, I'm here for you."

"I don't know what to do with her. Maybe I should leave her alone. She'll be seventeen this year and then eighteen next year. Probably she will get a scholarship and study abroad or maybe she'll just leave to study in São Tomé. She won't need me anymore."

"How can you be so brilliant and so dumb?"

"Did you call me dumb?"

"I called you brilliant first."

"What do you want me to do?"

"Talk to her. Just do it. Be honest. You two have a lot to talk about."

"Can I go to your place later? I don't want to be alone."

"You have more important things to work on."

"Can we meet tomorrow then? Tomorrow night?" she said, as she tried to reach his lips. He had never looked so tall before, so unreachable. He didn't make any effort in her direction.

"Rob... We can't do this. This is hard enough for me. I can't..." his voice began to break.

"Okay."

* * *

AFTER A SHOWER, Rob mustered the courage to knock on Omali's bedroom door. Omali was lying down, scrolling through her cell phone.

"Can I come in?" Rob asked.

"It's your house," Omali replied casually, not looking up from her phone.

"But it's your room," Rob pointed out as she entered. Omali still didn't acknowledge her and kept scrolling. "Can we talk?"

Omali put her phone down as she rolled her eyes. Rob sighed, realizing that Omali's silent acquiescence was as close to consent as she would get.

"Can you tell me what happened?" Rob asked as she settled onto Omali's bed.

"I don't know what you want me to tell you. I told you everything. The guys were throwing a party. Some of us snuck out and went to the party. I drank a bit too much. Tried to hook up with some guys. I think I fell near the pool, and they left me there. Irina told you the rest. She went to look for me, she found me and called the clinic. I don't have a better story. That's what happened."

"What were you thinking?" Rob blurted out before catching herself, attempting to soften her tone.

"I wanted to hook up with guys. I'm sorry I'm a teen with hormones that push me to want sex. Are you going to victim-blame me again?"

Rob exhaled deeply, sensing Omali's deliberate attempt to provoke her.

"If anything had happened, I would've never blamed you. But even that term frightens me. Victim-blaming implies the existence of a victim. Mali, I don't want to get to that. To you being a victim. I never controlled your clothes or the way you choose to express yourself because I know it has no impact on your wellbeing. Things happen. The world is a fucked-up place. You can be completely covered, you can be naked, it doesn't matter. But there are things you can do to avoid certain situations, to avoid being in harm's way. And I know it's unfair. And I know you wish I was that feminist screaming that you have the right to be in certain situations without fearing for your life and well-being. I wish the world was a different place. But there is the theory and there is reality. In theory, no one should starve. Yet, millions are starving. I don't care about what the world is supposed to be. Not now. Now I only care about what it is. And it's a scary place for you, for us. So, we need to be smart. You're not compromising your freedom, you're surviving. So please, do not put yourself in certain situations. Especially when it's not worth it. That party was not worth it, that much I know. Nothing is worth your life."

Omali was taken aback by Rob's words, her usual confidence faltering as she struggled to formulate a response.

"I just wanted to have sex, okay? Everybody is doing it. I wasn't going to die."

"When you're in certain places, you don't decide that. We have control over very little in our lives. Do not abandon the little control you have by getting drunk and making stupid choices. That's what stupid people do. And you're not stupid, are you?" Omali remained silent. "I know you keep repeating that you want to have sex to provoke me. But I'm not against you having sex. Sex is a good thing. I started having sex at seventeen with my boyfriend. You'll be seventeen soon. It's only natural that you wish to explore sex and I wish you would come to me when you decide you want to do that, but I don't think you will. I just hope you're smart enough to use protection. But Mali, these guys? These lame guys who can't get a woman their age, so they prey on young girls... These guys?"

"I don't care."

"But you should care. I know the world is going to tell you differently and maybe the world will have more influence on you than I ever will but let me tell you something: sex is serious business. It's more than a physical thing. Sex is fun, for sure. But it's only fun when you recognize the seriousness of it. Sex is one of the most vulnerable things in someone's life, whether there are feelings involved or not. Sex is intimate. You're trusting the other person to love and respect your body and they are trusting you back. Do you really wish to share such a vulnerable experience with anyone? Let me ask you this: would you be friends with anyone? Share intimate pieces of yourself with anyone? Would you be friends with Vanessa?" Rob asked, knowing that the name of her classmate would elicit a reaction.

"God no," she hurried to answer.

"You know Vanessa for years, you've been classmates for years, and still, you wouldn't share vulnerable experiences with her. If you won't be friends with just anyone, how are you going to have sex with just anyone? At best, they won't see you as a person, just a disposable commodity, just as a hole for their satisfaction, just as a body. They won't care about your pleasure, they won't respect you and without respect, how can you have sex? At worst, they might be violent, they might abuse you, they might get you pregnant or give you STI... So much could happen. Protection doesn't work 100%. The more you sleep with different people, the more you risk getting an infection. It's such a vulnerable moment, physically and emotionally. You are so amazing, Mali. You're smart and kind, really kind. Only people who can appreciate you should have access to your body, to your friendship, to your company. If I give someone access to my body, what I'm saying is: 'I see value in you. I love you and I respect you and I trust you.' If you're out here giving access to your body to anyone, how do you see people? You can't love and respect everyone. So you might just see them as an instrument, a means to an orgasm. At this point, they are just a better version of your hands. It's sick to think of people like that. It's sick to be thought of like that.

"I didn't... I just wanted to..." Omali began tearing up.

"I know that hook ups are the standard now. Everyone is doing it, right? They sell it to you as women empowerment, as freedom. But freedom is also freedom to be different, to choose not to participate in something that does not serve you. And that definitely doesn't serve you. You don't need to do it just because it's the norm. I don't want you to see other people as disposable, as objects and I don't want you to see yourself as such. You're more than that. Your body is more than that. Respect yourself enough to not abuse your body and respect others enough not to use their bodies." She hugged Omali. "This is just advice. Maybe you'll completely ignore me, but I hope you don't. I hope you'll love yourself enough to know that not everybody deserves access to you, especially people who don't see the full humanity in you."

Omali brushed away her tears.

"I didn't even want to do that. The thought of it makes me disgusted."

"I'm glad you see it now."

"I don't even like men, these men. They don't even know how to... My friends who do it, they say these men don't... Like, know how to have sex. Most of them don't even have good experiences. But they still keep doing it. Having sex with these random men."

"Yeah, it's as bad for girls as it is for guys, but at least, guys get orgasms. Most of these girls get nothing. Maybe the ego boost of being desired is enough. But it's not that hard to be desired. I think these men know how to give a woman pleasure. They just don't care about these women they hook up with enough to want to give them pleasure. Most of them don't see women as people."

"I'm glad I was too drunk to do anything."

"I'm glad these guys didn't take advantage of that. But please, don't do that again."

"I promise I'm only going to drink alcohol at home."

"So, you're the one who keeps stealing my Campari?"

Omali chuckled. "At least I'm safe."

Rob brushed against her, smiling.

"I'm glad you understand, but I still want to know what led you to do that, Mali. You're so smart. You only do certain things when you're rebelling. What were you rebelling against?"

"You know… Irina's family is religious."

"Evangelicals, right?"

"Yeah. They want her to get married as soon as she finishes high school."

"Oh my God… She has a chess scholarship already, doesn't she?"

"Yes. But she is doing what her parents want. They said she isn't allowed to see me anymore. She is only allowed to spend time with her fiancée after school. It's a guy from their church. The son of the pastor."

"I'm so sorry."

"I told her you can help. She said you can't, and she didn't want to talk to you."

"I'm afraid she's right. I can't help. She is a minor. She is under her parents' legal protection."

"But you can claim they are trying to get her married."

"But they aren't going to get her married now. They are waiting for her eighteenth birthday. If she is consenting, there's nothing we can do."

"It's not consent if she is being coerced."

"How can we prove that? I have an image to uphold, Mali. Because of my position, I don't get to just… If she, when she is eighteen, if she decides she doesn't want to get married, she can just say no. I will help her."

"It's not that easy. You know that."

"I can't do anything."

"You never can."

"You're being unfair, Mali."

"I never ask you for anything. I'm only asking you this."

"I know you think I'm this powerful person, but I'm not. I can't go to their house and tell them how to raise their child, the same way I wouldn't want anyone telling me how to raise you." Omali remained silent. She wrapped her arms around her legs, turning away from Rob, her disappointment palpable. "I'm sorry, Mali. We can't save everybody," she said, and she left.

MALI

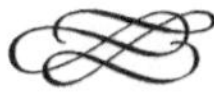

That Monday, Rob got to the office late. She barely had time to settle before Angelina breezed into her office.

"Where were you? I was getting worried."

"I told you I had my six months gyno consultation."

"Ugh, mine is coming. I'm so forgetful. I haven't been sleeping. My boy is on the new medication now. Everything is going great. He has been showing improvement in less than a week, but I read somewhere that some kids died in their sleep when they started the meds, so now I'm checking on him every fifteen minutes."

"I told you this new medication would work. There have been amazing results. And these cases must be very rare."

"Yes, but what if I'm the rare case?"

"You can't overthink everything."

"Yeah… I have my visit with Francis next week. I'm setting an alarm, so I won't forget," she said.

"And I've decided to switch to Angela as my gynecologist from now on."

"Why? Ohh… I see now. He's your ex and you still let him see your vagina," Angelina realized with a chuckle.

"It's not only that. He asked if I've had sex in the last three months."

"What did you say?"

"What do you think? I panicked and I lied. He's never asked me that before."

"Because he knew what was going inside your holes. He asks me that every time. He even asks if I've been with multiple partners and every single time I look at him like: 'really? You know I'm in a relationship. Yuri is your friend.' But I guess it's his job."

"He was like: have you had any type of penetrative vaginal and/or anal or oral sex these last three months?" Rob recounted with a cringe.

"All the above, your honor!" Angelina mocked her.

"Stop. I was so embarrassed."

"That's why Angela doesn't get to see my pussy. She is my sister. Actually, she is the one who said she doesn't feel comfortable with it."

"The next one is in November. I'll schedule with her."

"I need to do… Oh, by the way, how's Omali doing? I saw your text, but I didn't have time to answer back. Actually, I just forgot."

"She is doing better. I don't know. We had a conversation and I thought everything was going well and then she told me about Irina."

"She told you about Irina?"

"Yes. Why? She told you too?"

"Yes. I've known it for two years already."

"Two years? She said it started just now."

"I wouldn't say now. She has been dating Irina for a year already, but she had a crush on her since they met at school when she came to Príncipe."

"What are you talking about?"

"Irina and Omali's relationship. They have been together for over a year. Yeah, that's right. But only this year they had sex, so maybe that's why she said it's recent..."

"Wait, wait, wait, wait... Omali is dating Irina?"

"Didn't she tell you?"

"No, she told me about Irina's family. What... Irina and Omali?"

"Fuck, I thought she had told you. Now I'm going to have to tell her that I broke her trust."

"Please don't. I don't want her to be weird around me. If she chose not to tell me it's because she doesn't trust me."

"I told her you wouldn't have a problem with it. She knows you wouldn't."

"Yet, she told you, and not me."

"Because with me, there are no risks. Talk to her. I don't want to lie to her."

"I will."

Rob stayed there, reflective, overwhelmed by a sense of failure. She chastised herself for feeling this way, knowing it wasn't about her. Omali would come to her when she was ready. Yet, despite rationalizing, the feeling of inadequacy persisted. She was failing her sister, to the extent that Omali didn't trust her enough to confide in her.

As the day drew to a close, she made her way to O'Neil's place. He opened the door, coughing.

"Gosh, are you sick?"

"I have this persistent dry cough since last night," he said, his voice raspy. "Come in."

"You should've said something."

"It started yesterday. It has to pass soon because I'm heading to São Tomé on Friday."

"Oh, really? For how long?"

"I don't know yet. We'll visit the blue lagoon and explore many other parts of the island."

"Who is 'we'?"

"Maria and I. And some of her friends."

"Which Maria again?"

"Maria from the office in Cantagalo. She reached out and invited me to explore the island."

"So, a girl who works at my organization invited you on a trip. I'm sure the island is not the only thing she wants you to explore."

He chuckled. "Are you jealous?"

"Nope. You're single. You can do whatever you want. I'm thinking about your safety."

"How can I help you, then, Rob?" he said, coughing again.

"Is Alice home?"

"No, she's off to the Rolas islet with some tourists."

"Good. I'm going to tell you something and you need to promise not to tell anyone. Not a single soul."

"Tell me."

"Mali and Irina are girlfriends."

"Ahh," he exhaled, relieved. "She finally told you."

"What? She told you?"

"Yes. Months ago."

This revelation hit Rob personally. Sharing it with Angelina made sense; she was like family. But O'Neil? Why would Omali confide in him and not her? The questions swirled in her mind, but she fought to maintain composure, careful not to let her body or expressions betray her inner turmoil.

"Irina is having issues with her parents. Her parents are grooming her into getting married as soon as she finishes high school. Is there anything I could do to help? Legally speaking."

"You know I'm not a specialist…" he began, interrupted by a fit of coughing that seemed endless. She reached out and felt his forehead. He was running a fever.

"You need to be in bed," she said, guiding him to his room.

"I'm fine," he said between coughs.

"You're not. It looks like a viral infection. Do you have aches and pains?"

"Everywhere hurts."

"Do you have Vicks?"

"Yeah, Susana gave it to me. It's over there," he gestured weakly. She retrieved the jar.

"Take off your clothes."

"Ms. Frades... What are you trying to do to me?"

"Trying to help you get well."

She rubbed his body with Vicks, then wrapped him from head to toe in blankets. She made him chicken broth, and after he ate, she prepared a traditional mixture of warm palm oil and lemon, giving him two spoonsful of it.

"After taking this, you can't drink or eat anything, okay?"

When she left, he was already drifting off to sleep. She felt tempted to linger by his side, to monitor him as he slept, but she resisted the urge and made her way home.

As she walked, she grappled with the dilemma of how to broach the subject with Omali, unsure if she even had the right to do so. If her sister had chosen not to confide in her, perhaps there was a reason. Yet, that secret weighed heavily on her conscience, and pretending ignorance felt deceitful. She attempted to initiate a conversation with Omali several times, but she couldn't go through it. The topic seemed too daunting to approach directly. So, she postponed it repeatedly, allowing a week to slip by without resolution.

"You need to tell her, Rob. If you don't, I will," Angelina said. She was serious that time. She shared Rob's unease about the situation.

"I'll tell her, I promise."

That night, she prepared skewers of sea snails, Omali's favorite dish. Alongside, she fried silver bananas and made a fresh salad. The aroma wafting from the kitchen was enough to beckon Omali to dinner without the need for a formal invitation. They sat down to eat in silence, each lost in their own thoughts.

Rob's mind was a whirlwind of chaos. She had rehearsed the conversation countless times throughout the week, she had researched the situation, scouring online forums for guidance. Yet, when the moment arrived, words failed her once again.

"I was talking to O'Neil about Irina last week. To see if we could come up with a solution."

"I don't care about that anymore."

"But Mali..."

"She made her choice. She could've rebelled. I can't stand for her if she doesn't stand for herself. When she is eighteen, she'll have a choice. If she chooses to still go ahead with her parents' plan, there is nothing I can do."

"It isn't easy for her. They are still her parents. She loves them. She wants their love and approval."

"Not all parents are good parents. You left when you couldn't take anymore abuse. And you were seventeen. She is seventeen. You left and didn't look back."

"Not everybody is me. And I'm not the best example for conflict resolution."

"Sometimes there is nothing to resolve. Sometimes leaving is the only thing you can do. I told her she could stay with us. But she said she couldn't disrespect her family. Apparently, she has disrespected them enough already. I didn't know that being my...," she stopped herself and stayed silent for a while. "I used to hate you for leaving, you know? Not for leaving, but for leaving me behind. But I get it now."

"Omali... I didn't mean to leave you. I just... Mom was not... And then your father was just a bad person."

"Mom changed; you know. She stood up to my dad. Maybe it was too late. She tried to contact you so many times."

"I don't want to talk about mom. I want to talk about you. I know about you and Irina," she said, surprised by her own ability to voice the words. Deep down, it wasn't entirely unexpected. She was trying to protect herself, to avoid delving into the painful topic of her mother, so she sought to redirect the conversation elsewhere.

"Who told you? It doesn't even matter anymore. She broke up with me. She is dating the pastor's son. She doesn't even like him. All because her brother caught us kissing."

"I'm so sorry. I'm sorry this is happening. I'm sorry you didn't feel like you could come to me."

"Mom knew. She found my journal and read it. But she asked me not to tell anyone, especially not my dad. But dad found out anyway. He… He beat me. A lot," Omali revealed, her voice trembling. "I tried to call you that day from Mom's phone, but you didn't pick up. He beat me almost every day."

"Mom didn't do anything, as usual. She was always a pushover. She didn't love us enough to…"

"But she did. A few weeks later, she finally took a stand. After seeing my bruised face, Mom put an end to it. She asked him to leave. But only a few months later, she passed away." Rob fell silent, grappling with the flood of emotions. "Why didn't you visit mom at the hospital? She was there for four days before she passed. I called you so many times."

"I told you; I don't want to talk about mom."

"You never want to talk about mom."

"If you want to talk about mom, you can do it during therapy."

"I won't bring her up anymore. And I won't try to get Irina to change her mind. If no one cares, why should I be the only one caring?" she said as she left the table.

PUNISHER

The following week, Rob and Angelina decided to treat themselves to lunch from the food market. They settled onto their favorite rocky spot by the shore, savoring their meals and talking about life—their small, everyday lives. It had been a while since they'd indulged in this simple pleasure—enjoying a meal together and chatting about anything and everything.

"I bought us tickets for Titica's concert in August."

"I thought she wasn't coming anymore."

"She canceled for July, but it got rescheduled for August. I already told Yuri to take care of his kids. I'm going out to shake my ass."

"And now you have some ass to shake."

"Don't come for me. Even before, I shook my ass."

"Your bones, you mean."

They shared a laugh.

"Oh, by the way, when I was buying the tickets, O'Neil asked if Noite&Dia would also come. He wanted to take you to her concert."

"I doubt he cares now. He's in São Tomé with Maria."

“I saw the pictures. He looks happy. He has been posting her. Do you want to see?”

“I’d rather not. He’s not my problem.”

Angelina suddenly gasped dramatically, clutching her chest. “They are kissing.” Rob snatched the phone from her hands, unable to resist her friend’s antics. “You should see your face.”

“Don’t do that,” Rob said, ashamed.

“You’re stupid for not being with him. If you don’t, some other woman will. It might not be Maria, but it will surely happen.”

“It’s not that easy,” Rob said. Angelina rolled her eyes. “I’m serious, it’s not that easy.”

“You always do that. It’s irritating, honestly.”

“What do I do?”

“You complicate things. You complicate life. Life is hard enough; you don’t need to complicate it.”

“If you knew, you would be on my side.”

“No, I wouldn’t.”

“Yes, you would.”

“No, I wouldn’t. Because I know. I know why you aren’t together.”

“He told you?”

“Yeah. And that just shows that he’s willing to admit to what happened and do better. He is not hiding it. He’s taking accountability.”

“If you know, you should be on my side.”

“You think you’re always right, don’t you?”

“But I’m right. I don’t want to change him or to expect him to change.”

“He doesn’t need you for that. People change. He changed.”

“How can he change if he didn’t know what was wrong in the first place? And even if... The fact that somewhere in his subconscious, he might have thought that I’m not good enough because I’m black?”

"Your first boyfriend was a misogynist. You spent seven years with that guy. He wasn't an accidental misogynist because the world is misogynist. He was a proud misogynist who refused to see women as people."

"We were sixteen when we started dating. We knew nothing about life, and I thought I could change him. That's a mistake I won't make again."

"You started when you were sixteen. But you got older. And you still stayed with him. You gave him a chance. Why can't you give O'Neil a chance?"

"I don't want to be a pushover. I don't want to be like my mom. Did you know that Mali's dad used to beat her, and my mom did nothing."

"You're not your mother, Rob. And O'Neil isn't an abusive man. You're overcomplicating this and this is frustrating. No one is saying that you need to educate him. He admitted to it and said he'll work on himself and his blind spots. He didn't ask you to work on it with him."

"I'd rather not talk about this anymore."

"He's a good person, Rob. And you know I don't say this about just anyone."

"I'm serious. I don't want to talk about it."

"Of course you don't. You never want to talk about anything. Your sister has been begging you to talk about your mother, to talk about what happened. She needs you so that she can understand and process what happened, and all you do is tell her you don't want to and hire a psychologist."

"But… You are the one who suggested a psychologist."

"Yes, but I didn't think you would simply delegate your part in the process to a psychologist. You still need to talk to her. She wants to know why you left."

"She knows why I left."

"She wants to understand why, during the week your mother was in the hospital, on her deathbed, you never went to visit. She wants to know why you left her alone to deal with it. She was thirteen. Alone, at the hospital with your mother."

"Why can't she ask our brothers? They also weren't there."

"Because she loves you, not them. She needed you, not them. She cares about you, not them."

"You keep repeating that, but you said you understand me for not visiting."

"Your mother was never there for you, so I don't care if you visited her or not. But it's not about your mother, it's about your sister. You're so blinded by resentment that you don't care who you hurt. It wasn't about your mother at that point."

Rob's tears betrayed her. "You don't get to say that."

"Actually, I'm the only one who gets to say it. I opened my door for you when you left your mother. I opened my door for you when you came back from Europe. I was there. And I agree that you don't have to forgive. I also don't adhere to the concept of forgiveness. But while I move on, you don't. You keep ruminating, you keep hurting. And that's the thing, you don't mind hurting as long as you know the other person is hurting too. I saw it with your mother. And I see it with O'Neil. You may be in pain but knowing that they are suffering too brings you pleasure. You don't mind drinking the poison as long as you know the other person is going to die, even if you die too. You like punishing people. You punished your mother and ended up also punishing your sister. You're punishing O'Neil. You should be happy that your sister is not like you. Because she could want to punish you one day."

Rob remained frozen in place; her body immobilized as she grappled with Angelina's words. Her mind raced, consumed by a single question: *how did we get here?* What was intended to be a simple lunch with light conversation had unexpectedly morphed into a heavy dialogue. There had been no indication that such a conversation was on the horizon—then again, there never was with Angelina. Had she been harboring these thoughts for a while? Was this planned? What had Rob missed? She wasn't prepared for this discussion; she hadn't even had the chance for her usual soliloquy. The sudden turn of events blindsided her, catching her completely off guard.

"You shouldn't cry. This is good. Now you know," Angelina said, seemingly oblivious to the depth of Rob's hurt.

"I don't think I want to talk to you now," Rob responded, keenly aware that Angelina would miss her cues. While Rob was accustomed to Angelina's straightforwardness, it was typically directed at her actions rather than her character. What was she supposed to do with this revelation? She didn't know. So, she took the easier path: she avoided Angelina. The realization that someone she cared for deeply harbored such negative thoughts about her shattered her.

In the following weeks, Rob threw herself into organizing Angelina's and Angela's surprise party, though she still hadn't found the courage to address Angelina's words. Confronting them would demand an introspection she wasn't ready for—it meant facing her own deep flaws.

That day, the biggest challenge was finding a venue. The funds they had gathered from crowdfunding were limited. Thankfully, O'Neil and Alice offered their spacious house with a yard and pool. With that hurdle overcome, they had enough money left for food and drinks.

Rob arrived home a little late. She had been in charge of procuring seafood, so for the past weeks, she'd been purchasing fish and seafood and delivering them to O'Neil's place. Since they also had a generator and a large refrigerator, they could store the seafood safely.

Dinner was ready, and surprisingly, Omali was in a good mood. She had prepared fried fish and boiled cassava with okra and maquequê stew.

"It smells good in here," Rob said upon entering the kitchen.

"I'm going to set the table. Go take a shower. You don't want to eat cold cassava."

"Okay, okay. Oh, this letter was on the stairs. It's for you."

"Who is it from?"

"Irina."

"You can throw it away."

"Why?"

"Because there is nothing she can tell me that is going to change anything."

"But… You love her."

"You don't know that. Besides, since when is love enough for anything?" Omali responded as she turned her back to stir the pot on the stove.

Rob stood there for a moment, letting Omali's words sink in. It wasn't just the words themselves, but the way Omali had said them—empty, hopeless. She sounded different, lacking the usual lightness that was so characteristic of her youth.

After a short shower and getting dressed, Rob still couldn't shake Omali's words from her mind.

"How's the food?" Omali asked, surely awaiting compliments as her face had lightened up a bit.

"It's very good."

"That's it? No jokes?"

"No. It's really good. Thank you for making this."

"Stop. Don't make this weird."

"Can I ask you something?" Rob said, setting aside the fork she had been absently playing with.

"I'm not telling you how I made my stew."

"Why didn't you tell me about you and Irina?" Omali's face closed off, taken by surprise at the question. "You told Ange. You even told O'Neil. Why not me?"

Omali shrugged, signaling that she either didn't know, didn't want to talk about it, or simply didn't care.

Silence settled between them again.

"Ange and I aren't talking," Rob said before she retracted her own statement. "Actually, we're talking. Only at work."

"I noticed. I asked her."

"What did she tell you?"

"She said you are taking time to uncomplicate things, whatever that means."

Rob smiled sadly. "When I was seventeen, I used to date this guy. I invited him to one of my games. I used to play football. He asked if it was going to be recorded. I said no. He said: 'too bad. The only way I could watch women playing football is in double speed.' Ange went to cheer for me. My team lost. She took me to eat ice cream and I told her the story crying, calling myself stupid while the liquids from my face holes mixed into my ice cream."

"That's an image," Omali said, with a grimace of disgust.

"You know what she told me?" Rob continued. "She said, 'Stop crying.' And I said: 'But I'm so stupid.' And she said, 'Yeah, you are very stupid. That's good. You know you're stupid. You can change it.'"

"Did you change it?"

"No. I stayed with that guy for seven more years."

"I didn't tell O'Neil. I asked him to buy something for someone's birthday. He asked me specifics. I told him to buy her favorite game. And we were talking. He found out. I didn't even say her name, he just knew. He made me realize that Irina doesn't like gaming like I do. She games because she loves me, and she loves spending time with me. He encouraged me to also spend time doing things that she likes, to pay more attention to her. I found out she loves books. She wants to become a writer. He bought a writing kit. It was his idea. She writes on her computer, but she loved it. I wanted him to buy her favorite book, but he suggested an e-reader. She loves that thing more than life itself."

"O'Neil is thoughtful like that."

"We spent a lot of time on his computer, trying to find ideas of gifts for Irina. He helped a lot. He listens a lot. I told him something silly without paying any attention and he asked me to explain. I told him: 'You wouldn't get it.' Next day, he had researched it so he could understand what I was saying. He said: 'I might not have experienced certain things, but I can learn, and I can understand them because I want to. Of course I can understand you. We are friends, so when I ask you to explain, it's because I don't want to assume that I know what you're talking about. Not because I can't understand because our worlds are different.'"

"He really said that?"

"Yes. Word for word."

"Oh my gosh," Rob said, embarrassed.

"Yeah, I told him that normal people don't say things like that."

"He's not one of these white men who come here to abuse children, I promise. But oh my God, he doesn't make it easy for me to defend him," Rob said.

"He's obsessed with you. Always pressing me for stories about you. You two should be together."

"Why don't you ever ask me to buy things for Irina? I know I don't have O'Neil's money and reach, but I could help."

"I did. When you traveled last June, I asked you to buy earrings. I don't wear earrings. It was for her. Remember at the shopping center in Geneva? You asked me what I wanted, and I said earrings for Irina. You never noticed. But he noticed."

"I tend to think that I'm so perceptive. I might be worse than Ange."

"No, you're not. I told Ange and she didn't understand. I had to spell it to her: 'Irina is my romantic girlfriend.'"

"She is clueless. I love that about her."

"I didn't tell her because I trust her more than I trust you. I told her because it's easier to talk to her."

"I don't make things easy, do I?" she asked rhetorically. "Why don't you want the letter?"

"What? Oh, Irina's letter?" Rob nodded. "I already know what she's saying."

"And what is it?"

"She spoke to me in school. She said she regrets everything. She said she'll not marry him and that we could go to university together as soon as she is 18."

"That's great."

"That's great for her. But I'm done."

"What do you mean?"

"How many times am I going to let people hurt me? I'm not blaming her, but I was so desperate that I put myself in harm's way because she wouldn't listen, she wouldn't reconsider. I'm done. She can do whatever she wants."

Rob absorbed her sister's words, allowing them to settle in her mind. She took a deep breath.

"I know what I'm going to say is going to be hard to hear, but it'll help you. You didn't put yourself in harm's way because Irina wouldn't listen. You did it because you are incapable of processing your feelings in a healthy way. And people change. Irina was as confused as you were. Her world was shattering. Can you imagine being her? Imagine I find out you like women. And I try to punish you for it. I reject you, call you names, tell you that within your faith, you're a sinner, you're dirty and you'll never know heaven. She was alone. And she was afraid to lose the only family she has, even if her family is messed up. The fact that she took the decision to go against her parents took more courage than I'll ever have in my whole life. She's uprooting herself to live her truth. She must feel so afraid and so lonely. She needs you so much, Mali, so much."

Omali's tears glistened in her eyes.

"Oh, no. I'm sorry, Mali. I didn't mean to make you cry. I'm so sorry," Rob said as she walked over to Omali for a hug. Omali wiped her tears away.

"I'm fine. I don't know what happened."

"I didn't mean to make..."

"It's not your fault. Don't make this weird."

Rob returned to her seat.

"I'm sorry."

"I find it amazing that you are capable of saying these things and do not realize that they apply to you."

"You're talking about O'Neil?"

"Yes."

"It's not the same."

"He ghosted you, Rob. He was stupid. He's a man, what did you expect?"

"How does he do it?"

"Do what?"

"Charm everybody? I hate that about him."

"Where is the letter?"

"It's in your room."

"I'll talk to her."

"Good."

They finished eating and cleared away the plates.

"I like having these conversations with you. Sometimes I forget you're sixteen," Rob said as she transferred the remaining stew into a container.

"Almost seventeen," Omali corrected.

"Yeah, almost seventeen. For a moment, I felt like we're sisters close in age who could talk about anything."

"But you can talk about anything with me."

"No, I can't. I would love to, but I can't. And the fact that I feel like it sometimes is not a good thing. You should be a child, a teen."

"Like drinking, partying and having reckless sex or something?"

Rob chuckled. "A normal teen." She paused, the words she was about to express too heavy, so heavy that it seemed that her mouth couldn't support them. "When I left... I didn't leave you. I was leaving that place. I was trying to save myself. I didn't mean to leave you. And I'm so sorry for leaving you alone to deal with mom at the hospital when she was dying. You didn't deserve that. That week all by yourself."

"Don't exaggerate. It was four days. Ange was there. Angela as well. Yuri visited. Aunt Carmen visited; Aunt Daniela visited."

"You needed me. And I left you alone. I was a coward. I'm sorry. If you ever want to talk about it, I'm here. I love you, Mali."

"You're not going to die, are you?" Omali said, her stubborn tears persisting in flooding her eyes.

"What? No. You can't get rid of me."

"Mom said she loved me for the first time, and the next day, she had the stroke. Four days later, she was dead."

"You're not going to get rid of me that easily. I promise."

"Good."

HAPPY BIRTHDAY, ANGE!

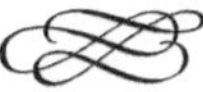

Rob attempted to squeeze in moments during her days to start a conversation with Angelina, but she consistently found reasons to put it off. She knew that delaying the inevitable was not a sound strategy, yet it seemed to be her only recourse at the time.

As Friday approached, the birthday celebration loomed. Angela and Angelina had traveled to São Tomé to visit their mother and were slated to return on Saturday. This provided a convenient pretext to keep them occupied while the surprise party preparations were underway. Their mother was surprisingly in on the plan, feigning illness and persistently urging the girls to visit her.

It was all hands-on deck, with tasks ranging from scaling and preparing fish and shellfish to baking cakes, sweets, and savory snacks, and making calulu, quizacá and izaquente. The tasks were assigned through a raffle system to ensure fairness. Scaling and cleaning the fish was the least desirable assignment, and unfortunately, Rob found herself in that group alongside Fehér, Daniela, and Jacinto. Armed with sharp knives and large plastic bowls of fish and shellfish, they sat isolated from the main house, swatting away flies as they worked. Minutes later, O'Neil appeared, disrupting Rob's laughter at Fehér's joke. Upon seeing him, everyone couldn't help but feel a twinge of jealousy towards the lucky guy who had snagged the decoration assignment.

"So you came back here to mock us? The poor and smelly proletarian?" Fehér said.

"I brought water for the poor. And some beignets," O'Neil retorted, holding up a bag of treats with a grin.

He handed out the water bottle and the beignets and stood there for a moment watching everyone rush to eat the beignets.

"Can you put it in my mouth? My hands are dirty," Rob asked, her eyes locking with his as she took a bite out of the beignet he held. "Thank you," she said.

He settled onto a nearby rock, not too far from her, and observed the bustling activity.

"You're trying to escape your royal duties? Wait, don't tell me, you enjoy mingling with us commoners?" Fehér teased.

"Don't mind him. He's just compensating for his lack of football skills with jokes," Daniela said, shooting Fehér a playful glare.

"This was low, auntie," Fehér said.

"Your mother cried when Fehér died. We all cried. You too, Rob, don't even try to deny," Daniela said, noticing Rob's attempt to distance herself from the conversation.

"Oh, so you were a Benfica supporter too?" O'Neil asked Rob.

"She was a die-hard benfiquista. Used to play football herself. Fehér's mother was her team coach. When Fehér passed away, Joana swore that if she ever had a child, boy or girl, she'd name them Fehér, and they would be a football star. Guess her prayers went unanswered, 'cause years later, she ends up with this fool who can't even make a pass," Daniela recounted, drawing laughter from the group.

"When I accepted to help, I didn't think I was also coming to Fehér's roast," Jacinto quipped, joining in on the humor.

"You'll see. I'll become a stand-up comedian and make you all eat your words," Fehér said.

"Maybe you'll have to eat your own words 'cause you won't have money for food," Daniela shot back, sparking another round of laughter.

"Fehér, looks like you've got competition. Better be funnier than Daniela during your sketch," Jacinto teased.

Rob and O'Neil exchanged glances every time they laughed.

"Since you're here doing nothing, come help me," Rob said to O'Neil.

"I'm the elder here. If anyone is going to be helped, it's me," Daniela interjected.

"I'm trying to get a job at Rob's organization, so I need to be in her good graces," O'Neil explained as he settled beside Rob, grabbing a knife to help scale the fish.

"Just say her fish is fresher than mine," Daniela teased.

"Dani! Don't say those things," Rob said, feeling mortified. "My pH is perfectly balanced, thank you," she added defensively, her cheeks flushing with embarrassment.

In the end, they were all grubby, smelly, with fish scales clinging to their faces, arms, and legs. O'Neil reached out to brush a scale from her cheek, a futile gesture given their state, but it made her smile. Together, they carried the fish to the kitchen for preparation by the cooks before heading to the beach.

"Shouldn't we shower first?" O'Neil asked.

"The fishy stench sticks. So, first we'll bathe at the beach, then we'll shower," Rob explained. Fully clothed, they waded into the water, washing away the pungent odor. Once cleansed, they left, but Rob stayed there, floating in the gentle waves. O'Neil stayed with her. Eventually, they settled on the shore, sitting in quiet companionship, side by side.

"This is nice," he said.

"What?" she asked.

"This. Here. You."

His words carried a deeper meaning as he was set to leave the following day.

"Thank you so much for your help. The construction is progressing well and hopefully, I'll secure another donation next year to finish it all and get it all working."

"You're going to get it. I already put in the request. And it's going to be doubled next year."

"Thank you so much."

"I didn't do it because of us. I did it because I really believe in your project. Come to think of it, that's the first time I've done something significant in my life."

"Come on, you work for The Universal Fund.

"You know how charities work. The billionaire creates their own charity, donates to it, gets tax breaks, and then the charity chooses projects to fund. You know, less than 1% of the money that goes into the charity actually gets donated."

"Yeah, James told me. He didn't like that. That's why he used the small influence he had to help me."

"This was an opportunity for me too. For the first time, I'm doing something that makes sense so thank you, Ms. Robinson Kwame Frades. You changed my life in more ways than one."

"What are you going to do? When you get back?"

"I don't know. I know I can't go back to HR. I feel like I would die."

"Stay here then. You've helped me so much, even with legal issues. You can stay here."

"No, I can't. I'm hoping distance will help. Being here, near you, every day… That would also kill me."

"I'm sorry for being radioactive," Rob joked. He smiled. "I get it, pheromones. But then again, maybe being near me, you would adapt and be immune to them. That's the whole premise of living. Adapting."

"I don't think I'm the fittest for survival."

She wanted to say more, to express herself further, with a torrent of thoughts pressing against her tongue. But she didn't.

"Maybe we don't have to…"

"Hey! You two, we need help in the kitchen!" someone called out.

"I guess we have to go," he said, getting up.

"Yeah."

After each taking a quick shower, separately, they regrouped to assist with the final preparations.

As the evening approached, Yuri set out to pick up Angelina and Angela from the airport. A pretext was necessary to get them to O'Neil's place without raising suspicion. Rob concocted a plan to feign an emergency at O'Neil's, providing the perfect excuse. Upon their arrival, everyone went quiet, even the twins.

"Why is it so dark in here? Don't they have a generator?" Angelina said.

"Rob?" Angela called out.

"Surprise!" The group erupted in unison, flooding the room with light and raining down balloons.

Fuck!" Angelina clutched her chest.

And then, laughter echoed through the room as they all joined in the celebration. Smiles were abundant as they danced, laughed, ate, and chatted. That night felt like one of those memorable adolescent nights that lingered in the mind long after. Rob knew that thirty years from then, she would still recall that night—the smells, the tunes, the faces. There was something about it that felt pivotal, as if it marked a turning point where choices mattered more than ever.

At the end of the party, she sat at a table, sipping bissap, and nodding along to the conversation without really engaging. Her eyes were fixed on him—his back, his shoulder, his neck. She observed his movements without him noticing. Though he had danced a few times with other women, despite his lack of skill, he had been sitting at that table for a while now, drinking a beer and seemingly oblivious to her presence.

Around 2 a.m., the DJ announced the final song of the night. The room had nearly emptied, but she remained seated, solitary, her attention fixed on his back. As the song played, her heart raced. In that instant, she felt like a teenager again, swept up in the possibility of anything.

"This is Rob's song," Alex said as he entered the room in search of her.

"No, it's not," she said.

"Yes, Mágico is your song. Come on, dance with me. It's the last song," he persisted.

"No, I don't feel like dancing," she said. Eventually, he relented and left her be.

She sat there, watching him. Waiting. Hoping he would ask her to dance. But he remained stubbornly still. So, she mustered her courage, took a deep breath, and approached him.

"Dance with me?" she asked, extending her hands. He hesitated for a moment before finally accepting them.

"You know I can't do kizomba. Your friends tried."

"We can just hug and move slowly to the sound of the music."

Slowly, she wrapped her arms around him. The warmth of his body against hers sent shivers down her spine. His natural scent, mixed with the woodsy, floral perfume he wore, created an intoxicating blend that made her feel lightheaded. She rested her head on his chest, and closed her eyes, losing herself in the moment. His hands held her waist firmly yet tenderly, anchoring her in his embrace. In that dimly lit room, everything felt natural, soft, and magical, just like the music playing in the background. As O'Neil's heartbeat echoed in her ears, she couldn't help but feel a slight flutter of worry at its intensity. She held him even closer. The world around them had faded away. In that moment, nothing else mattered except the two of them, together.

As they stepped off the dance floor, they made their way to

the backyard, nearby the beach. A shiver ran through her body. The sweat from all the dancing had left her feeling chilled.

"Here, take this," he offered, handing her his shirt.

"Gravana this year is really cold, isn't it?"

"I wouldn't know. This is my first time here, and it seems like it'll be my last. I don't have anything to compare it to."

"I bet your parents are happy that you're going back to Europe. Leaving this Godforsaken place that no one knows," she teased, hoping to coax a smile out of him but successfully failing.

"My parents are happy when I'm happy."

"You're rocking that tan, you know. You'll be turning heads left and right."

He took a deep breath. Her efforts to break the silence weren't yielding the desired effect. But then again, she wasn't sure what she was trying to accomplish. The need to fill the void between them was pressing, as silence felt too loud, too revealing. They settled onto the sand, their gaze fixated on the ocean, all powerful and still peaceful. A lump formed in her throat, threatening tears. One escaped, trickling down her cheek, but she hastily wiped it away.

"You know what's crazy?" he began. "I came here with the intention of winning your heart. Yet, somehow, I'm the one whose heart got stolen again, and it's not through any fault or effort on your part. I thought I loved you before—six months ago, I truly believed that. But what I'm feeling now, what I've been feeling… I can't put it into words. It's as if I can't breathe without you. This is maddening. I'm grateful to have you in my life, and at the same time, I wish I didn't know you, so I wouldn't have to feel this pain. But then again, I wouldn't know that love could be this… Overpowering. The way you're passionate about things… How am I supposed to go on living without that in my life? I don't want to leave tomorrow. I'm afraid I'll lose my mind. But I can't stay either. Being near you and unable to hold you, to kiss you, to tell everybody that I love you —it's also killing me.

And you know what's even more frustrating? Having to pretend like everything is well."

"If only we could be strangers again," she said. "I would have fallen for you... All over again. It would have been simpler, meeting you now, without the weight of our past. I guess 'convenient' is the word."

"I'm not sure love is meant to be convenient."

"I've arranged for someone to take you to the airfield tomorrow," she said, changing the subject.

"It's not necessary. The airfield is nearby."

"You and Alice have too much luggage, and I can't drive."

"You won't come to say goodbye."

"I can't."

"It's for the best," he conceded, falling silent for a moment. As she rose to leave, he spoke again. "You're a coward, you know that, right?"

"Yeah, I know."

MÁGICO!

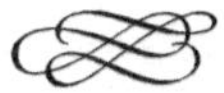

That night, her footsteps led her to Angelina's house. She paused before the veranda, debating whether to knock but before she could decide, the door swung open, startling her.

"You're not going to knock?"

"I thought you were already sleeping. Can I come in?"

"No. The twins are sleeping and if I'm going to scream at you, better do it somewhere else."

Angelina went back inside and returned with two cloths and four beers. She gave two beers to Rob and handed her one of the cloths to cover herself as they walked towards the beach.

"It's cold this Gravana, isn't it?" Angelina asked.

"I was just saying this. Last year it was very hot and there wasn't even kua kua. This year, it's very cold. I hate all of this climate change bullshit. A couple of days ago, they said it again, that islands like ours will be underwater by the end of the century. Sometimes I just don't get why we're bothering with all this, building all this infrastructure, knowing it's all going to vanish just because white people had to fuck up the planet. We're not the ones responsible for this mess, and we'll be the first to suffer the consequences."

Angelina smiled. "Yeah."

"Don't laugh."

"We have this conversation every time you're feeling a bit lost or nihilistic. And then we get back to doing what we have been doing."

"But isn't it frustrating? What's the point?"

"The point is not having people dying of hunger or lack of medical care while we can do something about it. We can't do anything about the planet. White people did that, and we are going to just suffer the consequences. That's a reality we can't change. But we can change the outcome for a pregnant woman who might die tomorrow because she needs urgent care that we can provide because we've built the infrastructure for it. I was that pregnant woman once. I'm here with you. So, it's worth it."

"I'm sorry. You're right."

"Besides, look at Tokyo, the city waiting to die. While they wait, they are living, aren't they?"

"Well, they don't have anyone to blame. They sit on top of three tectonic plates. We do."

"But the point is, they're still alive."

"How can you be so hopeful?"

"I have kids. Without hope in the future, I would die and take them with me. I don't want them to suffer."

"You're a great mom, Ange." Angelina looked at her, her eyes widening as tears began to streak down her face.

"Thank you. I don't feel like I am. I've been perpetually afraid since I had them. I don't ever know if I'm doing the right thing."

"You have twins. One of them has a medical condition. You're doing great."

"This really means a lot."

They stood on the sand, gazing at the ocean as the wind tousled their dresses.

"I missed you," Rob said as she settled onto the sand.

"I was always here. You didn't need to miss me," Angelina replied, joining her.

"I know. But I'm a coward."

"Stop missing people who are alive and near you. Just go to them. Stop complicating everything."

"I'll never miss you again. I'll just go to you," she said, brushing up against Angelina.

"See? You can uncomplicate things."

"Who was that girl with Francis?"

"Julia. His new girlfriend."

"Oh. I didn't know he was seeing someone."

"Yeah, Angela told me. He has been going to São Tomé every weekend to see his girlfriend. It's been a bit of a shake-up at the clinic."

"He moves on quick."

"You started exchanging fluids with O'Neil pretty quickly too."

"I'm happy for him."

"She is a biologist as well. A marine biologist. I think you know her. She works at the institute for conservation of sea turtles in Lobata. We donated to them last year."

"You know a lot about her."

"Angela tells me everything. It's actually a good thing that you two didn't work out. She wants kids. He also wants kids. He now can say it because he has someone who shares the same life goals."

"Yeah… I talked to Mali."

"I know. She told me."

"She tells you a lot of things, doesn't she?"

"I have a friendly face, I guess," she said as she casually picked up a crab from her leg and returned it to the sand. A brief silence ensued before she continued, "I know you gave a lot of yourself for my birthday party. Thank you."

"It was a team effort."

"Yeah, I know. But I also know that you did more. So, I'll make things easier for you since you won't start the subject. O'Neil."

"I don't know what to say about him."

"Is he still leaving tomorrow?"

"I can't make him stay."

"Here you go, complicating things again. Life could be so simple for you. At least in this aspect. I know you're used to struggling. We are used to struggling. Everything's been a struggle since we were kids. But this doesn't have to be."

"I asked him to stay."

"Asking him to stay here without you is asking him to torture himself."

"You think I'm punishing him, that I like to punish people."

"You do. Maybe that validates you in some way because you feel important to the point of making people suffer. But I don't think that's all there is to it. Because you're miserable. You're not even enjoying seeing him suffer anymore. Is it shame? Are you ashamed? Is it pride? It's not humiliating to be with the person you love and who loves and respects you. You're not a clown for giving love a second chance."

"If..." Rob began, her voice faltering despite her efforts to keep herself composed. "If I couldn't forgive my mom, how can I forgive him? Wouldn't that be like admitting I didn't love my mom enough?"

"Oh my god, that's what you've been struggling with? I don't know whether to beat you or hug you. Rob... No. That just means you're older and wiser now. You're turning thirty-three this year. You've grown and evolved." Angelina placed her hands on Rob's shoulders, drawing her closer. "You can't change the past. You can't save the seventeen-year-old you. You cannot save the twenty-five-year-old you. You can't rewrite the actions of the you from three years ago who chose not to visit your mom. But you also don't want to be forty and regret this moment, wishing you could save the thirty-two-year-old you.

"I think you'll beat my ass if I'm still like this at forty."

"I sure will. Let's leave all of this in the twenties. Next year starts a new decade. You want to be happy in twenty thirty. Even if we'll soon be underwater, let's be happy for now."

"Thank you, Ange," she said, resting her head on Ange's shoulder.

They finished their beers and ended up falling asleep there, on the beach, like drunk teenagers. They were stirred awake four hours later by the sound of Angelina's cellphone.

"What time is it?" Rob asked as Angelina searched for her phone.

"It's... 7 o'clock."

"Fuck! O'Neil's plane is leaving soon."

"Go then. Go," Angelina said. Rob swiftly collected her phone and the empty beer bottles from the sand. "Leave the bottles. Just go!"

She dashed off, her tired feet feeling the aftermath of all the dancing from the previous night. But then she turned back.

"I can't drive. Please, take me, Ange. I'm too tired to make it on foot in time."

Angelina and Rob retrieved the pick-up, and fifteen minutes later, they arrived at the airfield. Rob bolted out of the car, sprinting towards the fence. Her frantic pace slowed as she approached a cluster of people standing near the field, waiting for the plane. Amidst the crowd, she spotted him: he wore a blue shirt, white Bermuda shorts, and sunglasses. The sunlight highlighted the golden tones in his hair, while his exposed arms and legs revealed how naturally hairy he was. As she closed the distance, she mentally rehearsed the words she wanted to say, but nothing coherent seemed to form in her mind. She simply walked forward, uncertain of what would escape her lips. Finally, as she neared him, he glanced in her direction and removed his sunglasses.

"Hey!" she said, pausing to gauge his response.

"Hey?" he said, confusion etched on his face.

"Hey Alice!" she said, buying herself a moment to gather her thoughts.

"Hi Rob. O'Neil said you wouldn't come."

"Yeah..." Rob glanced downward, her nerves palpable. "Can I... Can I talk to you?" she asked him, her gaze shifting to the people around them.

He nodded and followed her to a quiet corner near the gate.

"So... I'm here," he said.

"Please, don't leave."

"We talked about this, Rob. I can't just be your secret fun time. I want more and I deserve more. I hurt you, so I don't get to expect anything more from you. It's best for me to just leave."

"That's what I'm saying. I want... I want you... I want us to be together."

His deadpan eyes were never more expressive, widening up as if he had just seen—or heard—the most important thing ever.

"Are you serious?"

"Yeah..."

"Are you doing this just to make me stay or do you really mean it?"

"I'm doing this because I love you. And I'm tired of fighting against my own happiness."

He hugged her tightly, lifting her off the ground in his embrace. Then, he leaned in to kiss her, but she turned her head away.

"So no kissing in front of people still?"

"I haven't brushed my teeth yet. I slept at the beach. I'm dirty, sweaty, smelling like food, drinks and sweat. My breath is terrible."

"I don't fucking care, just kiss me."

She kissed him briefly, a reserved gesture that conveyed her feelings without drawing undue attention in a culture where such public displays of affection were uncommon.

"Are you good now?"

"Yes, I'm good," he said, with a satisfied smile.

After breaking the news to Alice that he wouldn't be leaving with her, they bid her a warm goodbye at the airfield. They asked Angelina to take his luggage, opting to walk back on foot together. As they strolled hand in hand, he couldn't suppress his laughter.

"What?" she asked, her laughter blending with his infectious chuckles.

"It's just… It's just… It was so anticlimactic.

"What was?"

"Our airport romantic scene."

"What are you talking about?"

"You know those movies where one lover chases to the airport to catch their beloved before they board a plane?"

"Yeah, what about them?"

"This didn't feel like that."

She burst into laughter. "Oh, what were you expecting?"

"I don't know. You running to me; the gates already closed. You persuading the guards or turning them into your allies with a heartfelt speech about love, they let you through, you sprint through a bustling corridor, strangers lending a hand, until you finally catch up to me just before boarding, and we share a kiss while everybody applauds."

"Oh, buddy, that's the wrong country for that. We don't have a gate. We have a fence. People wait for the plane at the field."

"Yeah, but you could've made an effort if you were chasing a guy to the airport. And the crowd didn't collaborate."

"Poor baby, you didn't get to have your romantic scene," she teased.

"I deserve my romantic scene," he said with a sigh.

"If you want, I can leave you. And then, we can arrange something like that next year when I go to Geneva," she joked.

"Don't even joke about this," he said, pulling her closer to his side.

The following week, O'Neil's departure was inevitable. He was still an employee at The Universal Fund. In fact, they agreed that he wouldn't leave his position at TUF. He intended to request to become a permanent monitor on ground due to the prevalent risk of corruption in the country. This way, he could maintain his salary, be close to her, and continue to help her.

She boarded the plane with him to São Tomé. They spent two nights together at a hotel before he finally departed for Europe. His first stop was Lisbon, followed by Geneva a few hours later. Although it was only for two months, as he disappeared behind the gate, her heart constricted. She felt the urge to chase after him, to plead for him to stay. He would have loved that his romantic airport scene. But that did not happen. She remained outside, waiting for two hours until the plane departed. It felt reminiscent of seven years ago, her heart aching profoundly. She knew things were different now, yet her heart hadn't caught up.

She trudged back to her hotel on foot. She planned to stay awake to await his arrival in Lisbon, eager to talk while he waited for his connecting flight to Switzerland. However, fatigue overwhelmed her, and she drifted into sleep. The following morning, she awoke to his text, informing her of his arrival in Lisbon and his wait for the next flight. She dialed his number.

"Hey!"

"Hey!"

"How was the night flight?"

"Awful. A baby cried the whole eight hours."

"I'm sorry."

"I'm fine. I chugged two cans of energy drinks."

"Can I tell you something?"

"What is it?"

"I know you love me and what we have is real but for a second there, I felt like I would never see you again. You would disappear on me again. Am I going to feel this way every single time you go? I trust you, completely, and I still feel this way."

"I guess the solution would be for me to become super clingy. You're going to be so disgusted that you'll be happy seeing me leave."

She chuckled. "I'm serious."

"I'll never do that again to you. I know you know it, but your body still holds onto that fear. I'm just going to have to prove to you every day, by coming back every time. And eventually, one day, you won't feel this way anymore."

"Good. I'm going to miss you, my coelacanth."

"Your what?"

"I'm heading to the airport to catch my flight back to Príncipe. Call me when you get home."

"My home is wherever you are. But I'll call you when I reach Geneva. Safe travels."

"Safe travels. I love you."

"I love you."

THE END...

www.ingramcontent.com/pod-product-compliance
Lightning Source LLC
LaVergne TN
LVHW091302150826
845673LV00006B/1512

9782487170018